Taming Lucca

Book one: Red Devils MC

Michelle Woods

Woods Publishing & Design Inc.

Edited by: Mary Bogart Crenshaw

Publisher: Woods Publishing & Design Inc

Cover Designer: Woods Publishing & Design Inc.
Contact: woodspublishingdesign@gmail.com

ISBN 13: 978-0692627204
ISBN-10: 0692627200

To My Family–
For their love and support

Prologue

Τ he city behind the wall was the only protection that people had from the lawless world outside of it. Only while they hid in their ivory tower the world outside had reset itself. It was no longer lawless and it was now ruled by another Law: An outlaw's law. Bikers living outside the wall had created their own set of rules, ones that were made and enforced by gangs of bikers who weren't about to let anyone change the world they now ruled.

In the year 2075, the world was well on its way to being disease free. Technology had advanced and society was soon to be ruled by the upper class. Only Mother Nature had another plan.

When the government discovered that the world would lose more than half its land mass to the ocean from a massive tidal wave, they built the city behind the wall. It took them three months and only the rich, the privileged, and their servants were allowed to retreat behind it.

At four thousand feet high and two thousand feet wide, the wall was able to take the relentless pounding of the ocean that would slam against it. When the wave came, those unable to escape behind it fought to survive.

The world outside the wall became lawless and dangerous.

Michelle Woods

As the years passed, the city behind the wall was ruled by the upper class, the Hillies. The Hillies kept the lower Slum class subdued with fear, and crimes were punished by forcing the accused into the lawless world outside the wall.

Outside the wall life flourished again and people forgot about the horror they'd lived through before the Outlaws took over. Now their only fear was the constant fighting for dominance between rival gangs and they all prayed that the bad guys didn't win the fight.

Chapter 1

Molly Daniels pulled on the gray coveralls, sighing in despair. She really hated the damned things but she needed her job. Checking her hair in the mirror, she smiled at the cute twist she'd managed to tame her frizzy black hair into; it was a good look. Lifting the small bottle of mascara, she applied a light layer, wishing as she inspected herself that it wasn't the only makeup she owned. Taking one last look at her reflection, she let out a derisive snort. The shapeless coveralls were lumpy around her hips and baggy over her slight chest, making her look dumpy.

Molly rolled her eyes; the coveralls weren't a good look for her. She sighed, turning to see if the side view was more flattering. Her heart sinking when that view was no better, she really wished she wasn't required to wear these stupid coveralls. Wearing them today when they were not at all fashionable or attractive was disheartening. She had a date with Luzen tonight after work and she would have liked to look at least halfway decent when they went out.

Ha, what else could she wear anyway?

Molly let out a snort because the one dress she owned was second-hand with a simple flair skirt and had patches sewn onto the worn areas. It was just as well, she supposed, that

Michelle Woods

she had to wear the coveralls since her wardrobe was sadly lacking anyway.

Examining herself one last time, she decided it was the best she could manage with the tools available to her. She headed down the hall to the kitchen for breakfast. Her mother was standing by the counter loading ration cubes into lunch bags for Molly and her father. Molly continued into the kitchen, sitting down at the table in front of a bowl filled with goopy oatmeal. She frowned with distaste at the contents of the bowl.

She was so tired of oatmeal. But it was cheap and easily available in the Slums, so she ate it every morning without complaint, even if it did stick to the roof of her mouth for hours afterwards.

"Morning, Mother," she said, and took her first bite, grimacing in disgust at the gritty taste.

Molly watched as her mother set the filled lunch bags on the end of the counter. She began to clean the dishes in the sink. Looking over her shoulder at Molly, she smiled, although it didn't reach her eyes.

Molly stared at her mother's fitted skirt that hung to her ankles and the flared button-up blouse that was a popular fashion in the Hill district while absentmindedly eating her breakfast. Molly wasn't surprised that even standing in her slum kitchen, her mother was immaculately groomed, her slightly graying hair forced into a clean bun, which was also popular in the Hill district right now. Her mother always dressed in the latest fashions. Molly was unsure how she managed it. She almost suspected her mother stole the clothes from somewhere because it was all they could do to buy food most months, much less clothing like her mother was wearing.

"Morning, Molly. Your father tells me that you have another

Taming Lucca

date with that boy from the Hill district today. He said that the boy wants to take you to a restaurant in his part of the city. I wish you wouldn't go." Her mother paused, her eyes clouding with concern as she looked at Molly.

Molly didn't fool herself that it was concern for her own well-being. Her mother loved her in her own way, but she always put her own needs first, followed by Molly's father, and if she had anything left, that's what little concern Molly got from her.

"He's a Hillie, dear, and you two dating is like a bird dating a fish. It won't work. Even if this boy isn't concerned with his reputation, his class will never accept you as one of them. You're not in his league. You know…."

Molly raised her hand to stop her mother's tirade. It was the tenth time that they'd had this conversation, and she was over it. Luzen Colden, the man her mother referred to as that boy from the Hill, was twenty-four. He wasn't like the other class snobs who thought that those living in the Slums were little better than lepers.

Luzen was sweet; he brought her flowers and even some candy once. They'd been together for ten months, and today was the day he would ask her to marry him. She just knew it. When he'd asked her to go out he'd seemed nervous about her answer, and when she'd agreed he'd been overjoyed. He'd also told her last week that he loved her and that tonight was a special night. Molly smiled remembering his smile and the way he'd gazed at her.

She was twenty-two years old. She was well aware that their City wasn't perfect, but sometimes people could understand that classes didn't matter. Her Luzen was one of those people. Molly had been a gear head most of her life, and she'd been looked down on by many in the upper classes during her short lifetime. Even before they were together Luzen was

Michelle Woods

kind to her, and to the others who worked on her team, if a little clueless about their true circumstances.

If he asked her to marry him, it would be her chance to escape from this demeaning class and move into their upper-class world. Where she wouldn't have to eat lumpy oatmeal every day, she thought with disdain.

Eating another tasteless lump of the stuff, she cringed. When she became a Hillie, as the Slum residents called those who lived behind the gates, she wouldn't look down on her old class as many who'd moved into the Hill district did. She would be kind as Luzen was, only she'd know what it was truly like to be living in this squalor. Looking around at the dirt floor, the slanted walls, and the old almost unusable appliances, she felt a feeling of hope settling in her stomach. Molly would be grateful to escape this place and, quite frankly, her mother.

"Please, not before I go to work. We can argue about this when I get home. Where's dad this morning? He's supposed to be on shift at seven too," Molly questioned between disgusting bites of goo, trying to change the subject.

"He's helping Mrs. Rohan with that generator of hers, it stopped working last night. She had no power for her water system, so he went over to help her fix it." Her mother looked at her with condescension. "And I wasn't trying to argue again, dear. I just want to talk to you about this boy. You need to face the facts about your relationship with him, it isn't g——"

Molly ignored her mother's comment, smiling. She had a feeling of excitement run through her and her mouth watered because Mrs. Rohan grew oranges. When her father helped her fix the old generator, she paid him with fresh fruit. So maybe tomorrow, she could have something besides oatmeal and nasty ration cubes, which tasted like cardboard, to eat.

Molly ate the rest of her oatmeal in silence while her mother

Taming Lucca

finished cleaning up the small kitchenette, muttering about ungrateful children. Molly stood and took her lunch from her mother with a cursory kiss to her cheek. Glad she was able to get out of here before her mother started in about her and Luzen again, Molly grabbed her bag from her room.

"Don't wait up. I will be late tonight. Tell dad I'll see him at work," she called out as she neared the door.

"I really wish you'd reconsider about that Hillie, but what does a mother know——" her mother's voice followed her out the curtained door into the streets. Molly shook her head because she was really tired of hearing the same old song and dance.

She felt her shoes sinking into the mud as she walked towards the gates watching the children, who ran by holding toy guns made from trash. They went scurrying over piles of rubbish and ran into houses made from aluminum siding, calling out to each other as they laughed and played. Molly couldn't help but wish for their innocent wonder instead of the cold reality of what surrounded her. She sighed, looking around at the Slum district. Seeing all the rundown buildings, the muddy streets, and the poverty that filled this district of the great city behind the wall, she just wanted to escape.

She looked up at the massive buildings beyond the gates seeing the way that they gleamed brightly in the sunlight. Those buildings weren't made of aluminum siding, she thought sourly. No, the Hill's massive towers were made of steel and they gleamed because the clean windows of the buildings reflected light. Their streets weren't filled with piles of rubbish, and their fancy tech allowed them to lead very different lives. Molly stared at the shining example of the differences between the Slum district and the Hills, trying not to allow her resentment take over. The Hillies treated them like lepers, always looking down on them just because they

Michelle Woods

were born in a lower class. She shook her head, trying to clear her envious thoughts. This line of thinking wasn't helping her get to work on time.

She headed to the barrier between the Slums and the Hill districts. As her boots made wet plunks in the mud, the early morning light bouncing off the buildings nearly blinded her. She crossed to the gate where she entered and stepped onto the cobblestone road leading into one of the twenty cubicles where she was scanned every morning for germs, vermin, and weapons before she was allowed to enter the Hills. Scanning her badge, she waited impatiently for the machine's lasers to move from her head to her toes.

A mechanical voice chimed in an annoying whine, "Slum Mechanic 452 free from germs, now cleared for entry. Proceed to manual inspection." Molly gritted her teeth upon hearing the whiny computer pronounce her fit to step into the Hill.

Screw you too, she thought petulantly.

Stepping out into the second area of clearance, a small courtyard, she glanced around. Slum district workers were waiting in the small courtyard beyond the entrance gate and were forming a line. Molly sighed as she walked towards the second gate, her mind wandering.

Spotting her friend Racheal, a busty blonde with a dynamite figure covered by a similar pair of green coveralls, Molly sucked in a quick breath, envy eating her up. She didn't have any baggy areas that made her look dumpy in her uniform. Racheal was just stepping out of the cubicle to her right. Seeing Molly, she smiled and waved before coming over to greet her.

"Hey Doll, I hate these early shifts. I wanted to work nights, but the lottery gave me this shift again. How was this morning with your mum?" Racheal questioned with a knowing look.

Taming Lucca

Molly let out a heavy sigh, her shoulders drooping.

"You know mother. She was trying to convince me to stay home again. Ugg—I don't know why she can't just stop with this don't date him crap. 'He's a bird, you're a fish.' It's all crap. I know why she really wants me to stop dating him." Molly mocked her mother in a high nasally voice that she knew sounded nothing like her but it made Molly feel better. She again looked at Racheal's uniform and her blue eyes narrowed. "I really hate how great you look in these damned coveralls, you know," Molly muttered as they moved up in line as the person in front of them stepped forward.

"Yep, I know it," Racheal said, preening a bit. "You know your mother is just thinking of you getting hurt and that's what causes her to act that way," she added with obvious disbelief in her tone of voice. Racheal had been her friend for over six years and she knew that Molly's mother didn't care for much other than her father and the Hills.

"Ha, my mother cares for little that doesn't affect her. The only reason she cares at all about me and Luzen is because if I do marry him then I would be living better than her, and she can't stand that. I know she's always trying to pretend she's better than everyone else in the Slums because her mother was a whore who got pregnant with a Hillie's baby," Molly hissed, quietly venting while scowling at her friend, who smiled with delight at the angry outburst and slung her arm over Molly's shoulders.

"Okay, okay, I know she isn't a warm fuzzy type, but I'm sure she loves you and wants you to be happy," Racheal said, although Molly could tell she didn't believe it any more than Molly did by her tone. They moved again with the line of people waiting to be allowed into the building two at a time for manual inspections. After a few minutes, they finally reached the front of the line. "Maybe really deep down," Molly said,

Michelle Woods

her eyes rolling because it wasn't very likely that it was true.

They had arrived at the front of the line and she showed her ID badge to a guard who inspected it with a scanner before returning it, and said in a firm voice "Clear 452."

Molly stepped into the building, entering the left door. She grinned when she met Lt. Tucker's smiling blue eyes surrounded by bushy white brows as she walked towards him. Carl Tucker had been a handsome man when he was younger and it showed in his handsome face and wide shoulders. He was her favorite guard, a man in his late fifties with gray hair and a slightly heavy frame; he was always friendly and seemed to love his job.

He'd been recently promoted to Lieutenant within the guard, as the two new stripes on his right shoulder denoted. He wore a white shirt and black slacks, the uniform all the guards wore, complete with a stun stick and laser gun attached to his utility belt.

"Hey, I thought you weren't doing entry scans since your promotion?" Molly questioned as she raised her arms to allow him to scan her again with the wand scanner.

"Well, they were short-staffed, and I wanted to slip you that manual I promised."

Lt. Tucker reached into his back pocket and discreetly pulled out an old manual for a turbine engine. This was her secret passion, and she had about thirty-five of these old manuals stashed away at home.

Carl knew about her obsession, having discovered her rummaging through some old manuals a few years ago in the office of an abandoned building in the Hill district. That first meeting could have gone very badly had Carl not been the kind man he was. He could have arrested her and she might have been tossed outside into the wild territory beyond the wall. She felt a shiver run up her spine at the thought.

Taming Lucca

Reaching out she took the manual from him, looking down at it in fascination.

"Oh, I love it. Thanks," she said, stuffing it gently into her coveralls. "How's Berta doing?"

"Purring like a kitten after you finished fixing her. I took her for a spin outside the wall just yesterday," he whispered to her as he finished scanning her.

"Well, keep her tuned like I showed you and she'll be fine."

Feeling better after talking to Carl, Molly moved to the exit as another man entered through the door behind her. She walked out into the hall from the little room with a wave over her shoulder. Berta was Carl's sweet Harley fat boy, which had been built back in the 2000's. It was a pre-disaster motorcycle. The man loved older technology as much as she did.

"Clear mechanic 452," Carl called out to the computer when she reached the door, which let out a loud click as it unlocked, and she left the small room and headed to the water plant.

Chapter 2

Molly spent the rest of the day working on one mechanical breakdown after another. She glared into the toolbox as she replaced the wrench she'd been using to tighten the bolts on the generator because nothing seemed to want to work properly today. As soon as she managed to get one mechanical issue fixed, another popped up, worse than the last. It was as if the machines were trying to side with Molly's mother to prevent her from meeting Luzen for their date at six. By noon she was exhausted. That was when the airflow generator decided to break down.

She'd requested parts for it over three weeks ago, and they still weren't in. It was hard to fix the machine without the required hoses. Molly bit the inside of her cheek, her frustration mounting. She went on a search for something she could use to make the repair at least temporarily. Entering the cleaning closet, she found some tubes and decided they would work. She used them to patch the one that busted, but she knew it was only a temporary fix.

Molly wiped her brow with a greasy hand, smearing it with a dark smudge. She was glad that she'd finally managed to get the machine fixed, although without those hoses, the patch she'd done wouldn't last a week. Getting to her feet, she tossed the tools back into her box and checked the time.

Crap, she only had ten minutes to get to the dock where she was to meet Luzen. She tossed the toolbox back on its shelf in the hallway before running to the employee bathroom where she quickly changed into a clean pair of coveralls from the employee locker and washed her face.

She lifted her hands, trying to tame her hair back into what had once been a very attractive twist but was now a mass of frizzy black hair piled on top of her head. She attempted to smooth it back into the twist for about three minutes. Finally giving up, she quickly pulled it down and braided it, all the while bemoaning the loss of the cuteness she'd created with the twist she had perfected for an hour that morning. She glared at her reflection. She should have brought her mascara, she thought, noticing with dismay that she had washed it off with the grease a few moments ago.

Molly checked the time again and seeing that she only had three minutes left to get to the dock, she let out a groan. This would have to do, she decided, because there was nothing she could do to fix the way she looked in time to meet Luzen. Sighing, she went tearing out of the bathroom and sprinting towards the dock.

Luzen stood by a hover car taxi looking at his watch; she ran down the ramp to meet him.

"Sorry, the airflow water generator was acting up again. Any idea when the parts will be in? It won't last much longer without them," she asked breathlessly, coming to a stop beside him.

"Molly, my dear, no need to apologize. A good work ethic is one of the things I love about you. Don't you look lovely." He smiled and kissed her on the cheek. Molly felt a light blush stain her cheeks at the compliment.

Luzen continued. "And I have no idea when the parts will

Michelle Woods

be in. They can't even be ordered until Thornton Davis takes a look at the generator to verify your assessment."

He waved her into the waiting taxi not even noticing the tensing of her shoulders as anger filled her. Molly knew she was a damned good mechanic and the idea that someone had to verify her assessment made her want to punch something. It was one of the things that maddened her about the plant's Hillie management. Any part a Slum worker requested for the water plant had to be verified by a Hill mechanic before the parts were ordered.

It was beyond stupid because half of the mechanics from the Hill had been trained by the Slum mechanics to start with. Trying not to allow her anger to show, she spoke carefully.

"Thanks. I'm just wondering when he would be coming for the review. We could lose that generator and then there would be a shortage of fresh water for the Hill." Or more likely the Slums, thought Molly sourly, her hands balling on the seat beside her.

The hover car flew towards the lower Hill restaurant and bar sector. Luzen patted her hand as if she were a child, his smile a little indulgent when he informed her, "Not to worry, my dear, it will be soon enough. Now, let me tell you about my day. We had our manager meeting today and they talked of increasing the wage for Slum workers by two credits per week, isn't that wonderful."

Molly bit her tongue to keep from yelling at him. Two credits would not make the fifteen a week they were currently earning a fair wage for any of the mechanics on her team. It would maybe buy one meal for most of their families. Molly unclenched her fists, trying to regain control over her rioting emotions because many of them had three or four children to feed.

When everything you earned went to fill your belly, birth

control, which was fifteen credits every few months, was too costly. Molly should know, she'd taken a chance on more than one occasion because she didn't have the credits for the birth control shots. Two credits wouldn't do much to help them provide for their families and it was quite frankly insulting that Luzen thought this was good news.

If the managers would raise it to ten credits as the teams had asked, it would make life less stressful for many of the workers at the plant. It was hardly an unreasonable wage to ask for when the managers made a thousand credits a week. The wage difference was supposed to be because the cost of living was so much higher in the Hill district than it was in the Slums. Gritting her teeth, she realized this was one thing she hated about Luzen. He had an utter lack of understanding of what life in the Slum district was really like.

"That's nice," she replied to avoid a fight on the night he might be proposing. Barely able to control the need to throw something at him for being so clueless, she tried to smile, but was sure it looked more like a grimace.

"Yes, I know it's much lower than they requested, but it is progress, right?" He beamed as if she should be grateful for the pittance.

"Progress. Right." Molly knew by his frown that she hadn't been successful in keeping her irritation with him from her tone. Smiling brightly to lighten the tension, she placed her hand over his, even as her stomach burned in anger and her mind screamed that it wasn't progress so much as a way for them to keep the classes separated. He lost his frown as the car came to a gliding halt outside of a restaurant called Crave. He assisted her from the car, leading her to the door and holding it open for her to enter ahead of him.

The restaurant was made of red brick with little windows that looked out into the streets of the city. Molly felt a little

Michelle Woods

thrill because the small tables she could see through the window were cozy and romantic. They entered to find a small hall lit with little candle lights along the walls and red floral wallpaper. Molly realized with glee that it must be a pre-disaster design. She loved the old fashioned designs the best because the newer ones were too static, usually done in grey tones that left much to be desired. Molly felt Luzen take her elbow, guiding her along to the podium when she stopped to look at a painting on the wall. A woman watched them approach. Molly was too busy looking around the room at tables with their white cloths and the little candle lights to notice the frown of disapproval the woman gave them.

"A table for two, please," Luzen told the woman behind the podium when they neared it.

Molly's attention was drawn back to the podium by her haughty-voiced reply. Molly almost felt the way the woman looked her up and then back down with contempt before turning to stare at Luzen with a sour expression.

"I'm afraid that we do not serve Slum workers here, sir."

Luzen looked puzzled, his brow furrowed as he scratched his neck, seemingly unable to fathom the woman's reply. Molly lips pressed into a tight line. She was so tired of being treated like she was less than others because she was born in the Slum district; it was maddeningly annoying.

"I see. Well then, where would you suggest we eat then?" he asked, his face contorted with a look of true bewilderment. Molly glared at him, her mind unwilling to accept the fact that he didn't have a clue that it was wrong that she couldn't eat here because of where she lived.

"That place next door serves them if you want to take her there, it's less——" she paused. "Upscale," she finally settled for with a sneer.

"Ah, very good, then we shall go there," Luzen said, unfazed by the woman's obvious snobbery. Molly was infuriated with the injustice of the treatment. She felt her teeth ache because her jaw was clenched so hard.

"Well, my dear, I had hoped to show you my favorite restaurant. But it can't be helped. We will have a lovely dinner at the small diner next door instead." He took her arm and began guiding her out the door. Molly wanted to protest the treatment she'd received. To rant at the woman or at the very least tell her to go to hell, but she didn't want to ruin their night so she allowed him to lead her away instead. Her head pounded with the knowledge that Luzen hadn't even bothered to protest the way she'd been treated.

Molly tried not to allow her anger to get the best of her. It wasn't that he didn't care, it was that he had been raised believing that this type of treatment of Slum district citizens was normal. It would be different when she was his wife, she was sure of it. He wouldn't allow such insults to be levied against her once they were married. Satisfied with her train of thought and glad that she hadn't let her mouth run away with her, she walked into the door that Luzen held for her at the diner next door.

Molly noticed immediately that it was definitely not upscale. The paint looked old with several spots that needed retouching. She had seen places in similar states of disrepair in the upper Slums, which was really the whore district. This was still better than anything the Slums had to offer, though. They walked towards the back when told by a gruff man to sit wherever. Luzen chose a booth along the wall near the small counter.

A woman in a red apron came over, barely glancing at them as she demanded, "Whatcha want?" She then seemed to remember something and said "Oh ya, the special is fish soup with crackers."

Michelle Woods

"Hmm, Molly will be having the special and I'll have a steak medium with potatoes, please," Luzen replied for her, looking at the menu.

"Drinks?" the woman probed.

"Ah yes, water for the lady and I'll have a lemonade."

"Ten minutes then," the waitress grunted, then turned and walked away.

A little surprised and frustrated that he hadn't bothered to ask her what she wanted, Molly plastered on a fake smile and lectured herself that he was being polite. He was probably embarrassed about what had happened at Crave a few moments ago. She needed to relax and enjoy having real food; at least it wasn't oatmeal.

After that the dinner seemed to be flowing smoothly. The conversation streamed naturally and everything seemed to be back on track for him to propose. The special was actually quite good, and she ate it with gusto while they talked. She laughed at a story he told about a lost part that was found on the roof of a building nearby where a parts delivery man had left it on his lunch break.

Luzen excused himself from the table after they had eaten to use the restroom. Molly sat back looking around the room at the tacky décor. It was mostly gaudy art and odd little sayings that were pinned up all around the little diner.

When she looked towards the door she saw a woman dressed in a sleek red dress and heels sitting in the booth behind theirs. She was chatting loudly with her friend. Molly tried to ignore their conversation but the woman was so loud that she couldn't tune it out. What she heard caused anger to boil up inside her, reaching the point when she knew her mouth was going to get her into trouble because she'd had enough contempt directed her way for one night.

"Did you see her outfit? So common. If I were her, I'd be

Taming Lucca

embarrassed. I can't believe that someone let her in here. How dare they allow Slummies to eat here at a proper establishment? I bet she steals something before she leaves, and it will serve them right."

Molly's hands dug into the plastic table holding it so tightly that she could see her fingers turning white. Even as she lectured herself to just let it go, she knew she couldn't. Molly took one more deep breath, trying to make herself agree that they weren't worth it. She knew, even as she stood and moved to stand beside their table, that she was making a mistake. But she was tired of the treatment she'd been getting all night from these stuck-up people who thought they were better than her because they were born in the Hill district. She just couldn't take any more of it without saying something.

"Excuse me, is there a problem?" Molly asked the women snidely.

Red's face contorted into a snarl and she looked down her nose at Molly before asking coldly, "How dare you talk to me? You are not worth my time and you certainly shouldn't be allowed in here. Let's go, Tara. This is beyond unseemly." Tara, a little brunette wearing three inch heels and a sheath dress in gold, glared at Molly with disdain and stood.

"Indeed, let's leave. This place has gotten very Slum like."

"That's funny, that was just what I thought when the two of you entered." Molly smiled sweetly at the brunette.

Yep, her mouth was going to get her into trouble again. She really needed to learn to put a muzzle on it.

"Well! I never. How dare..." Red screeched.

"Is there a problem here, ladies?" interrupted a gruff male voice from behind Molly, who still stood near the table the two women had vacated. A dark light of glee entered Red's eyes as she moved around Molly and clung to the arm of the man who had spoken.

Michelle Woods

"Oh, thank goodness you're here, sir. This creature has stolen my credits. It was horrible." Molly had turned to look at the woman, who was simpering to the rotund man who had spoken to her and Luzen when they arrived. When he talked, the fat jowls that hung from his face wiggled. She was watching Red and didn't notice that Tara had slipped a wallet into her pocket. Her mouth hung open at the woman's bold-faced lie.

"Sir, that's not true. This woman is making that up. I am not a thief," Molly cried, outraged at their gall. Moving forward a few feet, she looked at the man who was clucking to Red, who still seemed to be distressed. Knowing that she hadn't stolen anything, she didn't know what the woman thought she would accomplish with this display.

"Well then, you won't mind if he searches you, will you?" asked Tara from behind her as she moved to stand by her friend. She really should have guessed what was about to happen next but she wasn't thinking clearly.

"Fine," Molly replied, holding her arms out.

She was grateful that she'd left the illegal manual at work in her locker. The manager extracted himself from Red to check her pockets. He walked over, giving her a once-over with his beady little eyes before he began patting her pockets. She was surprised to see him pull a red wallet out of her lower back coverall pocket. Molly stared in open-mouthed horror at the red wallet.

How had that gotten into her pocket?

When her gaze met Red's, she saw the delight on her face, and with a sinking feeling in her stomach she knew they had planted it on her. What was she going to do now, she wondered.

"This looks a little better than you can afford, miss," the man growled.

Taming Lucca

Filled with horror and fear when she realized how poorly this looked, Molly stuttered, "I–I didn't ta–take that! One of them must have slipped it into my pocket. I'm not a thie––,"

He didn't look convinced and Molly could feel the panic inside her begin to rise. If she was arrested for stealing they would throw her outside the wall and that was a fate worse than death. Everyone knew that outside the wall was a lawless hellhole filled with criminals and murderers and Molly didn't want to be tossed to them because these two bitches accused her of stealing.

"That's enough. We don't allow thieves in here," he interrupted gruffly, his eyes narrowing to beady slits. "Rhonda, call the guards," he yelled to the waitress who'd served her and Luzen their dinner.

Molly watched in horror as she took out her phone to begin dialing. She was getting ready to bolt when he grabbed her arm in a bruising hold and began dragging Molly towards the back where there was a door marked employees only. She fought, pulling against his hold, still trying to explain that she had not taken that wallet.

"Wh-whats going on here?" Luzen asked, having returned from the restroom.

Molly's shoulders sagged and she stopped fighting the man and almost began crying in relief. Luzen would get this mess straightened out. After all, he loved her. He would know that she hadn't stolen anything and fix this mess.

"Luzen…" Molly began but was cut off by the manager's gruff voice.

"It seems your date has robbed this woman." The rotund man gestured towards Red, who was still pretending to cry on her friend's shoulder.

Molly almost rolled her eyes at the crocodile tears the woman was shedding. It was ridiculous and she couldn't

Michelle Woods

believe that the idiot who worked here had fallen for them. It really went to show that some men let sexy attire convince them to believe anything.

"I did not! Luzen, you know I would never steal," she told him, outrage at the accusations levied against her evident in her tone. Tugging against the painful hold on her arm, she desperately tried to escape the man's grip.

"My dear, I——" Luzen stared in horror at her before he looked at Red crying in her friend's arms, seeming unsure how to respond. He shifted from one foot to the other, his face contorted with an unknown emotion. He seemed at a loss and Molly wondered how even after all the time they had spent together he was unsure how to react to this situation. It made her seriously rethink the idea of marrying him.

"I removed the wallet from her myself. She stole it," the man holding her said, still slowly tugging her towards that door in the back.

"Look—you know I didn't steal it, Luzen," Molly said before crying out in pain when he tightened his hold on her arm and jerked hard. He was steadily dragging her towards that room off to the side of the counter marked employees only despite her resistance.

She saw Luzen's eyes fall on Red, who had turned. His eyes were pinned to the front of her low cut dress. Red got an evil gleam in her eyes then before she wrapped her arms around her waist, pushing her breasts up, almost revealing her nipples. Molly couldn't believe that the hussy was trying that trick.

Surely Luzen wouldn't fall for that?

He stared at the woman in the red dress, watching her breasts heave with her pretend sobs. Molly watched him swallow, and she saw him subtly adjust his member that she could see was hardened. "Molly, I'm shocked. I can't believe that you would do such a thing," he said, never taking his eyes off those large breasts that bitch was using to ruin Molly's life. How the hell was this even happening? How were men so stupid when it came to fancy clothing and big boobs?

Luzen seemed mesmerized by the woman's tits and began moving toward Red, saying in a mollifying tone, "My dear, please don't cry."

Molly couldn't believe that he was comforting that woman with lust in his eyes while she was getting dragged away so they could lock her up.

How dare he!

How could he say that he loved her and then look at that woman while she was in danger? Then suddenly he was looking back at her and she saw that his lip was curled with contempt. Her mind reeled as she watched him wrinkle his nose in aversion. But even that didn't prepare her for the blow of his next words.

"I should have listened to mother about you, Molly. She insisted you Slum workers were no better than the ones who live in that squalor refusing to better themselves. And to think that I was going to ask you to meet my mother to prove that it wasn't true. I'm disgusted."

Luzen then took the woman into his arms, hugging her, rubbing her back and telling Red that it would be okay. Molly saw the little smile that Red hid in his shoulder as she pretended to whimper and cry like a baby. She was sure that Red could feel his hardened member pressing into her as he glued himself to her. Rage poured through her veins as she realized that this was not going to end well for her.

The sight of him pressing against another woman while she was in trouble destroyed her. Had the last months meant nothing to him? Didn't he know her better than this? She was supposed to marry him. Her chaotic mind ran over the

Michelle Woods

time they'd spent together over the past months and she was shocked that he was treating her this way. That was when she focused on his last words to her.

Wait, had he said meet his mother?

Impotent rage filled her when she realized that's what this date tonight had been about, not as she had thought, a proposal, but meeting his mother.

How could this be happening to her? She couldn't believe that she was being locked up all because even when she knew she should have, she hadn't shut up and ignored the two women. How could Luzen think that she could be a thief after ten months spent as her lover?

"I'm not a thief," Molly screamed as the manager thrust her towards the room, still holding her arm. The woman who'd been their waitress opened the door to the room, and the man shoved her towards it. She almost fell from the forceful push he gave her towards the now open door. Desperate, she glanced at Luzen again, sure she'd heard wrong. He couldn't believe that she was a thief, could he?

When her eyes landed on Luzen her breath froze inside her chest. He was holding the woman in the red dress, patting and rubbing her back, and she was rubbing against him. Molly could hear him murmuring to her softly in a tone she knew well from their time together. Disbelief hit her hard, making her stumble when the fat cook shoved her again.

"My dear, don't cry, I'm so sorry. This is awful. I should have listened to my mother about her. She acted so sweet. I just don't understand––" Whatever he finished that with was lost in the shuffle as the cook shoved her into what appeared to be the cleaning closet and she stumbled, falling against a shelf.

He slammed the door as she made a mad dash towards it, only to smack against the closed door. Feelings of desperation consumed her because she had no idea what to do. She was trapped in a room with no windows and no way out except a locked door. Molly knew that she didn't want to wait for that door to be opened by a guard. If that happened, then she was going to jail. She began screaming out her innocence as she pounded on the door.

"Let me out. I didn't do it—please, let me out—please."

Molly pounded her fist on the door for over ten minutes with tears streaming down her face. When her hand began to ache and she knew they weren't going to let her out, she fell to the floor. Her voice was hoarse and her hand stung from beating on the door for so long. Her arm throbbed where the man had grabbed her and she looked at it through her tears. It was bruised already and Molly felt a hiccupping cry slip out.

Tonight wasn't supposed to be dismal like it was turning out to be. She'd thought that she would be engaged by the end of the evening and instead she was sitting on a cold concrete floor. It didn't look like she would be getting out of the Slums any time soon.

Molly knew that by now the guard was on their way here to pick her up and that meant she was going to be thrown into prison. She didn't want to be thrown out of the city into the lawlessness that existed in that world. Being thrown out of the gates into a world filled with bikers and other criminals wasn't something she could fathom.

"Please," she begged leaning against the door, knowing no one cared, her heart filled with hopeless despair. Molly sobbed so hard her chest ached and when the guards came she was too upset to even try to escape.

Chapter 3

Lucca "Bone" Brighton stared at the little putz. Bone eyed the man, seeing that he was wearing a button-up shirt and khaki slacks with a freaking belt. The buttons on his shirt were done up to the top and Bone would bet his life that the man hadn't been laid in years. The little fucker was trying to tell him that the load of food they'd just brought in wasn't good enough. Bone looked at Tank to see if this was really happening because he was surely dreaming this. No one told the Red Devils that whatever they brought to the table wasn't good enough. Certainly not a suited up snob without the sense God gave a peanut.

Tank just shook his head and ran a hand over his face to hide the slight smile he was wearing when he noticed Bone's frustration with the man. Bone glared at him for a moment before looking back at the whiney son of a bitch who stood before him. He really needed to get the hell away from this place. The fuckers who hid behind that wall were all a bunch of pansy-assed idiots.

"Well, I can't authorize a full payment for your inferior goods, you understand," the little man was saying with a sly look on his face.

To be fair, at six three a lot of people were little to him, but

Taming Lucca

this guy barely reached his chest. Bone wondered if he knew how close he was to eating a bullet as he stood there with that look on his face. Running a hand through his brown hair with a slight nod to Tiny, who was in the bed of the truck, he shook his head at the man.

"All right then," he said, watching the man smile in glee, thinking he'd just negotiated a lesser price from the Red Devils. Shit, the little bastard had no idea who he was fucking with right now. It was sad really that the man didn't have a clue what was about to go down. Tiny covered the bed and jumped down, signaling Reina, who was driving the truck, to pack it up. His men started their bikes, and he headed towards his bike, Tank and Tiny walking ahead of him.

"Wait, where are you going?" Mr. Putz asked.

"Taking my inferior goods home. Wouldn't want to burden you with them," Bone said as he continued to walk away.

"But––but we agreed to a lower price for those goods," the little man stuttered out as he followed Bone towards his bike. Fuck, the putz must have a death wish because annoying Bone took life duration to zero quick. Bone made it a point to never take anyone's bullshit, ever.

"Nope, you said your piece, and now I'm leaving," he said flatly. He was almost to his bike, and if that little fucker was still on his tail when he reached it, he might just kill him even though he would probably regret it afterward. After all he wasn't a complete asshole, he just didn't put up with anyone's shit.

"No, wait, we'll pay full price. Please wait, we can't have a shortage," the little man whined.

"Great," Bone replied and he whistled for them to stop leaving and start unloading this crap so they could get the hell away from this place. The people who lived behind that wall were hiding from the world and thought they were special

Michelle Woods

with only that little bit of life. He didn't know how they could stand it being cooped up behind those walls, never venturing out to see the world. He couldn't imagine never seeing the world or riding his bike down a lonely highway just feeling the wind and the vibrations of the engine beneath him. It was unfathomable.

He loved being with the club, but sometimes a man just needed to ride. How they could stay in that high-walled prison and think they were living life to the fullest even with all their tech was beyond him. Heck, if it wasn't for the Red Devils MC, those idiots behind the wall might have to come outside the walls to actually work the land for their food, and that would be tragic. He waited near his bike, feeling impatient to get the fuck out of here, and let Tank take care of the money. This place made his skin crawl with all the fences and the button-ups. Bone shifted, pacing back and forth in front of the bikes waiting on Tank to get the credits.

"Bone, we're set. Tank got the payday," Rash called as he exited the small cubicle that housed the office where payment was rendered.

"Let's ride," Bone barked to his brothers before he climbed on his bike and roared out. Tank pulled up close not long after, and they all headed home. He knew they were as ready to get back to the clubhouse as he was. Church was tomorrow, but tonight was a celebration. Dog had decided to marry his old lady after two years. It wasn't what Bone would want for himself, but if it made Dog happy he was all for it. An old lady and marriage weren't for him though.

Nope, he liked having his freedom. That way he could bang whoever he liked, whenever he liked.

And since he'd never understood how a man could break the woman he professed to love by cheating like his old man had, there'd be no old lady for him. He'd watched his dad do it to his mother, one of the sweetest women he'd ever met, over and over. It had broken her heart a little more every time. He could still remember lying awake at night listening to his mother cry in great wrenching sobs when his father chose to stay at the club rather than come home with them. When he was young Bone hadn't known what made his mother cry like her heart was breaking but once he was old enough to understand, he had hated his father for it.

He'd promised himself on one of those nights when he was fifteen that he'd never do that to a woman he cared for, not ever. He knew that his father had loved his mama, but he'd promised over and over that he wouldn't fuck around again. Then a month or sometimes only days later he'd be back at the club with a sweetbutt doing it again.

Bone knew he was cut from the same cloth because no woman had held his attention for long. He still took that vow he'd made seriously so there would be no old lady for him unless he was willing to give up all other women for her, and that was not likely to happen.

Bone pulled up in front of the clubhouse. Damn, he wished these heavy thoughts weren't running through his head today. Both his parents were long gone now anyway.

Climbing off his bike, he looked off in the direction his parents' cabin had been before he burned it down one night while he was drunk and pissed off that they were gone. His mother had died from cancer ten years ago. The cancer had been stage four by the time the doctors had found it. Even though there was a cure for it, she'd died before they could get the drugs that would have cured the disease back to her.

Bone's father had worked his ass off to get those drugs but after the disaster, some drugs needed to treat illnesses were only available in the city behind the wall. They had stockpiles of drugs in that place, with cures for everything from cancer

Michelle Woods

to Ebola, as well as the equipment to make more of each drug. They didn't share the information or the drugs, and if you couldn't pay the price then you were expected to just die from whatever disease you had.

When they took her to the hospital in the city to find out why she wasn't getting any better, the doctors had offered to heal her. Of course, the treatment was only offered for the right amount of credits, and his father, Tailchaser, hadn't had the credits. Bone and Tailchaser had raced to get the credits, trying to get them back to his mother in time to save her life, but it wasn't meant to be and she had died before they arrived with the payload. It still made him ache when he thought about it. He missed her every day, but he wondered what she would think of the life he now led. He was sure she would have wanted him to get an old lady and settle down by now. He felt a grin split his face when that thought burst to life inside him.

His thoughts circled around to his father, his eyes moving over the burnt rubble as he clenched his fists. Tailchaser had never been the same after Bone's mother had died; he'd taken more risks and drank heavily. What had surprised Bone was the man never touched another woman after his mother died, which hadn't made a damned bit of sense. He died two years later when the Jackals had started the turf war over Juice, a designer drug the Jackals made and sold. They wanted to run it through the Devils' territory, but drugs were not something the Devils allowed in their town. Yeah, the Devils were assholes, but they didn't run drugs anymore.

When the world first went to shit, the Red Devils had done whatever was necessary to make sure the club survived. But now that they were settled, they didn't work the drugs anymore because it was just bad for business. Some of their affiliated clubs still ran the stuff, but the Devils didn't want

Taming Lucca

that shit around their families.

Damn, Bone thought as he ran a hand through his hair trying to wipe these thoughts away, he needed to get laid; that would take his mind off this shit. Walking into the clubhouse with Tank and Tiny, he looked around, smiling. The women had transformed the club while they were gone.

The chairs were in the main room and arranged in rows, with an aisle that was covered with pieces of red and black cloth in long strips. They were sewn together to make a runner down the middle of the aisle. An arch that had been made forty years ago by Duck for his old lady when they got married was up in front of the fireplace. Some of the brothers or prospects must have helped with that chore as that thing weighed at least three hundred pounds and there was no way the women were strong enough to have carried that. There were flowers from Aunt Mae's garden woven around the arch in reds and whites.

Damn, their women were amazing; they always took care of their own. He sure hoped they would have a feast ready for the bonfire tonight after the wedding. He loved Aunt Mae's cooking and couldn't wait to see what mouthwatering dish she'd come up with for the event. Tank went to a couch that was pushed against the wall and plopped down with a sigh, his freakishly long legs stretched out in front of him

"Shit, this is pretty. I can feel the estrogen taking up all the air in here," Tank muttered in a disgusted tone. "Hope Dog can still get it up after he spends a few hours in this mess."

"Shut the fuck up, Tank. I have no problems with my dick, asshole," Dog said as he came out from the game room above them.

He was already dressed in a button-up and slacks instead of his normal jeans and t-shirt combo. Dog was leaning over the banister to yell at Tank, his eyes narrowed and his hair wild as

Michelle Woods

if he'd run his hands through it several times. Bone wondered if he was nervous about the wedding. He knew he sure as hell would be if he was in Dog's shoes. That thought made him let out a light snort because that was never going to happen he knew; he just wasn't the type.

"Ah…the proud groom. If you can't get it up tonight and Terry's horny, I'll be happy to help ya out," Tank thundered, looking up and waggling his eyebrows at Dog, who hung over the railing yelling.

"Just fucking try it, asswipe. My girl would take your nuts off." Pride filled Dog's voice as he came down the stairs towards them, stopping beside the couch and leaning on the wall with his hands in his front pockets.

"She's already got yours. What's she need mine for?" Tank was laughing as he took in the look on Dog's face, which now sported a dark glower complete with tightly clenched jaw and a glare that should have fried him on the spot. Tank didn't seem to be fazed by the look as he continued to shake with mirth.

"Damn it. Take that back." Dog stood straight, and stared at Tank, who was laughing so hard, he was almost rolling around on the large couch.

"Shit, if I didn't know better I'd say Tank has a thing for Dog's balls," Tiny chimed in from the bar, where he sat leaning back against it. His eyes where focused on the fight that was quickly brewing between Tank and Dog. Bone let a small smile curl his lips because Tiny always knew what to do to diffuse situations like this; it was one thing he loved about the man.

Tank stopped laughing, sitting up to glare at Tiny. He was getting up off the couch likely to punch Tiny when Aunt Mae peeked out of the club's kitchen door at them.

"Stop running your flaps, and go get washed up for the

wedding. You all need to be here in forty minutes. I want you fresh as new flowers," Aunt Mae called from the kitchen, causing all four men to look sheepish. None of them had realized that she was even in the clubhouse. Shit, Dog better hope Terry wasn't in there with her or Dog's balls really would be in Terry's pocket.

"Shit," said Tank, standing up quickly, his gaze no longer focused on Tiny.

Aunt Mae had practically raised him after his mother had died when he was ten. He nearly ran to do her bidding. He was always like that with Aunt Mae. When she told him to jump, he asked how high and proceeded to follow her instructions to the letter. It was funny as hell, but Bone couldn't blame him; if his mama was still alive he would likely do the same with her.

Followed by the laughter of the rest of them, Tank jerked out the door with an obscene gesture over his shoulder. The rest of them left the club for their respective cabins, while Dog went back upstairs to one of the bedrooms in the clubhouse to finish getting ready. He'd stayed there last night at Terry's insistence so he wouldn't see his bride before the wedding.

Twenty minutes later, Bone stood before the slightly fogged mirror in his bathroom combing his hair with a bit of gel to keep it neat. He'd pulled on a pair of black slacks, a white dress shirt, and his colors. Setting the comb down, he tugged at the collar trying to loosen it without unbuttoning the top button. He hated wearing this fancy dress up shit. It always made him feel like he was caged or hemmed in. Bone tugged harder, finally giving up when it didn't help. He didn't want to rip the damned shirt before the wedding because he only owned one. Only for one of his brothers would he wear this

Michelle Woods

stupid crap, he thought with disdain. Hell, at least it wasn't a suit.

Dog was wearing one with his colors on over the suit coat because his old lady had asked him to wear one today. Dog wouldn't deny Terry anything; that woman made him too happy. Yes, Terry did have his balls in a jar somewhere, but Dog didn't give a fuck. It was a beautiful thing when a man gave his old lady the respect she deserved. So yeah, he would wear a dress shirt and honor his brother's choice to marry his old lady. He grinned to himself when he thought it because respecting his brother's choice didn't mean they wouldn't give Dog shit about his balls.

Checking his appearance, he had to admit he looked damned good even if he did feel like he was wearing a monkey suit. He ran his hand down his clean-shaven jaw checking for missed spots. Finding none, he left the bathroom.

Time to get this shit on the road, he thought as he headed out his cabin door to head to the clubhouse. Pulling up outside the clubhouse, he climbed off his bike seeing Trick a few feet away in a similar get-up. Bone wasn't surprised that Trick didn't look any happier than he did in the tightly buttoned clothing. None of them wore this shit unless they had to, unlike those dickheads who lived in the ivory tower beyond the wall. He grinned, walking beside Trick up the porch steps and stopping near the door, waiting on the women coming up the steps behind them.

"Heard about the putz. Surprised he isn't dead." Trick laughed as he held the door for Brandy, Stick's old lady.

Bone was too distracted to answer Trick for a moment when he noticed how weary Brandy looked. About to ask what was wrong, he noticed Stick talking to a sweetbutt near the corral where the cows were munching grass. Damn, that was a disaster waiting to happen, he observed as he watched

Taming Lucca

Brandy walk into the clubhouse with a small pained smile and a stiff back, while pointedly ignoring the scene nearby. Those two were hopeless, like his mama and dad had been, he thought with contempt.

"Yeah, it was hard to let him keep breathing. If he'd walked to the bike, I was gonna take his head off with the twenty," Bone finally answered Trick when he was able to pull his attention away from an almost instant replay of his fucked up family's past.

Bone looked farther down the walkway and saw Stacy, Lisa and Reina coming from the row of cabins that most of the club members lived in. Bone nodded to them and Trick shook his head. The two of them waited, holding the door for the ladies and then entering after them while they chatted about the run.

Inside, the clubhouse was filled with people who were standing around chatting or drinking beers while waiting for the wedding to start. A couple of the prospects were hanging around on the porch near the door talking. Bone nodded to them before he entered and headed upstairs to find Dog and Tank. Along the way he nodded or spoke to brothers, old ladies, and some of the kids. The kids ran around laughing while Aunt Mae and Katie chased them. They would be herded away after the wedding for their own party. The bonfire party was only for club members, prospects, some of the old ladies who would go with their old men, and the sweetbutts who kept the men entertained.

He finally made it to the stairs, taking them two at a time, and entered the game room where Dog was lounging on a couch smoking a cigar.

Tank stood near a large pool table laughing while he and Dog smoked. "That's true, we all hate these damned monkey suits. Shit, if you'd get your balls outta that jar she's got them

Michelle Woods

in, we'd all be better off."

Tank wore a button-up shirt too, except he had rolled up the sleeves to show off his ink. Tank didn't like to cover up the tats. Bone couldn't blame him. If he had lost his two older brothers the way Tank had, he would want to show off his tribute ink too. On each of Tank's upper arms were what looked like the flames of hell with each of his two brothers riding their bikes out of the fire. It was an appropriate tribute to them as a bomb the Jackals had set off in a bar the club ran over in Dixie had killed both men last year.

"You're just jealous, motherfucker!" Dog threw a pillow at Tank. He caught the pillow laughing, almost dropping his cigar before his face cleared of laughter, turning serious.

Tank looked at Dog, a faint smile on his lips. Bone noticed only because Tank not cutting the fool was a rarely occurring event. "Yeah, I am. If I'd met her first in that bar, brother, I would have kept her, you know. Terry's one fine woman. I'd love to find one like her to patch."

"Yeah, I know, man. She deserves so much better than an asshole biker like me, but I'm not giving her up for whoever that dick is. She's mine! Today she'll make me the happiest man on this earth. I thought that I'd never marry, but Terry's family won't accept my claim on her till we're married. They don't understand our way of life and what my patch on her back means to us. They keep telling her about nice young men they want to convince her to date. I want her family and every other person on the planet to know that woman's more than taken. She's owned!" He punctuated this statement by pounding a fist on the couch arm.

"Damn, man. Owned. Really?" Bone raised a brow, letting out a light chuckle at his brother's possessiveness. "Well, count me out. I never want to keep a woman longer than it takes to bang 'er a few times." He sat on the edge of the

Taming Lucca

couch, his face contorted into a slightly odd smile because the thought made him a little antsy. His skin twitched and he was damned glad he didn't have to worry about that happening.

"Bone, just you wait. Your day's coming. You won't be able to ignore a woman who means more than your hard dick, and when that day comes I'm gonna laugh my ass off as you spin in circles trying to patch her," Dog informed him with a wide grin and narrowed eyes. Bone felt his words flow down his spine with a small shiver.

"Not gonna happen, brother."

Bone tugged at his collar; damned thing was itchy. He checked his watch. "Show time, ladies," he said as took Dog's outstretched hand and jerked his brother to his feet.

Dog stubbed out the cigar in a nearby ashtray and straightened his suit with a dopey smile. He walked to the door.

"Fuck, get that dopey look off your face, man, you're acting like a chick. Before Bone and I know it, you'll be asking us if we can have a sleepover, or to braid our damned hair," Tank complained in true Tank fashion, making Bone chuckle. Dog just shot him a bird over his shoulder and walked down the stairs heading to the altar, where Preach stood ready to officiate the proceedings.

Bone and Tank stood at the altar with the happy couple. Bone watched Dog and Terry holding hands while Preach bleated out the ceremony in his loud gruff voice. Terry's head was tilted up towards Dog, her eyes holding a soft glow of happiness, while Dog looked down at her in adoration. The joy on the couple's face almost made Bone wish he was the kind of man who could be with one woman for the rest of his life.

Michelle Woods

He glanced around the room seeing a hot little blonde in the front row wearing a red number that was very low cut. She was staring at him and when she noticed he was watching her, she pushed her heavy chest out towards him. Bone felt his cock stir as he watched her tits almost burst from the top of the low cut dress. Nope, still not a one-woman man, he realized. He smiled, giving her a little wink before moving his eyes over the rest of the family.

Turning back to the altar, he glanced at the dress Terry wore. It was a low cut wedding dress that showed her large cleavage off to perfection. It clung to her until it hit her hips where it flared out into a bell-shaped skirt, with a deep V in the back of the dress covered by Dog's property patch clearly worn on her back. Preach was wrapping up the ceremony, Bone realized, when Dog leaned closer to Terry.

Preach pronounced them man and wife, telling Dog he could kiss his bride. Dog didn't hesitate, he pulled her close and in seconds was kissing her deeply to the catcalls and whistles of the rowdy crowd. Her blond hair was flowing down Dog's arm where he'd bent her over to lay one on her. Bone laughed, letting out a whistle of his own because yeah, even at a wedding they weren't a calm bunch.

Dog pulled away from Terry to begin dragging her down the aisle. Bone laughed as Terry giggled and allowed herself to be led away without a fight. At the door of the clubhouse, Dog scooped Terry over his shoulder with a gleeful shout and took off running towards their cabin to the sound of the shrieks of his old lady, and the laughter and jeers of their family.

Waiting for the crowd to exit the clubhouse, Bone eyed the petite blonde with large breasts as she smiled and waved a little at him as she was led away by Toad who was apparently her date. Too bad, he'd thought maybe he might get to know her a little better. Maybe see what those tits looked like bare. Shifting to alleviate the pressure his zipper was putting on his cock, he hugged a cute sweetbutt who came over to give him a kiss.

Tank moved up beside him leaning in to whisper in his ear. "Jackals are on the move again. Two prospects just got back and said they spotted them moving Juice in the nearby town of Cutler. Want to get a crew together to take care of it?"

Fucking Jackals! Couldn't even give them a single night of peace from their stupid shit. Bone considered what to do for a long moment. They needed to shut those bastards and their designer drug trade down, but tonight was a celebration that the club had been looking forward to for weeks and the men needed the break.

"Nah, tonight we party. Tomorrow we take those fuckers down," Bone told him.

Tank nodded, smiling before he winked at Bone and took the arm of the sweetbutt who had kissed him and took off with her. Fucker.

Damn, he thought, walking out of the club towards the bonfire, grabbing a beer and taking a seat on an old bench seat. Bone watched the fire for a long time, seeing the rowdy crowd cutting up and having a good time. It was about an hour later when a woman came and sat down beside him. She wore a skintight lime mini dress. Her hair was curled and hung to her shoulders in dark brown waves. She looked up at him through her lashes, leaning forward and giving him a nice view of her rather large tits. Bone felt his cock stir, hardening to press against his zipper when he eyed those creamy mounds of flesh.

"Bone," she purred, her hand moving to rest on his hardened cock. "You promised last time that you'd rock my world, but then you had to leave before the party started. I was so disappointed." She leaned towards him and her right nipple peeked out of the tight dress.

"Hmm––well, we can't have that, can we, sweet?" he murmured. Bone reached out his hand pulling the top of her dress down, baring her breasts fully. "Nice tits," he murmured as pulled her onto his lap and took one of her tight nipples into his mouth sucking it roughly.

She moaned and arched her back, thrusting her breasts towards him. His hand cupped the tit he wasn't sucking on while his other hand slid over her thigh.

"Oh, yes, suck my tits harder, Bone," she begged.

Bone ran his teeth over the tight bud of her nipple before sucking the peak hard. He then moved to the other doing the same. Hearing her let out a cry of needy pleasure, he moved his hand up to slide his fingers over her little bud, rubbing it with his thumb.

"Fuck me, just fuck me."

Bone grunted when she grabbed his ears and began to wiggle on his lap trying to find release. Fuck, she was hot for this. He wasn't overly excited with her bouncing around in his lap like she was but he was horny enough that he was ready when she made a few adjustments before taking his cock out.

Bone slid a condom into her hand. She quickly sheathed him in the condom then slipped his cock into her warm wet pussy. Seconds later, she was bouncing up and down, riding his cock hard while he sucked her big tits.

As he neared his orgasm inside her clenching cunt, he thought 'this is the perfect life,' a sweetbutt riding his cock and his crew partying around them. Feeling her come, he grabbed her hips and began thrusting up into her needing to find his own climax. He let out a thick groan as he came, hearing the blaring music from the big outdoor speakers and

Taming Lucca

the partying around the fire a few feet away ring in his ears along with her cries.

Chapter 4

Molly stared out the window of the tiny cell, her mind wandering over the past ten days she'd spent locked up in this little slice of hell on earth. She'd thought that life was rough living in the Slums, but this was so much worse.

The cell that she was in was so small she couldn't get up to move around. It was only large enough to have a small bed, which stretched across the room from one side to the other. If Molly stood up beside the cot she'd be out of room. Thank God she wasn't claustrophobic. Otherwise she likely would be mad as a hatter at this point.

The cot she sat on was just long enough that she could stretch out to lay down and the little window she was currently looking out was about one foot by two foot showing part of the upper slums, just enough that she could make out the little houses that lined the street. They were grey one-story flats that housed mostly mistresses for the Hillies who wanted a bit of ass on the side. Although some were for the nannies and teachers that the families in the lower hill employed, most were for the whores or the mistresses.

Molly sighed, rubbing a hand over her dirty cheek where it

Taming Lucca

itched. The stench of her odor filling the tiny room made her cringe. She hoped they would let her out of here soon so that she could at least bathe.

They'd fed her actual slop like they would give an animal every day. She would go back to eating nasty oatmeal in a heartbeat. She couldn't believe that they were allowed to treat prisoners this way. It was inhuman.

Molly had been told that she was allowed one family visit as they'd shoved her in here, but in ten days no one had come to see her. She pushed her greasy hair back from her face, tilting her head to the right trying to relieve the ache she had there from lack of movement for so long. Everything hurt.

It made her want to cry but after ten days she knew it would do her no good. She couldn't cry anymore, she'd cried and screamed herself out waiting for someone to come in and realize that this was all a mistake and let her go home.

The last time the guard had entered he'd said that in the morning she would be sentenced. Molly wasn't upset over that because it meant that she would get out of this cell and as far as she was concerned, that was a good thing. After ten days she didn't care if they did throw her out of the city as long as she didn't have to sit in here and rot with the smell of her own body odor assaulting her.

Hearing the scrape of the lock on the door being slid back, she shuddered. Turning to the door, expecting her normal dinner of slop to be delivered through the feed slot, she was surprised to see a man standing the open doorway.

"You've got a visitor, Slummie," said the guard, a fat man with jowls and mean beady eyes who'd taunted her every time he brought her food to her.

"Shit, you stink," he said, waving his hand before his face as the smell exited the little room. He motioned for her to walk ahead of him. Molly gritted her teeth, wanting to snap at him

Michelle Woods

that of course she stank. Hell, what did the man expect, she hadn't been allowed to bathe in days.

Molly got off the cot, feeling pain in her legs and letting out a little moan. Damn, her bones ached from being cooped up in that room for so long. She was slow and the guard let out an impatient grunt before commanding her to get a move on it. She wanted to slap the son of a bitch in the face but she knew that would only land her in more trouble, so instead she moved into the narrow hallway.

He led her down the corridor to a room with only a glass partition. It had holes in it and a chair on either side. On the other side of the glass partition sat her mother, her hair styled neatly and her clothes immaculate. She looked like she was attending a garden party in the hills, not visiting her daughter's prison cell.

"You've got twenty minutes, then it's bath time, Slummie." The guard walked out, leaving her facing her mother, unsure what to say. Feeling resentful of being dirty and a little fearful, she waited for her mother to speak, watching the tight press of her lips and the way a muscle twitched near her eye.

Her mother glared for a long moment before demanding, "Do you have any idea how embarrassing this is for me and your father?"

Yes, Molly thought, her hands gripping the sides of the little chair she sat in, what an inconvenience for her mother her imprisonment must be. After all, it would look bad to her mother's ridiculous friends who were just as obsessed with the Hill district as she was. Hell, Molly admitted, as obsessed as she had been only ten days ago.

Shaking in utter astonishment at her mother's gall, she watched her mother through the glass wondering how this could be happening. What the hell had she done to deserve this lot in life?

Taming Lucca

Shaking away her thoughts, she focused on the woman who'd birthed her.

"I asked you not to go, didn't I! You went, and then you were stupid enough to try to steal some poor woman's purse. How did you think that would go, Molly?" her mother continued when Molly didn't say anything.

"I didn't take anything, Mother. They planted it in my pocket," Molly howled, tears she had thought dried up filling her eyes. Molly stared at her mother, who didn't seem to care that she was suffering. No, her mother only cared about how she looked in the eyes of the class she wanted so badly to be a part of.

"Really? If that's true, it's what you get for dating that man! You were trying to be better than everyone else and look how that went. You should have stayed with your kind like I told you to," her mother said, her tone haughty.

Ha, that was rich, as if her mother wasn't trying the same thing with her fashion choices and her obscene need to have anyone from the Hill like her. Molly felt her fists ball and her fingernails dug into her palms as she glared through the glass at her mother.

"Mother, don't you even care that I'm in prison about to be sentenced for a crime I didn't commit?"

"Oh, don't be so dramatic. You'll be out of here once you're convicted in the morning. Then you can live outside the wall. Stop acting like it's a death sentence." Her mother gave her a bored look, her perfectly groomed nails tapping on the counter that was attached to her side of the glass inside the little meeting room.

"Yes. I will be outside the wall. We all know who's out there, don't we, large groups of murderers, thieves, and bikers." She shivered with fear; none of those people were anyone she wanted to spend time with. Molly felt her stomach twist into

Michelle Woods

knots and her palms became sweaty just thinking about the life she would find outside the walls of the city. Fear made her tear up again but she forced them back with sheer willpower, unwilling to cry anymore over this debacle.

"Well, that's what going out with that Hillie boy has cost you. I tried to explain the way things worked to you, but you didn't listen. Now you know what I was trying to tell you but you'll have to suffer the consequences of your actions." Molly couldn't believe that her mother could stoop to this level of heartlessness. Molly eyed the woman beyond the glass, wondering how she could look at her own daughter with such disdain. It was as if she hadn't spent hours in labor to bring Molly into the world.

"Why did father not come to see me today? He wouldn't allow this to happen to me, he loves me," Molly finally found the courage to ask, after she realized that her mother really didn't care one way or the other what happened to her. Her mother was coldly watching her only child and was completely okay with her being thrown out into a world filled with men and women who might hurt or murder her. It was crazy.

"Your father was so heartbroken that you would do this that he has disowned you," her mother said coldly as she rose to her feet, brushing imaginary lint off her skirt. Molly watched, her eyes glued to the movements as she felt each word her mother said like a blow. "I think that we're done here. When you get outside the wall let this be a lesson to you and never try to act better than others when you're not."

With that parting shot, her mother banged on the metal door behind her and was let out. Molly sat there until the guard came to get her, staring at the door her mother had just exited through, shocked that her father had disowned her and her mother had just walked out with a 'well you deserve to be punished for trying to better your lot in life' without

Taming Lucca

even bothering to look back at her.

The guard took her to a room with a shower, real soap and an actual bed. She was grateful for the nicer accommodations but she felt like it was her last night on earth. Like in the morning she was headed to her death.

When he left, she stood in the shower defeated, her tears flowing down her face being washed away with the warm water that flowed over her. She knew, even as she washed away the grime that covered her skin, that she may not make it to her twenty-third birthday. The world outside the wall was lawless and she didn't hold much hope she would be able to survive it without any idea of where to go or what to do.

She didn't know how long she stood in the little enclosure washing her skin but she knew it must have been a long time because her skin turned red from the heat of the water. When she finally felt clean again, and her tears had long since stopped, she stepped out, drying off. Molly dressed in the clothes that had been laid out on the bed, a pair of dreaded grey coveralls.

Lying down on the bed, she watched the light from the window play across the ceiling, her mind reeling. What would tomorrow bring? How would she get out of this mess? Would she end up selling her body to pay for food because she had no other means to live? No, no, she wouldn't, she firmly told herself. She wouldn't allow that. She was a mechanic and a damned good one; surely someone could use one somewhere. Even with the dark thoughts swirling inside her, it didn't take long for her to fall asleep.

The opening of the door woke her the next morning. Molly blinked a few times before rolling to face the door. Expecting to see the guard who'd been tending her for the past ten days, she was pleasantly surprised to see that it was Carl entering the cell. His bushy brows were drawn, his eyes heavy with

Michelle Woods

sympathy, and she'd never seen a more glorious sight. At least one person cared what happened to her and she felt a warm glow fill her when she realized that he did.

"Ah, kid, if only I could save you, I would. You know that. They won't take my word that you couldn't have done this. I'm so sorry," Carl said, stepping towards the bed to take her into his arms in a tight hug. Molly couldn't stop the sobs of relief that burst from inside her. Her chest ached with the realization that this man who she barely knew cared more for her than her own parents did. It was heart-wrenching.

"I'm so, so sorry, sweetheart." He rubbed her back and held her while she cried for about three minutes before he pulled away.

"We have to go or they'll send someone else in to get you, but I need you to take this." He handed her what looked like a map, some credits, and a compass in a see-through pouch.

"You'll have to hide it until you're beyond the gate, or the other guards will take it. Listen, sweetheart, you know I ride Berta outside the wall. I'm friends with some bikers in the north, a town called Hampstead. They are always looking for mechanics, and you're a damned good one. Tell them that Clutch sent you and that he wanted them to take care of you. I don't know if you trust any of the other biker gangs out there, but the Blue Bandits are good men. I've ridden with them. So look for leather cuts with a blue reaper on them with the words Blue Bandits MC, Death Valley. Any colors besides that, you hide or run just in case, okay. The Bandits will keep you safe if you tell them Clutch sent you to talk to the Prez. Repeat it."

Molly didn't know what to say as she reached out taking the little pouch. She was glad that at least now she had a plan and somewhere to go, but she wasn't sure how to thank Carl for his generosity. His kindness almost tore her in two because it was more than her family had offered her. She'd always liked him and over the past four years she had enjoyed the time they'd spent together but she had never expected this much consideration from him.

"I can't take this," she mumbled.

"You can, cupcake. You aren't alone even if your parents are assholes. Now, repeat what I told you," Carl commanded, his eyes hard and his lips set into a grim line.

"Clutch sent me. I need to talk to the Prez," Molly said, fearful of the world beyond the wall. She didn't have much choice other than taking his offer really. If he was insisting, then she might as well take the helping hand that was offered even if it did sting her pride a little.

At least having some credits and a place to go made her feel that maybe there might be a safe place for her outside the wall. She wasn't as fearful with this little pouch in her possession as she had been the night before when she thought she had nowhere to go. Molly stuffed the little pouch inside the coveralls and down into her bra.

"Good girl, Molly. Let's get you to this pointless damned sentencing," Carl gruffly growled, his anger evident in the way he spoke and the scowl on his face. He hugged her one last time before sadly shaking his head as he got up off the cot. He helped her up and asked if she was ready. Molly nodded even though she was nowhere near ready for this because what choice did she have?

She followed Carl down the long corridor that led to the courtroom, her mind wandering over what would happen to her once she was thrust out into the world. Molly didn't know what tomorrow would bring, but with a plan and some credits at least the outlook wasn't as grim as it had been a few hours ago.

Molly looked around when they entered the courtroom,

Michelle Woods

seeing the grey concrete box she was to stand in. Anger made her ball her fists when she read the words written on it, but she walked over and stood in the box labeled 'criminal' without a word. She didn't want to get Carl in trouble by protesting.

Carl shut the little door to the box and gave her one last sympathetic smile before he whispered, "Remember what I told you, kid, and it will be okay, I promise."

Molly glanced around seeing the people who'd come for the trial sitting on the benches that lined the wall beside her to the left. She searched the faces for a familiar one but didn't see any so she turned back to face a man in a long robe who sat at a wooden counter. The robe was white and had a judge's emblem on the front. Molly had seen the long robes before but had never thought to be standing before one to receive judgment. Perhaps she would be able to explain her version of the story and they would let her go back to her life and she wouldn't have to use Carl's little care package.

The judge called the room to order with a little gavel. The sentencing took about five minutes and to her utter shock, Molly wasn't even allowed to speak. Red and Tara from the diner were allowed to speak and then the manager retold the story of grabbing her and shoving her into the closet.

The judge leaned on his desk the entire time with a bored expression that Molly found offensive. This was her life he was making a decision about; how dare he act as if it wasn't important enough to even warrant his attention. She would bet he didn't even listen to half of what was said as he doodled on a pad before him with an unfocused look in his eyes. When they were done speaking, he just snapped the gavel down with a "sentenced to life outside the wall."

That was it.

It was all over in a few minutes, and she was to be tossed out. Molly felt shocked by the quickness of the trial. Ha, that

Taming Lucca

hadn't been a trial so much as a formality. She'd been judged the minute those two women planted that wallet on her. As she was led from the room by a still scowling Carl, she noticed the snickers of Red and Tara as they watched her being led away. She wanted to jump across the room and slap them but she knew that would likely land her in more trouble, so she just walked on pretending not to notice.

Carl turned her over to another set of guards with a gentle squeeze of her arm to let her know she wasn't alone and she was taken to another room where they told her that she wouldn't ever be allowed back into the city. They read her a list of rules about being close to the walls and that she was allowed inside only to go to the hospital if she ever needed it and how to get a letter of acceptance for that. It was all ridiculous really because if she had to go through that twenty day processing she'd likely die before she was able to be admitted anyway.

Standing in the mud outside the gate only ten short minutes later without a clue as to how she'd gotten there, she glanced around looking out at the world she would now be a part of. Everything had happened so quickly, she was still reeling and she felt like her head was spinning.

She turned when the guard who'd been watching her for the last ten days pushed her away from the gate they had shoved her out of, laughing as she stumbled and almost fell.

What a jerk!

She wanted to kick him in the shins but she didn't want to give him a reason to stun her with his stunner stick. Molly stepped away instead, moving into the little market area beside the gate. Looking back over her shoulder at the City that had been her home for twenty-two years with dismay, she almost began crying again.

Molly could barely believe that just ten days ago she was

Michelle Woods

a successful lead Slum mechanic with a lover who she had thought loved her. Now, she was labeled a criminal and was standing in the mud with a vague idea that she could find a home outside the wall with a pack of bikers. With a sigh, she set out to find something besides these stupid coveralls to wear. If she was starting a new life, she wasn't starting it as a dumpy Slum mechanic.

Chapter 5

The market near the gate was a place for surrounding cities to sell their goods to the people who lived in safety behind the wall. It was the city's primary source of fresh foods and clothes. Having never been outside the wall, Molly was amazed by the colorful market. She walked down the row of stalls looking at everything, trying to absorb it all. Her eyes were drawn from one thing to the next with excitement and she couldn't believe how interesting watching the people who were chatting and laughing was.

Inside the city, women who weren't in the dreaded coveralls were expected to wear skirts or dresses because pants were for men. Molly had always thought it was dumb, but she knew what was expected of a proper lady and she'd worn them. Out here it seemed that women were allowed to wear men's clothing. Most of them wore a denim material like her coveralls only theirs were made into pairs of pants and were lots of different colors. Some even wore little half pants that only came to their mid thighs. Inside the wall this type of attire was talked about as scandalous in hushed whispers. In the city, no woman would have worn pants unless it was a jumper like her coveralls.

Molly walked down the rows of stalls until she found a

Michelle Woods

stall that sold backpacks. She stopped, picking up a blue one that had ties on the top to hold a bedroll. She would need somewhere to store things and the bedrolls also sold at the stall would give her a place to sleep besides the ground.

The man in the booth stood and walked towards her with a jovial smile, asking if she was looking to get a backpack today. His thick jowls wiggled as he talked about several more expensive products but she shook her head, telling him she wanted the one she'd picked up. The little man nodded, his bright smile unfazed by her refusal, and he began showing her the bedrolls and how they attached.

Molly found a manual propping up one leg of the shelf of one of the tables that she bartered with the man to buy as well as the blue pack and a bedroll. Her next stop found fifteen days' worth of ration cubes, some sunscreen, and four bottles of water.

As she filled the backpack with her purchases, she saw a stall with clothes in the row across from her and a few stalls down and headed for it. Walking closer, she noticed the guard who'd pushed her earlier standing a few feet away. Molly didn't want to get anywhere near him so she quickly ducked into the clothing stall before he turned. She was afraid he was looking for her and watched him from inside the little stall for a moment before she walked farther inside.

She walked down the row of colorful denim pants and looked at them with consideration. She wasn't from the city behind the wall anymore. Should she let go of the things she'd learned were right according to the Hillies or allow it to shape her view of this new world?

Still trying to decide, she heard a sound behind her. She turned to find a woman with blue hair, who appeared to be a few years older than her and was wearing a pair of the denim pants and a bright blue tank top. Scandalized slightly by the

Taming Lucca

tightness of the attire as well as by the tattoos that covered her left arm, Molly stared.

The woman seemed unfazed by her gawking and smiled brightly before coming towards her. As she got closer Molly saw that the tattoo said 'Property of Slim' in dark black ink. The woman was a little on the heavy side of ideal, with generous breasts and hips. She wore several jangling bracelets and black boots. Her smile made her seem to glow with an inner happiness that Molly envied.

"You need to try those on, they would look great on you. Now, let's see." The woman began tugging on Molly's coveralls, clucking her tongue when she had the coveralls tight to Molly's hips. Molly felt even more scandalized by this manhandling so she stood still, hoping the woman would stop tugging at her clothes.

"Sugar, you're hiding a hot figure under these horrid coveralls. If I looked like you, I'd be flaunting it all over the place." The woman let out a tinkling belly laugh that caused Molly's heart to squeeze inside her chest. Had she ever laughed like that with so much joy? She didn't think so. It made her realize that she'd never been happy a day in her life. Molly was astounded by this discovery. She understood finally why her life in the Slums had never been enough, which was kind of sad.

The woman began to usher her to the back towards a small dressing room that was curtained off near the back of the stall. As she went, she was grabbing several pairs of pants off the tables. When they reached the dressing room, she thrust the pants into Molly's arms. "Here, try on these jeans, then come out and let me see so we can find the right fit."

She jerked the curtain door closed leaving Molly alone in the room. Still a little surprised to find herself in this little cubby holding several pair of pants––no, jeans, she stared

Michelle Woods

at the curtain. Shaking her head after a moment of silent staring, she turned and set them down on a small bench behind her. She was about to pull the coveralls off when the curtain was jerked back open. Molly spun to look at the blue haired woman as she held out another stack of clothes.

"Sorry, almost forgot these. Now try them on and don't forget to let me see. Okay?"

"Umm––okay."

"Great." The curtain was snapped closed a second time.

Molly saw a full body length mirror in the corner hung on a post stuck in the ground near the bench where she'd set the clothes that she hadn't noticed at first. She watched her pale face in the mirror for a moment. She looked terrible, her hair was messy and it had frizzed, her eyes had dark circles beneath them likely because she hadn't been sleeping well, and her cheek had a little rash along one side. It was fading but it must be why it had itched so much. She would have to remember not to scratch it.

Removing her coveralls, she pulled on a pair of the jeans. Deciding they were comfortable, she picked up a bold red shirt from the other pile, putting it on as well. She stood for several minutes gawking at herself in the mirror. She couldn't believe it was her reflection staring back at her from the mirror.

The jeans were loose around her waist, but not baggy like the coveralls. The shirt fit her well; it wasn't tight like the blue haired woman's was, and it flowed nicely, showing a hint of her small breasts, but not clinging to them. With her black hair, the color made her look like she was glowing instead of pale and colorless.

"You got something on yet, Doll?"

"Urr––yes," Molly replied, unsure what to say to the woman. The curtain was snapped open again and the woman

Taming Lucca

stood regarding Molly with a slight frown.

"Hmm––the shirt's fine, but the jeans are not right." She pulled another pair of jeans from the pile, handing them to Molly. "Here, these are the size you need. Put those on with the shirt."

The curtain was closed again, leaving Molly slightly bewildered. She looked really good in these jeans, what did the woman mean these were the wrong size? She stood in front of the mirror for a few more minutes staring before she took them off and pulled on the pair the woman had suggested.

They felt less baggy, and her reflection revealed that these were much tighter. Dismayed, she decided that she was getting the first pair, not these. Before she could change back into the first pair the curtain was pulled opened by the blue-haired woman who cooed, "Ooh yes, those are perfect."

Molly looked down thinking perhaps the mirror wasn't working, but saw that it was working just fine. These jeans made her look like she was a whore. She looked up at the woman ready to tell her so when she saw a huge man step into the stall. He was massive, with tattoos covering his left arm with the words 'Lisa's old man' in thick black ink. His arms and legs were big as tree trunks with broad shoulders and hips. His hair was shaggy and long, and he had a shaggy beard that was a sandy brown color. He wore a leather vest with patches, a white tank under it, and jeans with leather chaps at the bottom. Molly stood frozen as the woman was rattling on about her needing several pairs of jeans, as well as a few shirts. The man reached forward and grabbed the woman on the butt, right in front of Molly as if this wasn't scandalizing. Molly stepped back, cowering slightly in the small dressing room.

"You'd sure better be Slim, or you're a dead man," the

Michelle Woods

woman said as she glanced back at the large man over her shoulder, smiling at him.

"Ha. You think I'd let a man get close enough to touch your ass, baby?" The man, who must be Slim, leaned over, his mouth kissing down the woman's neck.

That was when Molly realized that this man was the reason the woman looked genuinely happy. It was in her eyes when she turned them up to his. Slim's hands had slid around her waist to pull her back into his arms possessively. The woman's eyes met Molly's, noting her cowering in the dressing room. She began to pull his hands away while dodging the mouth still trying to kiss her neck.

"No, you big lug! I know better. But you need to go play with the boys, you're scaring the customers." Laughing, she playfully batted at his hand that was trying to grab her hips as she pushed him backwards out of the stall.

"Okay, baby. You don't have to abuse me. I'm sure the mouse is just timid, not scared. Although those people from behind the wall are scared of everything out here." He chuckled and took a step back every few seconds to allow the woman to push him from the stall. Almost at the entrance, he stopped, not allowing her to push him any farther and held her hips, gently bending down until he met her eyes.

"I only came in to tell you I have to head back for some club biz. I'm taking Trick with me, but Pretty Boy and Tanner are staying to help you pack up in a few hours. Do not leave without them, and make them help. No doing it by yourself, baby. I mean it, Lisa." The look Slim gave her was intense. Lisa's face was turned slightly with the way their bodies had shifted when she was pushing him from the stall, so Molly saw the way it softened. Lisa pulled his hand to her stomach holding it there.

"Slim, I'll be okay. Promise," she said softly, planting a kiss

Taming Lucca

on his chin.

Slim squeezed her gently, adoration clear on his face as he stared at her before he grinned widely, which Molly found frankly scary, and smacked Lisa's ass harder this time. Her hands flew to her butt to rub the sting away.

"You'd better be, woman." Slim turned and walked out of the stall, letting out a yell to a group of men standing a few feet away leaning on some poles. "Let's ride."

One man moved away to meet him and they walked away together. As they moved away she saw that they each had a patch on the back of their leather vests that said Red Devils MC with a little red man with pointy ears and a forked tail, and holding a flaming pitchfork. Molly realized that the man who made Lisa so happy was part of a biker gang.

Lisa watched Slim walk away, letting out a sigh when he was swallowed by the crowd. She shook her head, turning back to Molly with a smile lingering on her face. "Sorry, Doll. That man fries my brain with his hotness. Now, what were we doing? Oh right, getting your clothes."

She began to stack clothes by the register. Molly watched as the pile grew, her eyes widening. She could not afford all of the clothes Lisa was stacking up. She was dismayed to realize she would have to take the coveralls with her. She was only able to get one pair of jeans, a few pairs of underwear, and a shirt. She'd started shopping with forty credits. Now she only had ten.

"Wait, I can't buy all this. I'll just take one pair of jeans, some underwear, and a shirt."

Lisa looked at her with a puzzled expression. "You can't travel with just one set of clothing, sweetie, what if it rains?"

"I will take my coveralls too. How many credits will it be?"

"Oh no, Doll, you will not be taking those coveralls. I plan to put those poor things out of their misery tonight in a fire.

Michelle Woods

Besides, today's a special event, everything is buy one get three free. Isn't that lucky." Lisa beamed.

She gathered several things from the stack she'd been building. "Let's see, two pairs of jeans, three shirts, and five pairs of underwear." She looked at Molly's feet. "Oh, and a pair of hiking shoes and four pairs of socks, that will total out to be five credits."

Although she was grateful that Lisa was trying to help her, she couldn't allow her to give her all these clothes. She had gathered from the byplay between Slim and Lisa that she was pregnant, and families needed all the credits they could get. She would know having been raised in the slums.

"I can't allow you to just give me all this stuff. You have a family, and you need to eat."

"Oh Doll, aren't you sweet. That's not something you have to worry about, my man can take care of me just fine. Heck, if he doesn't, his brothers would look after me. Besides, I like to charge the uppity ones from the city twice as much." She laughed loudly, drawing the attention of the men who stood near the stall.

The one smoking smiled in their direction. Molly also saw that the guard from the prison was walking towards the tent. What a jerk that guy was, she thought angrily.

"If you get the chance you should charge that man double for sure." Molly's hand pointed out at the guard, then clapped over her mouth when she realized that what she'd said was very vindictive. She worried that Lisa would be mad that she was saying bad things about a city guard. Lisa only laughed that deep belly laugh again.

"So noted," she nodded solemnly. "I really like you."

"Thanks." Molly saw that the guard was now heading towards Lisa's stall, grinning with malice at Molly as he did.

She shivered; she really didn't like that guard, he was very nasty. Seeing her face, Lisa turned to look behind her. Seeing the guard heading their way, she let out a sharp whistle. The two men's heads swung towards her, and they came to attention. Lisa made a strange fisted hand motion, nodding towards the guard coming closer, and the men moved quickly towards the entrance of the stall blocking it. They acted casual, standing there with an unconcerned air as if they hadn't just run to the entrance of the stall. The guard tried to enter, but the hard arm of the bigger man swung out, not allowing him to enter.

"Sorry, Mate. Only one customer in the stall at a time, safety reasons. You understand, right?" the smaller man said as he stubbed his cigarette out with his boot after dropping it.

"That's ridiculous. I just wanted to warn that woman about the Slummie in there with her. She's just been thrown out of my city for theft. I'm sure she's stolen things from her already." He smiled gleefully at Molly over the man's shoulder.

A roaring sound started in Molly's ears; surely now Lisa and the two men would turn against her, allowing the guard to harass her, and they would probably help him. Her eyes filled with tears that she just barely held back. She wasn't ready to give up the slight friendship she'd created with Lisa yet. Why did this keep happening to her? She wasn't a bad person and surely she didn't deserve this.

"Really? Well, it's a good thing you're here then, huh," the big one said, not moving his arm from where it blocked the guard's entrance. "Except the rules prevent us from letting you in. Safety first and all that rot. Could be an accident with two people in there and we wouldn't want that, now would we?" he asked, tilting his head to look at the guard, whose face contorted into a scowl.

Molly grabbed her backpack, dug her money out and gave Lisa all the credits she had left. Then she gathered what she

Michelle Woods

thought was worth ten credits and began to move away with a quietly uttered, "Thanks and sorry for the trouble."

"Doll, this is way more than we agreed to. Take this back," Lisa said, shoving half the credits back into her hand, and scooping up what she'd left on the counter beside the register. "You also forgot these."

Molly stared at her in disbelief. "You heard what he said about me, didn't you?"

"Yes, but I'm a damned good judge of character, and I'd bet good credits on the case against you being a load of shit. Why don't you head out the back while the boys detain him," Lisa said as Molly shoved the money in the jeans pocket and the clothes in her backpack. "Thank you, Lisa." She hurried towards the back entrance to the stall that was covered by a curtain.

"Wait. If you ever need anything and you see one of the boys, tell them that you're a friend of Lisa, Slim's old lady, and they should bring you to her. Okay?" Molly nodded her head although she didn't understand the old lady comment; it made no sense to her, Lisa was only a few years older than Molly.

As she exited she heard an angry shout. "Hey, what are you doing, take your hands off me."

"Sorry again, mate. You can't enter an employee only area. Safety." Molly smiled as she began walking faster. "Hey, the Slummie went out that way."

"Well I didn't see her, did you, Pretty Boy?"

"Nope," came the flat reply before the voices faded into the distance as she hurried around another stall and mixed with the crowds of people shopping, a smile still attached to her lips.

Chapter 6

Wiping her hand over her sweaty brow, Molly stopped walking. She'd been traveling in the woods along the road for two days. Right now she was hot and exhausted. The sun was beating down on her fiercely and had been for over three hours. She decided to take another rest and sat down on the grass close to the road sign she'd just exited the tree line to read.

Lakeville, according to the sign, was thirteen miles away, which put her about three hundred miles away from the Blue Bandits according to the map.

Shoot.

It was going to take weeks to get to their town. She'd only gone about thirty miles in the last two days. She grimaced in disappointment. She thought she'd have gotten farther than thirty miles by now. Molly let out a defeated sigh and pulled the water out of her backpack drinking a large gulp.

Lying back in the grass, she was grateful for the small breeze that blew across the sweat on her skin, cooling her down. She should really move away from the road, it was never very long before a biker or car came by.

She was still too fearful of the bikers to look at their leather vests to see if they were Blue Bandits when they roared by

Michelle Woods

as she hid in the woods. Molly didn't want to go near the cars either because they could be filled with murderers or thieves. She didn't know who she could trust, so she hid and trusted no one. She was just getting comfortable when the loud rumble started.

Crap.

She jumped up, grabbing the pack from beside her, and ran towards the trees about three feet away. She prayed that they wouldn't see her before she got to the forest to hide. She was almost there when the roar became much louder; she ran faster, desperate to hide before they saw her.

Her backpack was bouncing around, things clanking together, and she hoped nothing broke. Gritting her teeth and sprinting into the forest at last, she continued running; if they had seen her she needed to find somewhere to hide. She was searching in front of her for somewhere to hide when she heard what sounded like water.

Running headlong over the thick brush, she didn't see the root until she was already falling. As she went down, her ankle twisted. Moaning in pain at the horrible wrench, she lay there stunned for several minutes. Her hands and knees stung, but her ankle was throbbing painfully by the time she was able to sit up.

Thankfully she heard the roar beginning to fade away so she must not have been seen by any of the bikers. Attempting to stand, she winced in pain as she tried to put weight on her ankle.

Shit, that hurt.

She sat back down taking off her right shoe, not surprised to find her ankle was already swelling. From the pain she'd assumed it would be. She lay back in the grass beneath her thinking that maybe she'd take a nap, and then try again. She closed her eyes, propping her foot on the root that had

Taming Lucca

caused the problem in the first place. It didn't take long for her to fall asleep because of the ordeal the last week and a half had been.

When she woke an hour later, she looked at her ankle. The swelling had gotten much worse while she rested. Her ankle was almost three times bigger than the other one.

Great, Molly thought, as she again tried to put weight on her ankle.

Crying out in pain, she almost fell back down before catching herself on a tree nearby. Shit, she needed to get the swelling down somehow. Hearing the water again, she looked towards the sound, seeing the small creek a few feet away. She knew it was her best chance.

There had to be something she could use as a crutch. She searched the ground, finding a long stick close by, so she picked it up. She checked its strength, and when she didn't break it by putting most of her weight on it, she used it to head slowly toward the water. The trip took almost twenty minutes, and she stumbled into about ten trees, scraping her hands even more than they already were.

When she was finally at the water's edge, she rested her ankle in the stream. Molly felt her head begin to pound from the heat and the pain in her ankle. Damn, this just sucked. The stream wasn't cold, but at least it was cool enough that it might help some. She watched as fish swam in the shallows. It was a shame that the water was likely poisoned so she couldn't catch them for dinner.

It would be nice to have something other than ration cubes to eat, but the storms that had raged sixty years ago hadn't only taken half the world's landmass with them into the ocean, they had also unleashed something they now referred to as water poison. It wasn't really a poison so much as a parasite that killed very quickly. It traveled the blood stream

Michelle Woods

to the heart, causing massive heart attacks.

You had to drink the little buggers, or they couldn't get into the body in sufficient enough quantities to harm a person. If the tiny things made it to their victim's heart, he or she was dead; for most people this took about forty-five minutes. Even sixty years later, they had only found a way to kill them in the body if they hadn't made it to their victim's heart.

The cities now filtered all the water through the water plants, which was then pumped into buildings and homes. Even in the Slums they had fresh water. She knew that towns outside the wall had to filter their water too because nobody wanted to die of water poisoning. The fish and some animals that hadn't died out from the poisoned water had found a way to live in harmony with the parasite but no human had ever been known to survive it after the forty-five minute mark.

A fish jumped up to catch a bug flying near the water and Molly again thought that it was really too bad she couldn't eat them. She let out a groan of disappointment before plopping back on the grass and allowing the cool water to soothe her ankle. Staring up at the trees that swayed back and forth above her with her hands beneath her head, she watched the shadows they cast for a long time before finally falling into a fitful sleep.

Molly awakened to the sound of screeching from a bird that had landed on the nearby rock she was lying beside. It was only a foot away, and she observed it hopping on the rock while calling out to another bird somewhere in the forest, who answered. It was red, and had what looked like a mohawk on its head with a bright orange beak. It was truly a fascinating site. Birds were rare in the city; they saw a few seagulls, but even those were not common. She lay watching until the bird took off, flying away in a beautiful display of color.

Sitting up, she checked on the swelling in her ankle. She

wasn't sure but felt that it had gone down a bit. Deciding that it hadn't gone down enough for her to try walking yet, she knew she'd have to stay here for the rest of the day. Maybe even the next day, she thought ruefully, glaring at her ankle. She was upset with herself for falling; if she'd only paid more attention. Grumbling to herself, she opened her backpack. Might as well eat some of the ration cubes since she wasn't going anywhere anytime soon.

When she pulled out the cubes, she noticed that the bottom of her backpack was wet. Very wet. Oh no, she thought with growing distress, not the water, please, she begged. She pulled everything out, finding two of the water bottles had been broken during her fall. She only had one left that was full, as well as the half empty one that she'd been drinking earlier.

Thankfully the ration cubes weren't wet, but the map and her spare clothes were soaked. She used the rock nearby to lay the clothes out to dry. Putting the map under a rock sitting in a patch of sunlight near her legs, she untied the bedroll and spread it out. Scooting over onto it, she took out a book. The man who sold her the backpack had been using it as a wedge for his table, and she'd given him an extra credit for it. Lying back in the grass with her leg propped up, she was grateful she had bought it from the man.

Molly shifted the pack on her shoulder with an irritated huff. The last sign had read fifteen miles to a place called Devil Falls. Molly was hot, tired and just about ready to give up on finding the Blue Bandits MC. She'd spent two days at the clearing by the river, now she was still two miles from the town of Devil Falls, and she knew that meant at least thirty minutes of walking. She had finished drinking the last of the water two hours ago. She would have to stop in that town

Michelle Woods

to fill the water bottles. She groaned, shifting the backpack again.

Fifteen minutes later she was hovering in the tree line staring at the diner called Tammy's. It was just off the road about a hundred yards away from where she was standing. Molly didn't immediately rush towards it like she wanted to. Instead she waited to see who was using the diner, needing to be sure that she didn't run into the bikers that had roared by a few hours ago.

She'd been hearing more and more bikes going by in the last few hours, which worried her; she might be getting closer to their home base, she thought with a gulp of fear. As she stood there staring at the little diner, she suddenly realized it didn't matter. She was already parched and without water, there wasn't much of a choice. It was get more water, or die from dehydration. She would have to take her chances. Standing and gathering her pack, she walked towards the small diner with her heart beating like a drum in her ears.

She really hoped that she could get in and out of this place without trouble.

Chapter 7

Entering the small diner, Molly was relieved to see that hardly anyone was there. There were two men with gray hair at the counter with their backs to the door and a waitress behind the counter. One man was very overweight; the other was lean and looked to be in good shape. Neither turned to see who'd come into the diner. The waitress, a tall woman with chestnut-colored curls, stood behind the counter filling saltshakers. She glanced up and stared at Molly, making her shift from one foot to the other nervously, before the woman said, "You can sit anywhere, Darling. Menus are at the tables, just yell when you're ready to order."

The larger man noticed the woman staring and turned to glance at her, then nudged the thinner man, who turned to stare at her too. Molly's heart squeezed a bit in her chest when she saw the face of the thinner man. He looked a lot like her father; well, if her father had longer hair and a tattoo covering the back of his neck.

This man's stare was piercing and he didn't look very friendly. Molly gripped her backpack strap hard, her palms sweating. Her stomach twisted into knots as she stared back at them.

Why was he still watching her, she wondered. Glancing

Michelle Woods

around at the typical diner décor, she spotted the bathroom with relief and headed towards it with a quick stride, trying not to show how nervous the man was making her.

"I just wanted to borrow your bathroom. Then I'll be going, but thank you," she told the woman as she walked past the counter. Her hands were gripping the pack tightly and she knew if they weren't they would be trembling. Molly just wanted to get into the bathroom, fill her remaining water bottles and get the heck out of here.

"Sure thing, Darling. Let me know if you change your mind," the waitress replied before she went back to filling the saltshakers.

Molly was almost to the door and glanced back to see if the man was still watching her. He'd turned around completely, and she saw to her dismay that he wore a Red Devils tee shirt. She also saw a cell phone in his hand, which worried her even more.

Shit, she thought, entering the bathroom and locking the door behind her. She looked in the mirror and almost sighed in relief when she saw herself. No wonder they had been staring at her; she had dirt smudged across her left cheek, and her hair looked matted in places. Her heart slowed and she felt the nervous energy that had overtaken her lessen.

Well, the next time she got kicked out of a town she would make sure she had a comb, she thought with a silent snicker. Shaking her head at her own silliness, she ran a hand over her face. Taking off her backpack, she realized that her shirt was ripped quite badly with a gaping hole present near her left hip, and her jeans had green stains from where she'd fallen two days ago. Damn, no wonder they were watching her like she was a sideshow attraction.

She certainly was a sight. The man had probably been calling someone to tell them about the homeless woman he'd

Taming Lucca

seen today. Deciding she needed to look more presentable even if she wasn't going to be entering any more towns, she opened the pack. She pulled the last pair of jeans out of the bag, then dug deeper to find a blue shirt.

Before she changed her clothes, she washed her hair as best she could in the sink and she used some paper towels to wash her face and arms. After pulling on her fresh clothes, she tore a strip off the ripped shirt so that she could braid her hair. Taking out the three water bottles, she filled one, then drank about half while filling the second and third bottles. Refilling the first bottle, she set it down while she checked the map, realizing that with a thirty-eight mile walk to the next town, she'd have to ration the water carefully.

Ugg, walking sucked.

She wished forty credits could have bought a car. Laughing at her joke, she put everything except the hair tie she'd made and one of the three bottles of water into her backpack. Running her fingers through her hair to comb it as best she could, she braided her hair quickly. Picking up the bottle and taking another quick swig, she opened the bathroom door, stopping dead just outside the door.

While she'd been in the bathroom, the diner had filled with five men in leather vests and jeans or leather pants. The one closest to her was talking with his back to her, and his vest had a Red Devil with pointy ears and a flaming red pitchfork. Her heart began to pound, drowning out their words, and she swallowed nervously.

Feeling her head spin a bit from the fear that flooded through her upon seeing the leather vests, Molly was about to dart back into the bathroom. Before she could, she heard the light click of the door behind her and held her breath but it was too late. All the men turned to look at her.

Damn.

Michelle Woods

The tall brown-haired man who had turned to face her caught her attention. She felt suddenly trapped by the man's intense eyes as they gazed at her. He stepped a few feet forward until he stood close enough for her to reach out and touch his bare golden abs. Thick ropes of muscles that looked hard lined his abdomen and she wanted to reach out and lay her hands on those sexy ridges.

Tall and sexy was all her brain could seem to process as she gawked at them. Molly was a little shocked that those thoughts were even in her head. Her palms itched as her gaze roamed over the man's bare skin. She wondered briefly what would happen if she just leaned over and started licking those abs.

Shaking her head to dislodge those thoughts, she gripped the backpack on her shoulder tightly. She was quite shocked that her thoughts were going there. Normally she had to know a man well in order to think about him in a sexual way. Yet here she was staring at this stranger wearing only a Red Devils vest and tight jeans with lustful thoughts running amuck in her head.

He had to be over six feet tall, she thought even as she continued to stare absently at his abs, and for her five three frame that was tall. Feeling the wetness between her legs grow, she knew her cheeks must be flushed.

He bent slightly to catch her eyes, and smiled a devilish smile. "Hey, I'm up here, sweet."

Again, she was shocked by her own behavior. She blushed furiously before looking at the man's face to see a ruggedly handsome man with a day's worth of stubble. A scar ran below the left side of his jaw, from his ear to the tip of his chin. His thick brown hair hung to just above his shoulders and he had a sexy grin on his face. He had thick arms with biceps almost as big as her thighs and broad shoulders. Molly

Taming Lucca

suddenly felt the need to fan herself she was so heated. Her body burned with desires she hadn't ever felt as strongly as she did in that moment.

It had taken nearly six months for Luzen to get her to even notice him as a man; of course, now she thought of him as that pompous ape who'd believe anything if it had tits. She almost laughed out loud with hysteria at that thought. Stupid Luzen, he was the reason she was here with this man and his golden abs.

"That's better, beauty," he said with a hint of amusement. "Duck said you were a little homeless looking. Wanna stay at my home? I can be real sweet," he said, and the men surrounding him laughed.

"No," Molly squeaked. He stood straighter, and his face darkened as he glared at her with distaste.

"Have you got a better offer? Or you just planning to stay homeless?" he asked, his voice cold.

"I w-was just leaving. I don't want any trouble." Her voice was shaky, and her hands trembled. Fear was getting the better of her. Carl's warnings were ringing in her head. 'Don't trust the other bikers with where you're going, Molly,' he'd said as he'd walked her to the sentencing. Following that with 'if they're rivals, they could try to hurt you thinking they'd hurt the club.' Remembering that dire warning, she was feeling a little dizzy and it had her heart pumping so fast she thought that she might pass out. She clutched the water bottle to her chest; the man's piercing green eyes followed. She needed to get out of here. She made to dart around the man but another man she hadn't seen sitting at the counter jerked to his feet, moving into her path to stop her.

"No, no, little sheep, not gonna get away that easy." He was even taller than the first man and looked to be bigger than Slim, the man from the market, had been. Slim was

Michelle Woods

slight and almost short compared to this man. This man could double as a mountain. He had raven-black hair and brown eyes with a thick beard that hung to his chest. He was wearing a tee shirt under his vest and jeans with leather chaps and the boots all the men were wearing.

"Please," she begged.

"Aw…so sweet. You beg so sweet, little girl. Would you beg like that when I was fucking you?" he asked, reaching out to grab her.

She stepped quickly back trying to avoid the hand reaching for her and ran into a hard male body.

Hands landed on her hips, and a sharp voice said "No, Tank."

For a moment, the man in front of her held his hands near her waist as he gazed over her head at the first man who held her hips in a tight grip. Then the moment seemed to pass and the man dropped his hands, then sat back down at the counter, leaning back as if he had not a care in the world. Molly felt strange and a little dizzy. She lifted her hand to her head trying to stop the spinning feeling she was suddenly trapped in.

She knew that the achy hot feeling in the pit of her stomach was desire for the man holding her, but the puffy almost dizzy feeling wasn't; the room seemed to be spinning slightly. She leaned heavily into the man behind her as the world swayed a bit and the man at the counter sat up looking at her. She began blinking, trying to focus her suddenly blurred vision.

"Where did you get that water?" the man at the counter suddenly demanded.

Molly blinked again and swayed into the man who held her arms. The room was out of focus, and no matter how much she blinked, it didn't seem to be helping. The chest behind her rumbled as the man spoke in what sounded like a roar, but maybe that was the roaring in her ears.

"You didn't fill that bottle in the fucking bathroom, did you?"

Molly turned her head trying to look at the man who was speaking so harshly to tell him that of course she had, what the hell did he care, water was free. Only all that came out were garbled sounds as the world around her darkened, then the water bottle fell from her nerveless fingers, rolling across the floor. She realized she was fainting from all the excitement.

"Fuck. Fuck. Baby, don't pass out, you have to tell us how long ago you drank that shit."

She could hear him yelling; she opened her eyes, seeing him hovering over her. So sexy, she thought again. "Seckey" was what she said in a blurred version of the word she was thinking. If she weren't passing out, she would have blushed at that slip of the tongue.

"Baby, tell me how long. Fuck, we can't take her to doc on the bike." She couldn't tell him; she was passing out, didn't he know that?

"Take my cage, Bone," a gruff male voice that crackled with age said.

She could feel hard arms wrapped around her, and she was being carried at a jarring rate. The man holding her yelled, "Tank, get the keys from Duck, and hurry the hell up."

She knew it was him because she could feel the vibrations of the words as they came out even though she'd closed her eyes. It was weird that she was still aware, even though she was unable to talk or move. She couldn't figure out why she was feeling so strange. Her head was still spinning, even though she was not moving, as if she were on a tilt-a-whirl. The hard arms holding her gripped her tighter, and she felt the chest that pressed against her.

A few moments later she felt herself shifted into someone

Michelle Woods

else's arms; she didn't like that this man didn't hold her as close as the first man had. Then just as quickly as she thought this, she was grabbed back by the first man, who gathered her close to his chest. She could hear muffled sounds as if her ears were working for a moment then fading out. She could only hear the roaring sounds for a moment, a slamming of a truck door the next, tires squealing as she was jostled, and a sexy male voice begging her to stay with him.

Chapter 8

Bone entered the diner with Tank, Rock, and Log. Tiny, Lucky, and Stick were outside talking to Tessa, a busty blond sweetbutt, and her friend Lena, who they'd found when they pulled up to the diner. Duck called to tell him that a dark haired woman that looked very young, twenty or so, had come into the diner looking like she'd been in a tussle. Duck said she wore a ripped shirt, was carrying a backpack, and was so small she was probably homeless, hurt, and hungry.

He'd told Duck they'd be over in a minute; the club could always use another sweetbutt or house mouse. Tank sat down next to Duck at the counter with his elbows resting back on it, almost crowding Duck off his stool, and stretched his legs out in front of him with a sigh. Duck gave him a bored look, then casually asked him, "Comfy?"

"Yep, sure am," Tank replied.

Duck didn't respond, he just reached out and swiped his elbows off the counter without a word. Tank smacked into the counter with a loud crack when the back of his head hit it on his way to the floor. Bone laughed as he watched Tank, who was a foot taller than Duck with at least sixty pounds on the man, get up off the floor rubbing the back of his head like a sissy.

Michelle Woods

"Damn, Duck. You trying to kill me?" he asked in a whine.

Duck just stared at him without saying anything. His eyes were narrowed into slits, his lips compressed into a tight line, and he looked mean enough to murder you in your sleep.

Fuck, that man was scary sometimes.

He was a retired Vice Prez who'd lived through the storm days, the days when food was dwindling, and mini-wars were fought over a safe place to stay. Whole towns had been burned to the ground during those dark days, and half the world had been a third world country before things had finally been reset. Life had been hard back then, and the men had to be harder in order to survive. Keeping their families alive was even more of a challenge and Freda, Duck's old lady, had lived to the ripe old age of seventy-two before she'd left this world. That was two years ago; Duck was seventy-six and he said he was only here because Freda would kill him for dying cause she left him. Freda and Duck were like Dog and Terry meant to be.

Duck had watched as the world was rebuilt, and had even helped rebuild it. Sixty years ago Mother Nature had decided she really was a bitch then proceeded to take back half her world by drowning it in the ocean. It had taken forty years to get things back to almost the way it had been before the floods.

Bone watched Duck silently stare at Tank. Duck wasn't much of a talker that was for sure, Bone thought, watching him pick up his coffee and take a long sip. Tank sat down at the counter a seat away from Duck, taking the same position but giving Duck his space.

"She still here?" Bone asked Duck when he had set his coffee down again.

"Yeah, the little gal's in the bathroom. Been in there for about twenty minutes." Duck looked at the door with an odd wistful expression on his face.

"I guess we wait then," Bone replied and leaned against the wall facing the front door, his back to the bathroom, while Rock sat in one of the booths along the window of the diner.

"Hey Bone, what happened the other day in Tidwell?" Fat Boy, another retired Red Devil, asked.

"That was a freakin' disaster. Jackals were laying down heavy fire. We lost Deke, and Boggie got shot in the stomach, still at doc's recovering. In the end, we killed twelve of theirs though. It was still a clusterfuck." He ran his hand through his hair. Tidwell was a town one the Red Devils' patched over clubs ran, and for the last few months they'd been having trouble with the Jackals. Bone hated turf wars.

"Boggie gonna be all right?" Duck questioned.

"Yeah, Doc said he was just gonna be laid up a while so his insides can heal enough that he can move around more. 'Bout a week I expect."

Bone didn't like it when one of his men was down because of those damned bastards who were trying to fuck with his club. Doc told him the other day that if it had taken them even ten more minutes to get Boggie to him he wouldn't have made it. It pissed him off royally that he lost one of his men and came damned close to losing another one. Damn those fucking Jackals.

They needed to nip this turf war in the bud so that they could get on with their lives. He absently watched as Lucky and Stick entered, his mind centered on the shit he was dealing with since the Jackals started trying to run drugs through their territory.

"Hey Linda, can I get a burger?" yelled Lucky as he slumped into the booth with Rock. "A lemonade too," he called a second later.

Bone snickered. "What are you, a damned pussy? A

Michelle Woods

lemonade. Fuck, wanna get a tampon too, asshole? Get a damned beer like a man." Tank let out a barking laugh, while Stick sat down on the back of the booth putting his legs in the seat laughing.

"Shit. Why are you letting a bitch in the club, Bone? Didn't Hairy tell you women had no place in the club unless they were free pussy or an ol' lady?" Duck boomed with a chuckle.

"Ya, he just didn't tell me grown men would turn into pu–" Bone heard a click behind him, and turned to see the woman had come out of the bathroom.

She was tiny, only about five foot maybe, and her dark hair was pulled back into a braid. She looked like a waif with her slightly baggy shirt and the dirty spot on one of her cheeks. Her eyes filled with panic when she saw him and his crew, and they darted around looking for an escape.

Bone was a little surprised when his cock turned to stone as he let his eyes wander down her body. Something inside him shifted and he found himself stepping closer to her, taking up some of her personal space. She wasn't his usual type; he usually liked his women busty and blonde.

He wondered what it was about her slender frame and wild eyes that got his engine roaring because he was harder than he had ever been and she was still fully clothed, which was a shocker. He looked down at her, taking in her small breasts. She was braless, and her nipples poked against the thin fabric of her shirt making him want to take it off and suck them till they were ripe little cherries. Her hair was still wet and he'd guess she'd washed it somehow in the bathroom.

Fuck, she really must be homeless.

For some reason that made his teeth clench and his body tensed. Bone stared at her, noticing her gaze trained on his abdomen with a slightly wicked grin, taking in the way some of the black mass of her hair had escaped and was curled around her ears that were small and pixyish. Her face softened, her lashes lowered to a sexy half mast, and she seemed to be flushing a little. He realized that she was as turned on as he was. He could tell by the way her lips parted and she focused on his bare stomach. Grinning like a fucking idiot, he ducked until he could catch her eyes.

"Hey, I'm up here, sweet," he teased.

She snapped her eyes up to meet his, and he saw they were a warm honey brown color surrounded by dark thick lashes. Damn, those eyes made his heart speed up as they scanned his face. What was it about her that turned him on so much?

"Now that's better, Beauty," he said, amused by her startled expression. "Duck said you were a little homeless looking. Wanna stay at my home? I can be real sweet."

He didn't question why he was offering her the privilege of living with him when he'd never offered that to a woman before; his cock had made that call. It still throbbed inside his pants, and his zipper was going to leave a permanent indentation if he wasn't careful. The fuckers sitting around laughed at him. He glared over his shoulder, but hell, they knew he wasn't sweet.

"No," she whispered, stepping away from him slightly.

He gritted his teeth; that word was his kryptonite. He'd been known to beat people half to death for saying no to him. His brothers stopped laughing, staring at her, waiting to see how he would react. Lucky for her she was a woman, and his dick was involved. Did she think she was too good for him? That thought pissed him off, causing his hands to clench into fists of rage. He noticed her trembling hands, and the way she shifted from one foot to the other while her eyes bounced around looking for an escape. Realizing that she wasn't trying to insult him, she was just scared half to death, he released his clenched fingers.

Michelle Woods

"I w-was just leaving. I don't want any trouble." She was shaking like a leaf. She darted to his left right at Tank, who moved, standing up to stop her from escaping.

"No, no, little sheep. Not gonna get away that easy," Tank teased.

"Please," she said in a soft raspy voice that had his dick jerking in his pants. The soft sound of her voice made him think of being balls deep in her and hearing her beg in that soft raspy voice. On the heels of that thought, he heard Tank's next words and was flooded with a haze of rage. His insides were clenching hard in anticipation of killing his best friend.

What the fuck was wrong with him?

"Aw…so sweet. You beg so sweet, little girl. Would you beg like that when I was fucking you?"

Bone watched as Tank's hands began to reach out for her, his words spoken low and husky, but what surprised Bone was his reaction. He was about two seconds away from ripping Tank's heart out. He stepped up behind her, his hands reaching forward to land on her hips while pulling her possessively back against him.

"No, Tank." His voice was hard, cold even, and he knew his eyes must hold the same coldness when he met Tank's eyes with his own.

Tank's hands froze in the air as he scowled at Bone. They stayed like that for several seconds, both unwilling to look away. Tank must have seen the determination to win in his eyes because he sat back down again, taking that casual pose as if nothing had happened. Bone was grateful; he knew he would have fought his friend for her if he hadn't stepped back.

It would have hurt their friendship, possibly messed with the club, a Prez and Vice should never be at odds, but he still wouldn't have been able to stop it from happening. Her soft body swayed a bit, and more of her weight settled against him. Bone settled her slight weight against him feeling odd. He wanted to rub himself all over her, to mark her. He must be losing his fucking mind. What the hell was he thinking, *mark her?*

Tank sat up alertly, staring at her intently, and sharply asked a question that almost made his heart stop. "Where'd you get that water from?"

Something about the way she moved when Tank asked that made him realize exactly where the water had come from. Suddenly he wasn't thinking about sex anymore and all his brain could think was 'fuck no, not the unfiltered water from the bathroom sink.' Bone felt rattled and a terrible pit of doom settled in his stomach.

"You didn't fill that bottle in the fucking sink, did you?"

Shit, how long did a water poisoned person have, like forty-five minutes? After forty-five minutes, the survival rate was less than ten percent. She turned to look at him, blinking owlishly with a hazy look in her eyes, which would have been sexy if the situation weren't so dire.

"Fuck. Fuck. Baby, don't pass out, you have to tell us how long ago you drank that shit."

She looked funny with the goofy smile that lit her face then, and she garbled out "Seckey." Whatever the hell that meant. He held her face in his hands, steadying her as she swayed again, blinking her eyes as if she were trying to focus.

Desperate, he asked, "Baby, tell me how long."

He caught her a moment later when her knees gave out. Scooping her up and heading to the door without a thought other than getting her to Doc as fast as he could, he stopped near the door when he realized he couldn't carry her on the bike. "Fuck, we can't take her to Doc on the bike," he said aloud to Tank, who was already holding the door for him to exit.

Michelle Woods

"Take my cage, Bone," Duck said, his hand digging out his keys from his front pocket.

"Tank, get the keys from Duck and hurry the hell up." He exited the diner with her, heading at a dead run towards Duck's cage, a rundown black Chevy. Tiny jogged up beside him, jerking the tailgate down without any questions, as Tank slammed out of the diner with the keys and jumped in, cranking the engine. He shoved her into Tiny's arms as he jumped in the bed, then grabbed her back, sitting down with her cradled in his lap. Tiny jumped in with him and hit the roof to let Tank know to go. The cage tore off with a squeal of tires.

Bone looked down at the woman; she seemed to be getting paler and when he checked her pulse it was weak. He felt an uneasy sense of panic overtaking him and he had no idea why. It was as if his body knew something it wasn't telling him. It would have ticked him off if he wasn't so afraid that she would die before they got her to Doc.

"Please," he whispered into her hair, unsure why he felt so desperate all of a sudden. "Stay with me, baby. It's going to be all right, just hold on. Don't leave me."

He clung tightly to her as the truck flew across the four miles to Doc's, the pit in his stomach twisting tighter with every shallow breath she took. Her face was beyond pale at this point and was almost chalky. He felt like an unmoored boat set adrift as he held her in the back of the jostling truck. Tank brought the cage to a screaming halt outside of the large cabin that Doc used as a makeshift hospital. Tiny and he did the shuffle of the woman again as they rushed her into the large cabin.

"Stacy, get Doc. She's got water poison, and I'm not sure how long it's been," Bone roared as he ran past the reception desk where the woman had been filing her nails.

Taming Lucca

"Shit, he's stitching up Rash. He got in another bar fight." She followed him into the room he went to and watched as he gently lay his burden down on the surgical bed there.

"Go get him, now," he roared at her again, making her jump and run from the room. Tank and Tiny were moving around the room gathering things from the shelves for an IV. Bone was unable to do anything except watch her chest rise and fall. He had to be sure she was still breathing because for some reason the fact that she lived seem paramount.

Stacy came back with Doc right on her heels. He stopped by the bed. His scope out, he placed it on her chest listening. Glancing at Bone he asked, "How long has it been? Survival rate is low if it's been more than forty-five."

He turned to Stacy, asking her to get ten cc's of Thylozeen, the drug that would kill the parasites that were currently invading her body. Bone felt his desperation ratchet up a notch as Doc said those words to him. He'd already known that they were running against a clock with water poisoning but he'd hoped he remembered wrong how long someone had before they died.

"We don't know," Bone said flatly.

Stacy returned with a syringe. Tiny had already started the IV, and Doc pushed the needle into her neck making Bone cringe a bit watching. It wasn't that he was squeamish, it was just that seeing Doc shove that needle into her made his chest ache.

"Put her on a drip, Stacy."

Doc checked her pulse, timing it on his wristwatch. After a moment he pulled a blood pressure cuff off a nearby table. Placing it around her small arm, he pumped it up then let it out. Removing the cuff from her arm when he was done, he took a look at her eyes using a penlight, and checked her pulse again. This all seemed to take hours as Bone waited for his

Michelle Woods

verdict but in reality it was only about fifteen minutes.

"Pulse is still thready, but I think you got her here in time. Nothing we can do now but wait," Doc told him when he stepped back. Looking at Stacy, he added, "I'm going to finish stitching Rash's head. Keep an eye on her pulse and come get me if it's too slow or if her color gets red."

Bone sat down in the chair next to the bed in relief feeling as if a two ton weight had just been lifted off his shoulders. Fuck, what the hell was wrong with him? He was acting like a fucking pussy over a woman he didn't even know.

Tiny and Tank leaned against the wall behind him silently watching him. Bone ran a hand over his head grateful that neither man commented on him losing his shit for the last fifteen minutes. He sat watching the tiny woman in the bed breathe wondering what caused the panic he'd felt over a complete stranger's possible death.

Was it her size that was making him feel irrationally protective of her? He was a biker, damn it. He shouldn't be so panicked about her dying on him when he hadn't even fucked her. Maybe that was it. He was freaking out because he'd been thinking of fucking her three ways to Sunday while those little bugs had been working their way to her heart. Yeah, that must be it because otherwise he was losing his fucking mind.

Running his hand through his hair again, feeling frustrated by his behavior but unable to leave her, he sat back in the chair waiting. Tiny shifted on the wall, and Stacy checked the woman's pulse again. Bone waited while she held her fingers to the pulse in her neck before taking her blood pressure again. His breath seemed frozen inside his chest as he waited for her to speak.

"Her pulse seems to be returning to normal now. If you want you can leave and I can call you when she wakes up,"

Taming Lucca

Stacy told him, stepping back from the bed. Bone racked his brain for a good reason he needed to stay with her because he wasn't moving from this chair. It came in a flash and he gruffly laid out his plan.

"Tank, go back to Tammy's diner with the cage and put a filter on the bathroom water. Ask Duck to drop my bike at the house. We don't want this happening again with someone else. I've got no fucking idea how she didn't know it wasn't filtered. I thought every-fucking-body knew that most towns don't filter the water in bathrooms due to the high cost. We need to know why she didn't know that. I'll stay here to talk to her when she wakes up." Tank raised his eyebrows but didn't comment. Bone shifted slightly when his piercing gaze landed on him; fuck, the man saw right through his bullshit excuse he'd bet.

Shit, he was still acting like a pussy.

"Stacy, any idea when she might wake up?" He tried not to seem too interested in the answer but everything inside him was focused on it. His palms felt sweaty and there was a slight ringing in his ears as he waited for the information.

"Not sure, usually takes about ten hours or so. She should be out of the woods in another hour, though."

"Good. Tank, bring my cage over in about two hours and we'll move her to my place." Bone knew that this would surprise all three of them, but he didn't give a damn. She was staying with him, and that was the end of that. He wouldn't accept any other outcome because the thought of her out of his sight for more than a second made his skin itch and his blood boil.

"Sure thing, Bone," Tank said after watching him for a long silent moment before getting up and leaving the room without asking questions. Bone was grateful the man knew him so well because otherwise he would be answering questions he didn't

Michelle Woods

have any answers for. He didn't know why he was acting like a fucking moron over this tiny woman, but he couldn't seem to help it. Tiny's head tilted and he stared at him oddly for a while but finally followed Tank out.

Stacy was the most shocked by his words, and as the two men left the room, she asked in disbelief, "You're going to allow her to stay at your house? You never allow any woman to stay there."

"Yep," Bone told her flatly, his voice warning her not to comment again. His sudden need to keep this woman close was none of her damned business.

"Huh, well, I'll be back in a minute to check her pulse." She walked to the door without looking back at him, her movements quick because he'd likely just scared her with his gruff reply. Bone didn't like scaring his people but today he couldn't say he was sorry he had. He didn't know what the fuck was happening to his normally rational self, he just knew he needed to keep the woman in the bed beside him close. It was the only urge he seemed to have at the moment and it freaked him the fuck out. Deciding it was just curiosity, he settled back into the chair to wait, watching her as she slept.

Chapter 9

Molly awakened to the sound of voices talking in another room. Her mind was hazy and she felt parched like she hadn't had water in days. Unsure where she was, she lay still trying to absorb as much information as she could about her surroundings before she let them know she was awake. Molly could tell that the bed beneath her was soft, and a pillow was propped beneath her head. She felt warm inside the thick bundle of covers that smelled delicious. Peeking out of one eye, she realized she was alone in the room.

Opening her eyes fully, she looked around discovering that she was in what appeared to be a man's room. It was rustic, almost bare, with dark cherry toned furniture. Several pairs of jeans and a set of boots lay on the floor near a half open door, where she could just make out clothes hanging up inside. A half used box of condoms was on the nightstand and the sight made Molly blush. The dresser along one wall had bullets littered across it and she could see that there were more condoms and a wallet lying on top of it as if he'd emptied his pockets and never cleaned it up.

Molly racked her brain trying to remember what had happened. She recalled being in the diner and feeling dizzy. She was assuming that she must have passed out.

Michelle Woods

Her head was filled with hazy memories that she'd been in a truck, but otherwise, she was unsure how she'd ended up in this room. Feeling itchy, she rubbed a hand over her stomach, realizing that someone had removed most of her clothing.

Molly felt panicked when she realized she was only wearing a shirt and her underwear under the thick quilt. Where the hell were her clothes? Had they drugged her? Was that why she felt fuzzy on the details of how she had been brought here?

Struggling to sit up beneath the heavy quilt, she found that she was exhausted by the effort. Falling back to rest against the wide blackened wood headboard, she panted fearfully wondering what was going on. Why was she trembling from the effort of just sitting up? Her insides were quaking and her entire body ached. She lifted a hand to her forehead holding it while she tried to figure out what had happened in the diner.

She'd been distracted by the brown-haired man's sexy abs, that much she remembered. Molly felt her cheeks heat when she recalled the way she'd stared at them as if they mesmerized her. Dear lord, what the hell? She wasn't the type to fall into lustful abandonment at the sight of a little male anatomy, why had this particular man affected her so strongly?

Hearing footsteps coming up the stairs, she realized that whoever had been talking downstairs was now on their way up here. Shit.

Molly wanted to jump from the bed and find something to wear so she could run. Only she wasn't even able to push herself up slightly on the headboard before she was too exhausted to do anything but wait. The tall sexy man from the diner came into the room, his eyes seeking hers. He walked to the foot of the big bed, staring at her.

"Good to see you're awake, sweetness." She watched him warily; he sat down on the bed by her feet. His hands reaching

Taming Lucca

out to cup them, rubbing the soles, and she knew she should tell him to stop. She didn't though because it felt too good. She watched him while clutching the covers to her chest.

"Before you passed out and almost died of water poison, I asked you some questions. I need to get some answers even though you likely aren't feeling well. Duck said you looked like you'd been in a tussle when you came into the diner. There were stains on your jeans, and your shirt was ripped. Tell me, did someone hurt you?" Bone's eyes traveled over her face while he spoke. "If they did, I promise to kill them slowly. And, by the way, what the fuck made you get water from the bathroom sink?"

She blushed when he said fuck because that word had always embarrassed her. She had rarely heard it, except when the men on her maintenance team were referring to visiting whores in the blue sector when they thought she wasn't around.

Wait, water poison?

Was that why she was so fuzzy on the details?

It must be. Damn, she was lucky to be alive right now she realized, her heart jumping into her throat, making her parched feeling increase. She blinked at him as he sat waiting on her to speak, his hands still gently rubbing up and down the arches of her feet in a slow soothing caress she wasn't protesting. It was odd that she couldn't bring herself to tell him to stop touching her. Molly didn't know what to think of her easy acceptance of his caresses.

He continued without pausing. "Don't you know that most restaurants on the outskirts of a town have unfiltered water in the bathrooms due to the cost of having it filtered? It can't make you sick unless you drink it, so why bother, everyone knows not to. Did you want to die or something? If it's because someone is after you or because they hurt you, you can tell

Michelle Woods

me. I won't judge you and if they hurt you, I'll happily kill them."

Bone gazed at the tiny dark-haired woman from the foot of his bed. His cock was thick and it throbbed painfully, making him feel like a fucking pervert. Hell, she'd almost died less than eight hours ago and here he was thinking of ripping the covers she held to her chin off her so that he could fuck her senseless. Bone liked her in his bed with her tousled hair and honey brown eyes staring at him and his dick, which strained against his zipper, liked it too.

Fuck, he really needed to get a grip on his body.

Bone was focused so intently on her that he noticed her blush bright red when he'd said fuck. He suddenly had a horrible feeling that his throbbing dick wasn't getting anywhere near her pussy anytime soon. Just fucking great.

Bone had scooped her up as soon as he'd been told by Doc that she wasn't dying and brought her here. He'd stripped off her pants after putting her into his bed and that was when his cock got hard; he'd been sporting a serious case of blue balls since.

What was it about her that made him so horny?

With her awake, his dick was protesting not being able to drown in her hot little pussy. Right now, though, he needed to find out who or what she'd been running from. She might have been running to someone, not that it mattered now because she wasn't going anywhere. She belonged to the Red Devils now. He'd claimed her and that was all there was to that because what he owned, he kept. End of story. He felt a shifting inside his chest when he thought of her as his and that was fucking with his head big time.

Bone's rioting feelings made him want to stand up and run away from the sexy dark-haired pixie in his bed but he waited for her answers to his questions instead. He'd never been a

Taming Lucca

frightened little bitch and he didn't intend to become one even if he was confused by his feelings of possessiveness in regards to her.

Bone did know that if someone had hurt her, he would kill whoever it was slowly, and laugh while they died screaming. She was theirs now, and it didn't matter that she hadn't been when it had happened. Nobody messed with family.

"What? I didn't drink poisoned water on purpose! And nobody hurt me," she squeaked, glancing up at him with wide eyes before she quickly turned them down. He watched her for another long moment, his eyes glued to the top of her head as she fiddled with the quilt, running her hand over the pattern on it.

Molly wasn't sure what to do. She was frightened by the way he stared at her with his hands still holding her feet and his dark eyes assessing her. He was asking her questions she didn't want to answer. She was afraid to tell him that she had fallen because she'd been running away from the sounds of motorcycles on the road. Aware that it was likely his club members she'd been running away from, she didn't think it would be a good idea to let him know that she'd hurt herself while running away from his friends.

"Don't lie to me, sweetness. I don't like liars. Duck said that you came in looking like you'd been roughed up, and your shirt was ripped. You also have scrapes on your hands and knees that I noticed when I was putting you in the bed earlier." He looked intently at her, seeming to be waiting for her to say something. Molly felt heat crawl up her neck to settle in her cheeks. Damn it. Why did she have to betray herself with a blush? Now he would know that she was embarrassed and he might try to press that advantage.

"I was running in the woods and I tripped, that's all. I'm not running from anyone and nobody hurt me, okay. I must

Michelle Woods

have ripped my shirt when I fell and I know that's how I scraped my hands and knees. It's also where the stains on my jeans came from so it's no bid deal." She looked up, meeting his intent gaze squarely so he could see the truth in her eyes.

Molly didn't think he fully believed her. He tilted his head, seeming to read her face, a frown furrowing his brow. His hands briefly tightened on her feet and he watched her carefully for any signs that she wasn't telling him the truth. Molly returned his stare steadily, not wanting him to think she was lying. Not that she was, everything she'd told him was technically true. She hadn't been running from anything other than the sounds of the bikes' loud motors.

"What were you running in the woods for? Did you take a ride with someone and they scared you?" he asked, his eyes lighting with a darkness she found scary and kind of dangerous.

She had a feeling his offer to kill someone for hurting her wasn't an idle threat. He meant it. Molly was a bit stunned by the level of violence that look promised.

"No, I just heard some noises that frightened me. So, I ran." She wasn't about to tell him the noise that frightened her was his crew of bikers. No way in hell was she telling him that.

"Fine, and the water?" Bone asked, watching her mull over how to respond to his inquiry. He could almost hear her brain working as if it were running around like a rat in a maze. What was she not telling him, he wondered, feeling a hard pit curl inside his stomach. If someone had frightened her, they were going to pay in spades for every second she'd been fearful.

"I didn't know," she finally settled on with a defeated sigh.

"How could you not know? Have you been living under a rock all your life or maybe you're from the prison inside the wall turned out for doing something awful?" Bone laughed at his joke.

No way was this timid little thing guilty of anything, other than maybe being too innocent for what he had planned for her. Only her eyes darted away from his, and she looked even more upset suddenly. Well, that was interesting. Bone watched her pale face and the way her hands curled on the comforter into a little ball along the edge.

"Well, I am," she said finally.

Surely she hadn't just said she was a turn out from the prison because the very idea was laughable.

"You are what?" he asked, waiting for her to clarify. Because she couldn't have just told him those idiots behind that wall had kicked her out for a crime when he knew she likely hadn't committed it, had she?

Molly exhaled loudly and then rushed to tell him. "I was released from the prison three days ago, but I didn't do what they said I did, I didn't," she said emphatically, and he wanted to snicker, because of course she hadn't. Anyone with a lick of sense could look at her and tell that she was an innocent.

"What's your name, baby? I'm Bone." He watched her shift on the bed, the covers falling to her lap. Bone couldn't help the way his eyes were drawn to the way the thin shirt revealed her little nipples. They were hard little buds and they pressed out as if they were begging for his attention. If he didn't think it would frighten her into trying to run from him, he would lean over and suck one into his mouth.

"Molly," she uttered before she bravely asked, "surely that's not the name your mother gave you, is it?"

"It's a road name. The club gave it to me when I first began riding with them." He watched her process that tidbit. Her brown eyes watched him for a long moment before she spoke again.

"I can't call you Bone. What's your real name?"

Michelle Woods

He leaned towards her, his breath teasing her lips. "I'll tell you," he whispered, knowing by the way her lips parted and her breath came in a quick little pant that she was just as affected by his nearness as he was by hers.

She looked at him expectantly, waiting for him to tell her. Her eyes filled with a dreamy haze that made his cock twitch in anticipation of the moment he would sink it inside her welcoming body. He grinned devilishly. "But only when I'm buried inside you."

She turned red, staring at him in astonishment before she exclaimed, "Tha-that's never going to happen!"

Embarrassment shined in her eyes as she stuttered it out, her mouth opening in astonishment at his audacity. Bone felt like he'd just been sucker punched because he knew her reaction to what he said next wouldn't be what his dick was hoping for. He leaned just a bit closer, his hands on the bed on either side of her as he forced himself not to jerk her into his arms so that he could ravage her.

"Don't bet on it sweetness," he growled, still hovering close to her. "Now, all that's left to talk about now is how you're going to repay me for saving your life. Personally, I think you should pay me back with exactly what we both want," he rumbled, his skin heated with the thoughts of her hot wetness wrapped like a glove around him. He watched her shift on the bed again, his dick jerking when her firm little breasts bounced a little, and his mouth watered.

Damn, he wanted to suck on those hard peaks.

"Wh-What do you me-mean, what we both want?" Molly stuttered in utter shock. He hadn't just told her to repay him by allowing him to have sex with her, had he? She wasn't a whore and she didn't intend to become one either. She felt her insides do a little dance and her body heated at the thought of him touching her. She shoved those feelings away. No, she

Taming Lucca

was not sleeping with him because she wasn't a whore, she reminded her runaway libido.

Bone's amused gaze met her shocked one. "Exactly what you think I mean, me buried to the hilt in your tight little pussy," he said, watching her flabbergasted expression.

Bone was pretty sure she wasn't going to allow him to screw her for saving her life, but his dick thought it was worth a shot to ask. After all, she might go for it. She wanted him as much as he wanted her and he was a man who took any opportunity to get what he wanted in the fastest way possible and he wanted her, badly.

"I will not sleep with you!" He could tell that she was desperately trying to think of something to say to him in response. Bone felt a smile tugging at his lips when she suddenly said, "I can do other things. Help out."

"Hmmm…well a good blowjob wouldn't be refused I suppose, but I had my heart set on fucking you," Bone teased. Aware that he was pushing her and that it might come back to bite him in the ass if she decided to run from him, he grinned, still watching her reaction. Not that he would let her get away, but it would be a pain in the ass if he had to chase after her

"What! That is not what I meant!" Blushing again, she almost screamed it at him.

"Huh. So, what did you mean?" he asked, sincerely interested in the answer now.

"I'm a mechanic," she said in alarm. "I can fix your bikes or cars. Or anything with a motor really."

Bone began laughing because the idea of her anywhere near his bike was funny as hell. She was likely to break it trying to prove herself useful. He wasn't sexist, he could just tell that she wasn't the type for that kind of labor. She was too delicate. She'd likely been a nanny or something while she was inside the cage they called a city.

Michelle Woods

"You think for a second I'm gonna let a woman handle my bike? Baby, you are too cute." He was laughing so hard he was bent over. Molly was thinking that it was a brilliant plan and that she could do that until she found a way out to get to the Blue Bandits. Right up until he started laughing at her before he'd uttered those last words. Her hands clenched into fists and she was angrier than she could ever remember being when he told her she was 'too cute'.

Seriously? What a sexist jerk!

"I'm a damned good mechanic. Why wouldn't you let me work on it?" Molly said through her tightly clenched teeth, her spine straightening as she felt her body tense with indignation. She could not believe that he would refuse to let her fix a mechanical problem because she was a woman.

Men! They were all bastards.

On the heels of that thought, she remembered Carl and felt slightly guilty for that unflattering thought but she quickly shook it off. Carl was just one of the rare few who weren't total assholes, she decided.

"Now, now, Molly, no need to get upset. You'll just have to work your debt off on your back in my bed I think." Bone watched her face turn bright red again and almost let out a snicker because he was enjoying teasing her.

He should show her some pity by telling her that he was going to have her be his house mouse for now, but he let it drag out a little longer. He wasn't giving up on getting her in his bed by any means, but he wouldn't force her either. He was going to allow her a little time to get used to the idea before he pounced. His dick protested with a jerk of disappointment in his pants.

"Bone, you here?" a loud male voice called out from downstairs before she could reply.

"Ya, I'm up here in my room," Bone called back before

Taming Lucca

looking at her, taking in the way her little nipples still poked at the thin t-shirt. "Cover up again, baby. Don't want anyone to see my goods," he said, watching her snatch the covers to her chin again. She glared at him with an evil-eyed gaze that made him chuckle because she looked so damned cute with her lips drawn and her eyes narrowed.

Slim stuck his head in the door, barely noticing the woman sitting in his bed. Bone stood ready to walk out of the room to talk to him, but stopped when he heard Molly speak.

"Slim," Molly gasped softly.

What the fuck? How did she know Slim? And why the hell was she all breathy when she said his name. If he didn't know that Slim was insanely in lust with his old lady, he'd already have him on the ground because of that little breath of sound she'd just made. Molly shouldn't sound that way when saying any name but his.

"Um, yeah, do I know you?" Slim questioned, looking confused while taking a longer look at her where she lay on the bed with the covers pulled to her neck. Bone stared at her too wanting to know what the hell was going on.

Molly had been so outraged at Bone's earlier pronouncement that she was a little slow to remember what Lisa had told her to say if she needed help. She didn't know why she hadn't thought of it back at the diner. Maybe it was because she was already fuzzy from the water poisoning when she left the bathroom? It didn't matter, she decided as she racked her brain, trying to remember what Lisa had said.

Finally it came to her. "Lisa–Lisa said to take me to her old man Slim if I needed help," she said with triumph. Bone had turned back towards the bed and she saw fury flash across his face at her announcement. His hands balled into fists by his sides, and the glare he gave her made her want to hide under the bed. She felt herself tremble and she clutched the covers

Michelle Woods

tighter.

"Shit!" Slim said.

Bone stared at the woman with deadly intent; he wanted to grab Molly and shake her. She had just invoked Slim's protection with that statement. He didn't want her to have anyone else to turn to. He wanted to be the one who protected her, kept her safe, the one she turned to when she needed help. Now she had just given another man that right, and he was not happy with that at all. His stomach clenched and his fingers itched to strangle his friend.

With a clenched jaw, he asked, "Where the fuck did you meet Lisa?"

"Th-the M-market," she stuttered.

"Shit! She's the mousey woman Lisa took a liking to a few days ago that was just turned out of the city. Lisa told me that she was being chased by some guard—" Slim said suddenly.

"The fuck you say! You said no one was chasing you, Molly. You lied to me. What the fuck?" Bone roared, cutting off whatever else Slim was going to say. Bone was pissed now because she'd lied to him. He felt like his head was going to explode. If that son of a bitch had hurt her he was a dead man.

"W-wait, no, I didn't and please don't say that word," she stuttered out, knowing she was blushing again hearing it slip so freely from his lips. "He was just following me at the market to cause trouble, but Lisa and two of your friends helped me get away."

"She means Pretty Boy and Tanner, I left them to keep an eye on Lisa," Slim explained as he stepped farther into the room.

"Well, that's good, but why was he after you in the first place, Molly?" Contempt filling his voice, Bone stared at her waiting for her answer.

Taming Lucca

"I don't know. I think he was just a jerk. He didn't like me because I lived in the Slum district. Or maybe it was because I was supposed to be a thief. I don't know." Molly shifted nervously while she clutched the quilt to her chest. Bone felt some of the rage slip away from him but Slim's next words brought it roaring back with a vengeance.

"Bone, she was promised protection." Slim grimaced as he said it, waiting for his reaction to that reminder. He turned with a murderous look in his eyes towards Slim, clenching and unclenching his fists. He wanted to rip him apart and it was really screwing with his head. He shouldn't be this attached to her, he barely even knew her for fuck's sake. Slim however had been like a brother to him for years; it was not normal for him to feel this way, but he did.

"Do you have a death wish?" Bone asked Slim with serious intent.

"No, but my old lady said I'd help her. You know that I can't not offer to protect her if she asks." Slim stood straighter near the doorway without flinching away from Bone. Bone had to respect him for that. Slim knew him and he was still standing between him and Molly. It wasn't smart on Slim's part but he could respect the other man for it.

Molly glanced between the two men noting the way they squared off in the middle of the room. Bone was really pissed, and they looked as if they were going to fight. Molly felt her heart begin to pound. They were making her nervous and she didn't think Lisa would thank her for getting Slim killed. The woman had likely not intended her olive branch to be used against one of the Red Devils.

"Wait, you don't have to fight. Just make him not force me into sex with him. I can do other stuff like wash clothes and housework to pay him back," Molly said quickly, trying to prevent the brewing confrontation. Slim's jaw dropped open

Michelle Woods

as he stared between her and Bone with astonishment.

"Fuc––I mean, shit. Molly, I wasn't going to rape you! That wasn't what I meant," Bone said, turning to her, running a hand through his hair in frustration. Bone watched her for a minute before he turned to look at Slim, whose mouth was still hanging open and his eyes were almost popping out of his head. Bone felt anger stir inside him again at the look Slim was giving him because that fucker should know that he wasn't into forcing women.

"Slim, you know damned well that I would never force a woman," Bone growled, his anger evident in the gruffness of his tone.

Slim shook his head. Closing his mouth, he smiled at Bone with glee. "No, I'm shocked that you just stopped saying fuck because she asked you not to," the asshole said.

Shooting him the finger, Bone looked at the woman lying calmly in the middle of his massive bed. "Shut the hell up, asshole," he grunted before turning to Molly. "You can do the housework and cook, but for now rest. Doc said you needed three days of bed rest to recover. I'll bring you some soup in a little while."

Molly was relieved that he wouldn't force her to have sex with him even as her hoo-ha protested with a violent ache. She felt a nervous ball of energy curling inside her, making her slightly nauseated because she had no idea how to cook anything. She bit her lip with distress, but how hard could it be. She could take an engine apart in twenty minutes flat; it couldn't be that hard to cook, could it?

"Let's go, asshat, she said she would stay," Bone said as he ushered Slim out the door, leaving her alone.

Molly settled back on the bed, her mind reeling from the past hour's events. It was strange how she'd been afraid of Bone at first when he'd entered, but for some reason she

Taming Lucca

wasn't now. She wasn't usually a trusting person. Yet, after one short conversation she was content to stay with him for now. Molly likely needed her head examined because she was letting her desires affect her brain cells. When did she become a bimbo and where was her backbone?

Laying back in the bed, she snuggled down in the covers that smelled of spice and man. She was going to be here a while it seemed, so she might as well take a nap.

Chapter 10

Bone followed Slim down the stairs, his head still whirling with crazy thoughts about Molly. At the bottom of the stairs, Slim stood in the brown rustic living room, turning to face Bone with a serious expression.

"I stopped by Vince's today on my way up to Titus with Lisa. He gave me some disturbing intel. Apparently, those assholes are getting bold."

Bone didn't need to ask which assholes he was talking about because the Jackals had been a thorn in his side for months now. It pissed him off that they were running drugs through Red Devils territory for the last two years, but in the last six months they seemed to be getting braver.

"They set up a Juice factory in Longville," Slim continued, his face grim.

"Fuck, that's only a half hour from here."

Bone couldn't believe they were setting up a half hour away from his town. The fuckers weren't getting bold, they were getting fucking stupid. It showed a lack of respect on a level that made Bone want to blow them off the planet. He felt his head begin to ache. Damn it, he was sick of these assholes moving in on his territory. They knew how the Red Devils would react; why the fuck would they chance this bullshit?

Taming Lucca

Scratching the back of his neck, he leaned on the stair railing.

"Yeah, I have all the information we need to take care of it. Do you want to wait till church, or move on it now?" Slim asked, standing next to the entrance to the kitchen with one boot covered foot propped on the wall. Pushing off the railing, Bone moved into the kitchen and pulled some soup out of the freezer with jerky angry movements. Needing something to do with his hands before he started throwing shit, he grabbed a pot from the cabinet above his head before slamming it on the stovetop. After running cold water over the bottom of the container of soup, he dumped it into the pot, turning on the burner.

"Do we have solid intel? We can't afford another fuckup like Tidwell," he said, remembering one of his men dying and another barely making it to Doc's because they'd gotten faulty intel on the Jackal safe house they were raiding in Tidwell. Bone didn't want another shitstorm like that one.

"It's solid."

Bone leaned on the end of the counter looking at Slim propped up on the wall just inside the kitchen. His mind wandered over the number of men they'd need for the raid as well as the number they'd have to leave behind to protect the club's home base. After some quick tallies of who would need to be where, he finally said, "Gather everyone at church in an hour and call the prospects that are over at the farm and have them come back to the clubhouse. I want it covered so there isn't any trouble while we're handling this shit in Longville."

"What about your girl?" Slim asked, crossing his arms over his chest.

"I'll have Aunt Mae stay with her till I get back. Have Pretty Boy watch the house to be sure. And call the retired members and see if any of them can help us out tonight, either here or with the cleanup. I'll call Duck and Tank, you text everyone

Michelle Woods

else and prepare your old lady."

That settled, Bone moved back to the stove stirring the pot with a spoon, trying to break up the lumps of icy soup so it would warm faster. He was concentrating on the task when he heard a snicker behind him and turned to watch Slim.

Slim nodded to him, pushing himself off the wall with a parting shot of "Never thought I'd see the day you were playing nursemaid to a woman."

"Shut up, fucker!" he said, laying the spoon down on the spoon rest with the intent to beat Slim's ass. Slim took off headed to the door, his laughter floating over his shoulder as he slammed out the screen door before Bone could reach him.

"Yeah, yeah, you'll be patching her before the week's out," Slim called from the porch.

"Fuck no, I won't! I just want to fuck her a few times, then I'll find her an old man," he growled at Slim's retreating form.

Bone knew even as he made the pronouncement that he already wanted to rip off the faceless man's dick and beat him with it. Slim was laughing while pulling out his phone and Bone slammed the door behind him.

Shit, he was so fucked.

Bone went back to the kitchen to make his calls and check the soup again. He felt like a freaking idiot standing in front of the stove making soup for the tiny firecracker in his bed.

Fuck, his cock was always getting him into trouble.

After talking to Aunt Mae, who said she would be over in about thirty minutes, he had called Duck and Tank. He filled them in on what Slim had found out about the Juice factory and asked them to meet him and the rest of the club at church. The soup was done by then so he put it into a bowl and poured some juice into a glass. Setting it all on a tray, he headed and back upstairs to Molly.

Taming Lucca

Entering the bedroom he almost dropped the tray, his eyes taking in her lying in his bed. Bone growled low and deep as his cock jumped to attention, throbbing painfully. He stared hard, unable to breath for a moment, his eyes glued to her body. While she was sleeping she'd kicked the covers off and she was sprawled on her back with one leg bent upwards revealing her panty-covered pussy.

Her shirt had ridden up and now rested just below her breasts showing him the nicely rounded curves. The panties, a periwinkle blue with little bows on the sides at her hips, had shifted slightly and showed half of the sweet little honey pot beneath. He wanted to grab those legs and wrap them around his shoulders as he buried his face between them licking her until she came screaming his name.

Instead he set the tray down on the table. Moving to the bed, he reached out, intending to pull the sheet back up over her before he was too tempted by her unintentional display, but at that moment she wiggled her hips a bit. His hand near the covers twisted around her legs and landed on her inner thigh.

Feeling the smooth skin beneath his hand made him want to come in his pants like a green boy with his first crush. Staring at his hand resting on her soft thigh like it owned that sweet little body, he was unable to stop himself from gently caressing her thigh. He rubbed his hand upwards just a tiny bit before sliding it back down the inside of her leg. He didn't allow himself to touch her anywhere else, and still he was so painfully hard that he wondered if his cock would burst.

He didn't know if he'd ever been this hard before, even when he was fucking a woman. The sensation of her silky smooth skin sliding beneath his finger was incredible. He groaned softly. Bone couldn't remember ever wanting anything as badly as he wanted Molly's legs wrapped around

Michelle Woods

his shoulders, or better yet his hips as he pounded her into the bed.

Fuck.

Her thigh suddenly stiffened under his caress and his gaze shifted up her body, slowly taking in every inch of skin his eyes cataloged, till his eyes met hers. He could see the fear filling the suddenly dark green depths. He reluctantly forced his hand to release her and quickly jerked the sheet over her. She seemed to let out a relieved breath as she watched him with wary eyes.

Molly woke up to find Bone caressing her inner thigh. Her body felt liquid and she almost moaned aloud as the hard male fingers smoothed over her skin gently. She didn't want him to stop, but she was fearful of the sensations he was stirring inside her. She wasn't a virgin, and she'd had sex with a few men, including Luzen, the idiot, but the feelings he stirred in her were unlike anything she had felt before.

For some reason her reaction to Bone's caresses made her body burn like it was dipped in fire. She had never, not even once in her twenty-one years, been turned on by a man like she was by him. Feeling his hand almost between her legs made her want to pull his hand closer and let him do very naughty things to her.

Molly felt her cheeks heat because she should be ashamed, she barely knew the man, and yet she wanted to allow him to take her any way he wanted. She'd professed to not be a whore and yet her body was betraying her. Her body wanted this man and her hoo-ha was enough of a hussy to allow him to do anything he wanted as long as she was able to come.

Molly knew that she needed to discover a way to get to the Blue Bandits fast, or she was going to end up in his bed. Her hands pulled against the sheet as she tried to gather her wits and prevent her raging libido from commanding him to just screw her already.

Geez, she needed to get a grip.

"Sit up," he murmured and he moved over to the dresser to pick up a tray. He set it down on her lap when she sat up in the bed like he ordered. Molly stared down at the tray; the soup smelled delicious and her stomach chose that moment to let out a loud rumble. Embarrassment made her dip her head as she lifted the spoon from beside the bowl, dipping it into the soup.

Bone sat down on the edge of the bed, his hand lifting to brush her hair back from her face. She realized then that he must have unbraided it earlier when he'd undressed her. She didn't know what to say so she just began to eat the soup, realizing after she took the first bite how hungry she was. She let out a moan of pleasure at the flavors that burst on her tongue from the well-cooked soup.

Bone couldn't seem to stop himself from touching her again as he watched her pick up the spoon to eat. He brushed her hair away from the side of her face, watching her sip some of the soup, grinning when she moaned while taking another bite.

"This is good," she said, looking up at him in surprise.

"Good. Make sure you eat it all, baby. You need to get your strength back and this will help."

He sat back against the headboard next to her wishing he could just stay here in his bedroom with her all night instead of leaving to take care of the stupid drug dealers trying to move into Red Devils turf. Knowing that he couldn't stay, he watched her eat and enjoyed what little time he could afford to squeeze out of the night to spend with her.

It was strange how he was content just looking at her when he'd normally be bored with any other woman, but for some reason she fascinated him. After she had eaten all the soup,

Michelle Woods

with little contented sighs and moans that made him want to push her back on the bed and see if she'd make the same noises while he fucked her, he lifted the tray and set it on the dresser again.

Opening a drawer, he pulled out his .22, laying it, his knife, and his brass knuckles on the top, leaving them there. Turning back to the bed, he walked over with the last item he'd pulled from the dresser, a spare satellite phone, which he handed to Molly.

"Baby, I have to go out tonight and I won't be back till midday tomorrow," he said, surprising her. He eyed her for a long moment drinking in the pale silky skin and the dark halo her hair made around her face. His eyes were drawn to her lips as he watched her, and he wondered how they'd taste. He knew that he wasn't leaving without a sample; he just wasn't able to go without a little something to take with him.

Molly watched as he took out a gun, a knife and some sort of metal from the dresser and began laying them on top of it. Even as she watched she wasn't frightened, which was strange. She knew that had it been any other man taking those things from the drawer she would have been freaking out right about now, but she just watched him waiting to see what he was doing. It was odd that less than a day ago she had been scared to death of him and his crew, yet now she just felt oddly safe here. She couldn't fathom why that was.

She was surprised when he held the phone out to her and told her that he was leaving. She wasn't expecting him to tell her where he was going and for how long.

"Okay," she uttered, still watching him hold the phone out to her.

Taking it, she saw it was one of the satellite phones the guards back in the city used. Molly stared down at it, surprise

Taming Lucca

overtaking her. These phones were expensive and would work anywhere.

Why was he giving it to her?

She knew how much one of these babies cost and it really was crazy of him to just hand her a sat phone when he barely knew her. The technology of these phones was from a time before the floods. Five years prior to the wave hitting, they had launched nineteen satellites made of a combination of almost indestructible metal that lasted about three hundred years into space that allowed cell phones to work all over the world without issues. Because they were no longer easily able to create the programming that went into the phones, they were now quite costly. It took weeks to make a hundred or so of them whereas prior to the disaster it only took days to make thousands of them.

"I want you to call me if anything happens, okay?" He looked at her intently as he handed her the phone, laying it in her hand then cupping her cheek. "Anything that scares you after I leave, you call Pretty Boy first and tell him to come here. Then you call me. We're both in the contacts. Got it?"

"Okay," she replied again, looking up into his eyes with an odd sense of being connected with him in some unknown way. He leaned towards her and suddenly his lips were pressing against hers with a light pressure. Then as if unable to stop himself, he grunted and his tongue licked across her lips seeking entry. Unable to stop her desire to touch him even knowing that she shouldn't allow it, she opened her mouth, feeling his tongue stroke against hers, slow and sensual.

She responded with an involuntary moan as her tongue met his in a tentative clash. He deepened the kiss as he moved onto the bed, his hand still holding her cheek. Her hands moved to his shoulders, the phone forgotten as it fell to the bed. She clung to him, set adrift with sensations of lust

Michelle Woods

bombarding her suddenly. He growled and began devouring her mouth, eating at her lips with hungry sounds of demand as his hand moved from her face and his arms reached around her, pulling her into his chest tightly.

She was overwhelmed with sensation, her heart pounding as his hand moved to bury in her hair, holding her for his invasion. Molly was shocked at the passion his demanding kiss unleashed. Her tongue mated with his in a sensual dance of give and take. His scent filled her head, leaving her dazed and achy, her body clenched as pleasure raced through her veins, her body becoming wet with desire. She was suddenly on fire.

Bone couldn't believe how sweet Molly's mouth tasted. She was moaning and rubbing against him as he pulled her into. Her little hands were curled against his shoulders clinging to him; her tight nipples poked his chest hard as pebbles. His hand buried in her hair while the other caressed her back.

He sank into her, his teeth nipping at her lips. Wanting to mark her, he consumed her with long deep strokes. His slowly kissed his way down her neck, leaving little nips and bites as he licked his way down toward her breast. He needed to taste those sweet buds with a need so strong it made him dizzy. Bone had never been so out of control with so little contact. His cock throbbed, aching inside his pants. He felt like he was starving for her and he couldn't seem to get enough. He needed more.

So wrapped up in his need of her, he didn't immediately recognize the dinging sound that seemed to be going off every few seconds. A groan of disappointment filled his chest as he realized the dinging was his doorbell. With a curse, he nipped a few more times at her neck before he pulled away, his achy cock protesting the need to let her go.

Molly was confused when Bone pulled away, his mouth

leaving her neck where he'd been kissing and nipping. Her eyes were hazy when she met his and she could see the unfulfilled desires in his. Her head spun with the dark sensuality she saw lurking in them and Molly worried that when she gave in to his commands she would lose herself. Fear and desire mixed together making her lips part as she stared at him when he slowly pulled back from her.

She heard a ding dong sound and realized someone was here, and that disturbing thought was followed by the realization that she had just let a man she had met literally hours ago kiss her senseless.

How could she have allowed this to happen?

She wasn't the type to let a man she barely knew have her and yet she'd been willing, even needy, only a few moments ago. She blushed scarlet again and as he began to move away from the bed, she murmured, "That can't happen again. It was wrong of me to allow it."

He turned to her with a hard look.

"It will happen again, babe." His hands reached out as he stopped at the dresser picking up the items he'd removed earlier. He holstered the gun at his back and hooked the knife on his pants. He turned to her again watching her for a long moment, his eyes running over her body possessively.

"Soon," he finally added.

Molly was overwhelmed with the heat that filled her body at that bold pronouncement. "No, I don't think so," she replied just as boldly.

"We'll have this conversation when I get back. Call me if you need me and remember, something happens, you call Pretty Boy, then me. Got me?" He paused in the doorway watching the sexy minx lying in his bed. He wanted to walk back over there and finish what they had started a few minutes ago. His dick jerked in agreement.

Michelle Woods

Damn, she was sexy when she got all bossy. And that adorable little frown which made her face look a little lopsided was cute as hell. He grinned, unable to stop the curling of his lips as he observed her back straighten and her eyes narrow.

"Yeah, I got it the first time," she parroted back at him in the same demanding tone he'd used.

"Good. Aunt Mae's here and she is going stay with you till I get back tomorrow. Behave while I'm gone." He walked out the door, heading down the stairs to open the door for Aunt Mae. At the foot of the stairs he paused, adjusting his hard cock into a more comfortable position and hoping like hell Aunt Mae didn't notice. Opening the door, he was surprised to find not only Aunt Mae, but also Lisa standing in his doorway.

"What are you doing here?" he demanded of Lisa, anger wilting the cock he'd been worried about Aunt Mae seeing. She'd better not be thinking she was taking Molly home with her because he wasn't about to let that happen.

Not in this fucking lifetime.

"I'm here to make sure she's really okay staying here with you, Bone," Lisa said with a fierce light in her eyes. Not having time to mince words, he flatly laid it out for her.

"Look, she stays. You don't want me to kill your old man to keep her, and I will." He watched her eyes widen slightly at his blunt statement.

Lisa nodded, her face twisted in surprise at his possessive declaration, but she didn't comment and he knew she'd leave it alone. "I'll be back in the morning. Thanks for taking care of her. Call me if anything goes wrong. And Lisa, thanks, she needs a friend, just don't take it too far." He was out the door heading to church before either woman could reply.

Chapter 11

Behave, he'd said to her as if she was an errant child in need of discipline. Her hands were balled against the comforter, her teeth ground together and she smacked her hand into the bed, anger burning inside her. She felt a muscle jumping in her jaw and she let out a little growl.

How *dare* he!

Molly lay there unable to find the strength to get up which made her anger and frustration even worse. She needed to leave for sure now; what had happened a few minutes ago should never have happened. Remembering the feeling of his lips pressed against hers and the way his hands had caressed her skin made her burn for an entirely different reason. Feeling the flood of desire that washed away the anger, she raised a hand touching her lips. They still stung a bit from his rough treatment of them.

She shook her head with disbelief at herself, feeling slightly breathless when thinking of his touch. She had never allowed a man to be so forward with her person so soon after meeting him. She had allowed Bone such liberties with her person because she was turning into a damned hussy and it was all that man's fault. Yep, it was his sexy abs. They stole every brain cell she owned and redirected them to her hoo-ha.

Michelle Woods

If he hadn't stopped, she wasn't sure that she wouldn't have let him push her back in that big bed and take her. Molly groaned as she kicked her feet against the bed letting out a frustrated sigh. Dear lord, she was losing her damned mind. It was official.

Bone, his name was Bone. What a ridiculous name. Shaking her head as she realized he was named after a body part, for goodness sakes, who wanted to be called Bone? Molly didn't know but he thought she would stay here and cater to his pleasure like a damned pet.

She was no one's pet.

She could hear footsteps coming up the stairs and wondered who Aunt Mae was. Molly was a little offended that he'd called someone to stay with her. She didn't need a babysitter; of course, she couldn't get up from the bed. She grimaced. Okay, maybe she did need a babysitter, at least until she got over almost dying a few hours ago.

She was surprised when the woman who came into the room wasn't a stranger. Lisa, from the market, walked into the room, a cheerful smile on her face, her blue hair pinned up in an artful arrangement that Molly envied.

A few seconds later an older woman who looked to be about sixty years old followed her into the room, and Molly knew this must be Aunt Mae. She wore a pair of leather pants and a black Red Devils t-shirt, and had shoulder-length gun-metal gray hair. She had wide hips and wore high-heeled shoes that looked dangerous. Molly couldn't help but stare at the woman because she wasn't what she'd been expecting when Bone said Aunt Mae. She'd pictured an old grandmotherly type and this woman was far from that. She was too flamboyant-looking in that outfit.

"Hey sugar, how ya feeling?" Lisa asked stopping beside the bed. Molly opened her mouth to answer but before Molly could get a word out, Aunt Mae's booming voice cut her off.

"You didn't tell me she was such a beauty." Her smile filled with an odd mixture of glee and what looked like motherly pride. That didn't make any sense, Molly thought, a little confused as to why the woman would feel motherly towards her. "No wonder our Bone's all worked up. 'Bout time I'd say," she said with a chuckle.

"Yep, bet she'll be patched by next month," Lisa said, laughing as the older woman moved to sit in the large blue armchair beside the dresser.

"Um—what's that mean, patched?" Molly questioned as she struggled to sit up on the bed, finally managing with a heavy sigh. Lisa looked at her and laughed her tinkling laugh again. "Oh honey, I forgot you don't have any clue about an MC." She tapped gently on Molly's legs to get her to move them. Molly bent them beneath the covers and Lisa sat down on the end of the bed, falling back across it with a groan.

"Damn, Bone has a comfy bed," she breathed in contented pleasure. Molly would have to agree but then anything was better than the ground or the cot she'd spent the last few weeks sleeping on.

"You're acting like such a rude girl," Aunt Mae clucked at Lisa with a smile, and Lisa responded by flipping the older woman the bird from where she lay on the bed. Molly expected the woman to respond with indignation but Aunt Mae just chuckled.

After a little shake of her head and a sigh, she continued. "Patched means you're a man's old lady, which is like marriage. See, I'm Slim's old lady."

Smiling widely with pleasure, she lay back on the bed looking up at Molly. Molly wondered with envy if that huge grin made her face hurt. She was still confused as to why being 'patched' meant married.

Michelle Woods

"So you're married to Slim then?" she asked her.

She became even more confused when Lisa said in horror, "Lord no. That's not for me. My mama was married to a man who beat her for twenty years. Thank God my Grams took me in when I was two, otherwise it would have been me too." Lisa made a sour face, and Aunt Mae interrupted.

"You're confusing the girl, Lisa. What she meant to say was that a lot of the women who are considered or actually married to a member of the club wear a property patch on them like Lisa's wearing. Show her," she said motioning to Lisa, who moaned at having to move, and rolled a bit so Molly could see the back of the leather vest she was wearing. On the back, it said 'Property of Red Devils M.C.' and beneath that was a patch with 'Slim' on it and the devil logo between them.

"That's, umm––interesting. So you're not married?" Molly asked, her brow twisted with confusion, still not really understanding this new tidbit of information fully.

Lisa chuckled as she lay back on the bed again. "Ha, don't let my old man hear you saying that. He'll freak on ya. He's been trying to get me to marry him for real ever since Dog and Terry got married by Preach. He says now that I'm knocked up we need to be married."

"Well, honey, it's already happened, you've been together for six years. You're not your mother." Aunt Mae looked sad as she watched Lisa. "He makes you glow, child. He's always made you glow."

Molly tried to push up so she could stand; she really had to go to the bathroom. She found that even sliding a few inches made her tired.

She exclaimed with frustration, "Why am I so damned weak?"

Then realizing she'd cursed out loud, she turned red, but it didn't even seem to faze the two women.

Taming Lucca

"Well, dang, Molls," Lisa said, looking at her with a raised brow. "You almost died yesterday, ya know. It's only because of what happened to Katie, Sal's daughter, a few years ago that Doc even had that drug on hand. That he did was damned lucky." She pushed up on her elbows looking sad to Molly.

"What happened to Katie?" she asked curiously. Despite the urge she had to use the restroom she wanted to hear more; this story sounded interesting.

"Well, she was about what, sixteen, Aunt Mae?"

"No, she was seventeen and that boy was barely twenty," Mae replied, her eye holding such a sorrowful expression that Molly wasn't sure she did want to know this story.

They didn't seem too happy telling it, but Lisa was already continuing. "Anyway, they were out at Devil's Ridge near the falls. They were skinny dippin' in the river, and they were messing about pushing each other under, only he wasn't ready at one point and he swallowed a bunch of water. He didn't realize he'd drunk so much of it I guess. They were lying on the bank when he realized what was happening to him. Katie managed to get him into the back of her truck. She flew hell bent for leather to get him to Doc's." Lisa grinned then, her smile making her face glow as Aunt Mae had pointed out a few minutes ago. She continued, "Damn, that girl can drive. She got him to Doc's in under ten minutes. And Devil's Ridge is twenty-two minutes at seventy-five miles an hour according to Trick." At this, Aunt Mae chuckled with merriment, finally losing the haunted look she and Lisa had both worn.

"Course she can, I taught her myself," she exclaimed, and Lisa's tinkling laugh rang out again, relieving some of the sadness that seemed to have filled the room. Aunt Mae winked at Molly when she glanced at her and Molly sent her a tentative smile in response.

124

Michelle Woods

"And who better than a former Indy driver."

"Indy driver, like those crazy vids they have of old races in the city?" Molly asked, her mouth parting in surprise. Surely they weren't talking about those crazy people who'd driven those tiny cars. The vids had shown wrecks where people had died in fiery crashes. She couldn't imagine Aunt Mae in one of those cars speeding down the roadway; that was insane.

"Yes, like those crazy vids. The world would be a hell of a lot more fun if we still had them races too," Aunt Mae grumbled.

Lisa shook her head at her and snorted a little at Aunt Mae's pronouncement before continuing. "Anyway, as I was saying before we went to crazy town with psycho granny over there," she pointed at Aunt Mae, who huffed in distaste. "Katie got him to Doc fast. But even though it was soon enough to treat the water poisoning, Doc didn't have the medication for him. Water poison is so rare these days. At least now that most people are aware of it and how to avoid it. So with Katie hysterically begging Doc to save him, and Doc not having a way to help, the boy died. Katie still hasn't forgiven herself, and she's twenty now, it's kinda sad. But ever since that night Bone makes sure we're never without that medicine. It expires, so they replace the drug every two years. Which is lucky for you because we hadn't had a case of water poison since Buck died."

"That's really sad." Molly's chest ached for the unknown girl who still felt guilty over something that wasn't her fault. It was also lucky. She would have died if it hadn't been for that horrible event.

Feeling her bladder urge her to get out of bed, she realized that she was going to need help getting to the bathroom. Like now. Feeling her cheeks heat, she tried her best to push up from the bed only to find herself sitting up but too shaky to stand. Frustration made her let out a little huff as she tried to move her legs off the bed without falling on her ass when she managed to get them beneath her.

Lisa saw her struggling to the edge of the bed and stood, moving to help her up.

"Bathroom, I'm guessing," she laughed and helped Molly walk the few feet to the bathroom. Molly turned bright red when Lisa helped her sit on the toilet, but she managed to get her underwear off without help thankfully. When she was done, Lisa helped her back to the bed.

Molly lay back exhausted feeling as if she'd just run ten miles when in reality she had only walked about ten feet. Aunt Mae was tucking the covers around her. "Now sweetheart, you get some rest. We can't have Bone get back and think that I didn't take good care of you. Are you hungry?" the older woman asked kindly.

Molly shook her head. "No, Bone fed me soup earlier."

"Ah, taught that boy right, Marian did."

"Marian was his mother by the way," Lisa interrupted.

"Yes she was, but stop being impertinent, Lisa. Molly, you rest up. Lisa and I will be downstairs if you need us. Just holler, we'll hear. We'll sleep in the guest room next door too, so we can hear you if you call out," Aunt Mae informed her before she and Lisa left her alone.

As Molly fell into a deep sleep surrounded by the masculine and cinnamon scent of Bone's bed, she thought about how strange it was that she felt more connected here with these people after only a few days than she ever had with her own family.

Chapter 12

Bone ran a hand over the back of his neck letting out a loud groan. Damn, he was tired. Looking around the warehouse, he saw the club moving around, stacking up the bodies, and clearing out the drugs.

It had taken them ten hours to empty out this damned warehouse. They'd spent four hours getting things coordinated and waiting till it was dark and it had taken four more to kill the thirty Jackals now laying in the pile of bodies along the wall.

Thankfully they hadn't taken large numbers of casualties despite the numbers they'd faced. Bone had been more prepared and he'd brought twenty-five men tonight. They'd had three members injured. Stony was the only one who was critical, but they had been lucky. With so many Jackals here tonight it could have gone very differently had they not had the element of surprise on their side.

Those damned Jackals had some major hardware in that back room. Tank was gleefully exclaiming over each new item as he took inventory. Tank and his damned weapons fetish; Bone felt a snicker as he remembered the moment they'd found the room filled with guns and ammo. The man had almost had an orgasm when he saw the two old school missile

Taming Lucca

launchers and the laser rifles with the enhanced scopes.

Bone rubbed between his eyes letting out a chuckled when he saw Tank walked out of the room wearing six guns and carrying two rocket launchers. Dog was walking out behind him, a sour expression on his face. Duck walked over to stand near Bone looking utterly disgusted.

"Told that damned fool that he can't carry that shit on his bike. Idiot," Duck said as he smacked the back of Tank's head, causing Bone to double over with laughter. Duck was about a foot shorter than Tank's 6' 5" frame; it was funny as shit when he beat up on Tank.

"Ouch, that hurt, damn it. I told you I'd give them to a prospect to take back in a cage, you evil old bastard." Tank was glaring at Duck. Bone was still laughing over the entertaining by-play between the two men when Tiny, Dog and Stick walked up to them.

"We got the drugs taken care of. The Dixons are coming to get it in about an hour," Tiny said, referring to a patched over club that lived on the coast. He stared at Tank.

"Compensating?" Dog asked with a grin.

"No, fucker. I don't need to. My dick's like the rest of me, more than enough." Tank glared at Dog while clutching the guns, looking ridiculous.

"Hey Tank, I think there's another launcher over in the corner, maybe you need that one too," Stick said, pointing randomly.

Tank's face contorted in disappointment as he looked down at his full hands. "I don't think I could carry it." Then with a sudden idea he looked at Stick. "You could carry it for me," he said, and everyone started laughing at his crazy ass.

"What?" Tank asked, looking confused.

"There aren't any more launchers, you dumb shit," Duck growled, hitting him in the head again and eliciting another

Michelle Woods

yowl from Tank, which made them all laugh harder. Deke, one of the prospects, came up to them.

"We've almost cleared this warehouse out. Do you want us to wait till the Dixons get here?" Deke asked, looking at Tank with an astonished scrutiny, causing Bone, who'd thought he was done laughing at Tank, to let out another snicker of laughter. Deke didn't stop staring in awe even when Tank let out a loud grunt of anger.

"Shut up, you're all assholes," Tank growled, stomping away with his new toys. They all watched him leave.

"Fucker's got not a lick of sense. Why didn't he just tell a prospect to get that shit for him?" Duck said as they watched him walk out the door presumably looking for someone to take his toys home.

"You know Tank, Duck. He doesn't want anyone playing with his toys," Dog said, still chuckling.

"Well?" Deke queried when they'd all settled back down enough to pay attention to him again.

"Yeah, your group can wait on the Dixons. Tell Rash to take the live ones over to the break house and lock them up. Tell him to set up a guard." The break house was a prison they kept for men who needed a little extra encouragement to talk till someone could get the information they needed from them. As Deke took off, Tiny looked at Bone.

"Rockers?" he questioned.

"Yeah, we'll vote next church. Pretty Boy too, I think." Both men had been assets to the club since they'd joined two years ago. Tiny nodded as Slim walked up to them; he was shaking his head in disbelief.

"Did you see Tank? He's a walking weapons factory. He looked like an idiot." That comment had them all snickering again.

Bone glanced at his watch checking the time, seeing it was

Taming Lucca

eight in the morning, feeling oddly worried that he hadn't talked with Molly. Would she wonder what had happened to him? Or was she content with Aunt Mae and Lisa? Bone didn't know why he was so concerned about one tiny little woman who shouldn't even be a blip on his radar.

Bone scolded himself internally for another minute before he gave in to the urge to call her and he pulled his phone from his back pocket.

"Be right back, need to make a call," he said to the others as he stepped towards the door.

As he walked away, he heard Dog say to Slim, "Damn, you're right, he checked on her before the job was over."

"Yep, now give me my hundred credits, asshole," Slim chortled with devilment.

Fuck, Bone thought, but he still dialed the phone he'd given Molly a few hours ago. She answered on the third ring with a faint "Hello."

"Hey sweetie, how are you feeling this morning?" Bone asked gripping the phone, his dick hard from her raspy voice; damn, that was sexy.

"Bone?" she asked, sounding as if she was just waking up, her voice less raspy now.

"Yeah, just wanted to be sure you were okay."

There was a long pause, which was kind of awkward, and he was about to just hang up when she spoke.

"Are you all right?"

"Yeah, baby, I'm okay." He felt his chest swell with some unknown emotion that had him rubbing his chest over his heart where an ache had taken up residence. He was a little taken aback that she was asking. He didn't know why the fact that she cared mattered but it sent warmth spreading through him when he heard her let out a sigh of relief.

"Lisa told me you were going to take care of some club

Michelle Woods

business and that sometimes not everyone returns. So——um, Lisa was worried about Slim. Is everyone else okay?"

Bone grabbed the back of his neck wondering what the hell he'd gotten himself into with her. Normally someone questioning him would piss him off but not with her. Instead he found himself relieved that she cared.

"Everyone made it, but a couple needed Doc. Slim's fine though. Is Lisa still there?" he asked, listening to her shift around. Imagining her lounging back against the headboard in just that thin shirt, her little nipples poking against it, and those blue panties was making his cock throb.

"Yes, she came up a little while ago to ask if I was hungry. They are down in the kitchen making breakfast."

"Good. We're wrapping things up here and should be home in a few hours."

"Okay," she whispered, sounding nervous.

"See you soon, baby, be good."

"Umm…sure, bye."

Bone noticed the hesitation in her voice as she hung up and it worried him. He was alarmed by his behavior. What the hell was he doing? He was obsessed with the tiny slip of a woman who he barely knew anything about and everything he learned seemed to fascinate him. He turned to see Slim and Dog watching him, having followed him out here to give him shit no doubt.

Fuck.

"Bone's so whipped he can't even make it ten hours without checking in," Slim remarked to Dog.

"Yeah, it's sad when a man loses his balls."

Tiny grunted, coming up behind the two men, putting a hand on each of their shoulders. "You two know all about that, don't you?"

"Asshole," Slim grumbled as he knocked Tiny's hand off

Taming Lucca

his shoulder, even as Dog turned and punched Tiny in the gut hard enough that he grunted in pain and doubled over.

"Damn, Dog, that fucking hurt," he managed to huff out.

"Good. My balls are not in a damned jar. My woman likes them attached," Dog roared, storming off. "I need a beer. You jerks are pissing me off."

"Better pissed off than pissed on," Tiny called to his retreating form, receiving a bird flung up over Dog's shoulder. Tiny was still rubbing his stomach when he asked, "What's his problem?"

Slim glared at him, shaking his head. Then he followed Dog's lead, punching Tiny in the stomach and knocking him flat on his ass before he followed after Dog.

"What did I do?" Tiny asked as he sat up, looking at Bone with a smile that let him know Tiny knew exactly what he'd done. Yep, his family was a bunch of dickheads.

Chapter 13

Four days later, Molly was almost back to normal. This morning when she'd woken up in Bone's bed again, she'd come down the stairs to argue with him only to find four men in the kitchen, and none of them were Bone.

She and Bone had been fighting again last night over whether or not she would be sleeping in his bed or the guest room, the same argument they'd had for the last two days. Molly had decided the second day she'd been at Bone's house, when she woke up with his huge boner poking her and his mouth covering hers, that sleeping in his bed wasn't a good idea. If his ringing cell phone hadn't interrupted them again, it would have been too late.

The decision also stemmed from a warning Brandy had given her. The phone call Bone had received had been some club business he had to leave to take care of so he'd called Lisa to come stay with her. When Lisa arrived she'd had Brandy in tow and after Bone left they'd all chatted before heading out to Tammy's, the local diner.

Brandy had warned her while they were talking that Bone wasn't a one-woman man. At first Lisa had protested that it wasn't true, but when Brandy had asked her in a demanding tone if she knew of a single woman he'd stayed with more than a few nights, Lisa shook her head. She then offered another protest that Bone had never acted possessive of a woman before. Brandy had given her a look before saying 'yeah, my old man, Stick, is that way too' and from the haunted expression on her face when she talked about him, Molly would guess she would know. Lisa had turned away, her expression sad and a bit remorseful as she changed the subject.

Bone finally relented with a grunt last night when he realized she was moving to the guest room even if he didn't want her to. Only when she'd fallen asleep in the recliner last night, he'd taken her to his bed again.

No one was ever here except her and Bone which is why she was surprised to be standing in her sleep shirt and a loose pair of boxers she'd stolen from Bone with four strangers staring at her when she got to the bottom of the stairs.

"Oh, good morning," she said, looking at the four men with dismay. One of them, she realized, was the mountain from the diner; the other three she didn't know. She watched them warily. The man from the diner was eating an apple and leaning on the kitchen counter while the other three men either sat or leaned on the wall.

"Mornin'. Name's Tank, that's Trick." He pointed to a man with short blonde hair that was standing beside the counter. He wasn't as big as Tank was, but he was probably six feet tall with a slender build. He nodded and smiled.

"Morning, nice to meet ya," he said as Tank pointed at the stocky man with black hair and a goatee standing against the wall to his right.

"That's Tiny."

Molly looked at him, watching as he gave a small nod. To these large men she guessed he would be Tiny; he was only about five seven or eight. Tank then pointed to the last man

Michelle Woods

sitting at the counter with his elbows resting on it watching her.

"I'm Dog. And you must be Molly." The man, a little taller than Tiny with chestnut brown hair and a wide barrel chest, spoke before Tank could introduce him, then looked at Tank and mumbled, "She is pretty, I can see why he's all worked up."

Molly realized he was talking about Bone. She twisted the hem of her shirt around her finger, feeling a bit nervous with so many large men watching her. She didn't know what to say to them as she stared at them wondering where the heck Bone had disappeared to. As if her thoughts of him summoned him, he entered through the kitchen door with his phone in his hand. His eyes rolled around the room until they landed on her. He smiled as he walked towards her.

"Hey baby, did you sleep well?" he asked as he placed his hands on her hips, causing her to jump a little in surprise. He wasn't normally so forward, although he did tend to touch her a lot now that she thought about it. That thought floated away when he leaned down and kissed her deeply, much to her surprise. He drew back with a wide grin and she realized that his kiss had been a way to mark her in front of his friends. Her fists clenched at her sides because how dare he do that? She didn't belong to him.

"Breakfast is in the oven, baby. I'll get it for you." He turned to look at the four men, growling at Tank, who'd been checking out her ass, "Get your eyes off what doesn't belong to you, asshole. You four head down, I'll be there in a little bit."

Laughing, the four men all filed out the door after some good-natured ribbing about them needing some private time to say goodbye, which caused her to blush and Bone to shoot them a bird. He watched her silently when they'd all exited

Taming Lucca

the room. Molly was feeling awkward and a bit angry over the very male way he'd tried to stake a claim on her. She wanted to tell him he was an asshole but decided when he set a heaping plate of bacon and eggs in front of her that maybe she could forgive him.

"Yesterday was the last day for you to be on bed rest. I guess you will start being my house mouse today," Bone said as he grabbed a bottle of orange juice from the refrigerator.

Molly stared at him as he pulled down a glass and poured juice into it. What the heck was he talking about? "A house mouse?" she asked, her brow furrowed.

He grinned. "Just means you'll cook and clean and shit."

"Oh." Molly had forgotten that she'd said she'd do that for him instead of share his bed. "Can't I be a mechanic? I really am good at it," she asked pleadingly.

Shaking his head, he leaned over, kissing her on the forehead. "No, I told you no way in hell are you getting near my bike so forget it. And have dinner ready when I get home at seven." He walked out without another word to her, just a little wave, and she stared after him feeling apprehensive about what he expected of her.

Four hours later she was standing in the kitchen staring into the refrigerator. It really was a remarkable piece of equipment that she itched to take apart to see how it worked. She was looking in the freezer, where she found meat labeled chicken and she decided to make that for their dinner. It looked easy to cook, and she placed it on a pan in the oven, cooking it till it was starting to turn a little black. As she took it out and poked it with a fork, she just hoped it was done enough.

She'd also found some fruits that she cut up. After placing it all onto two plates, she set them in the oven to keep them warm. Deciding that she'd done the best she could, she waited on Bone to get home. Sitting in the kitchen fiddling with the

Michelle Woods

idea of taking the refrigerator apart tomorrow and putting it back together before he came home, she wondered if she'd have time.

Hearing the door open, she hoped that she was well on her way to repaying him for his kindness. He came into the kitchen, walking up to her and taking her in his arms as he did every night, kissing her gently on the lips.

"Sit, I made your dinner," she said, a slight smile on her face.

He pulled back, grinning at her before sitting down at the counter. She pulled the prepared plates out of the oven and plopped one in front of him with a proud smile. She knew that it wasn't perfect but she had done well if she did say so herself.

"What the hell is this?" he demanded, taking in the fruit and chicken.

Her heart began to beat faster, pounding in her ears. What was wrong? Why was he mad at her? She looked at the plate. The fruit looked a little browned from the heat in the oven, but she hadn't wanted the chicken to get cold. Tears filled her eyes from embarrassment; it wasn't her fault that she didn't know how to cook. She'd tried to warn him she'd never cooked before, and she'd been so happy thinking she'd managed it, but maybe it wasn't right now that she looked at it.

Bone was looking at a plate of burnt chicken and several fruits that should never be mixed. It was disgusting. What the fuck? Had she done this to try and get back at him for his crack this morning about her not being allowed to touch his bike?

"Did you do this because you're still mad at me, Molly? Fuck, this shit is disgusting," Bone growled, his lip curling.

Picking up a fork, he pushed at the chicken, poking the fruits she had mixed up on the plate. He looked up; seeing her eyes were filled with tears instead of the glee he'd expected, he felt like an ass.

"Mol–" he began, but she just took off, running out the kitchen door towards the living room. "Fuck," he uttered under his breath as he watched her disappear.

He sat there for a minute staring at the goopy mess that was on his plate. He decided that he'd give her a few minutes to calm down before he would go find her. Who knew she couldn't cook? It was beyond him to think that a woman her age wouldn't even know how to make chicken. He used his knife to try and cut the blackened husk that lay on his plate. The knife didn't even dent the rubbery meat.

He would give her another minute or two to calm down and then he would go apologize. That was when he heard the front door slam. He jumped to his feet running towards the door, slamming it open to see her retreating form running away from the cabin.

Where the hell was she going, he wondered as he followed her out into the fading light of the sun. He was at the bottom of the porch steps when he realized he wasn't wearing his shoes. It took a minute for him to grab them, which allowed her to get a head start. Running up the path of cabins behind her, she was almost to Slim and Lisa's before he realized where she was headed. Fuck, he thought, as she banged on the door and was let in a moment later by Slim, who allowed her to pass without a word. He stepped out on the porch to wait for Bone.

"What did you do, Bone?" he demanded as Bone walked up the stairs.

"It was a misunderstanding, Slim."

"She was fucking crying, Bone. Lisa's gonna be pissed." Slim was leaning back against the house beside the door.

"I know," he said in frustration; he hadn't realized that

Michelle Woods

dinner was serious. He'd thought she was still pissed that they were fighting over the mechanic thing. He hadn't realized that she was really actually proud of the burnt chicken and every type of fruit he owned on that plate. It had been a disgusting mess.

He was pissed at himself for not realizing that she was serious and hurting her feelings by yelling at her. She was a woman. How was he supposed to know that she didn't know how to cook?

"She's just a little hurt at something I said not realizing it would upset her. Now go get her so I can talk to her, or I'm going in there, Slim." He ran a frustrated hand over his face. Damn it, he hated when he had to apologize.

"You think to tell me what to do in my own home, Bone. You may be the Prez but the minute she entered that door she became my problem, not yours." Slim pushed off the wall getting right in Bone's face.

"Look, I don't want to fight you, I just want Molly. When I get her then we'll leave," Bone growled.

"No. She stays here," Slim growled back.

"The fuck you say?" Bone said and grabbed Slim by the throat, slamming him into the wall.

Slim sucker-punched him in the stomach, and when Bone let go of his throat, Bone clocked him hard in the jaw. And then two of them were trading blows and rolling around on the porch seconds later.

Molly stood with Lisa watching the men beat on each other from the living room window. Molly watched as Bone knocked Slim in the jaw and blood shot out of his busted lip. She hadn't meant for this to happen. She felt a sinking sensation in her stomach and her ears rang a little.

Taming Lucca

"We have to stop them, Lisa, before they kill each other." She was shocked by the violence going on a few feet away. Lisa didn't seem fazed.

"Nah…they'll stop eventually but don't worry, if they don't, I'll call Tank. But they haven't taken out any weapons, so it's not serious." Lisa sat back on the couch with a little sigh.

Molly couldn't believe that they were beating each other half to death on her front porch and Lisa didn't seem to care.

"Now why didn't you tell me or Aunt Mae or hell, even Brandy, that you didn't know how to cook? We could have shown you a few things," Lisa queried.

"I didn't think it would be that hard. I mean chicken didn't look hard to cook, and the fruit was easy to cut up," Molly said absently, but she was still distracted by the thuds and grunts from the porch. She looked out the window again to see Slim land a hard right hook, knocking Bone back into the wall which seemed to wind him. He stood panting for several minutes, holding his jaw while Slim stood back watching him.

"Good, I think they might have worn themselves out finally," Lisa said, watching Molly as she stared out the window with longing at Bone.

She'd been crying when she'd entered, and Lisa had thought at first that he'd hurt her, but Bone had embarrassed her more than truly hurt her. Molly wanted to repay him so badly for helping her that she'd tried to do something that he told her he wanted even though she had no idea how to go about it. Lisa would bet that the only reason he wanted her to cook and clean was because then he could stuff her into the house mouse box, instead of admitting what he knew Molly really meant to him. Shaking her head at the game the two of them were playing, Lisa decided it would be a good idea to give Bone a reason to appreciate what he had by taking it away.

Michelle Woods

"We are going to teach you how to cook, Molls. You need to make him pay for hurting your feelings though, just so he doesn't try it again. You should go to Titus with me for a few days, that way he realizes what he's losing. I have to go get some stuff for the stall at the market. Slim's not going, he has to be here to help with the shop. Trick's shop is short a few mechanics with Vivi and Tick in Tidwell and Clove laid up." Lisa was looking at Molly to gauge her reaction to being separated from Bone.

Molly looked devastated before she nodded, looking at Lisa, and then asked, "Can I talk to him before we leave?"

Lisa snorted out a laugh at that question. She was pretty sure that no one would be able to stop Bone from seeing Molly. Hell, he'd just beat the hell out of her old man for even suggesting it. Molly, however, had no idea the power she was wielding when it came to Bone, at least not yet. Lisa would bet that despite what Brandy thought, Bone was going to end up owned by this little slip of a woman. She'd bet her last credit on it.

"Of course you can, doll. Now, why don't we go out there and tell them our plan," Lisa said, rising from the couch. Molly's eyes lit with glee and she followed Lisa to the door.

Bone was leaning against the house panting. Fuck, his jaw hurt like a fucking bitch. Slim had landed a hard one with that right hook of his. His lip was bleeding, and his eye felt like it was starting to swell. He'd needed to get his ass beat though; it at least made him feel a little better over being a dick to Molly, even if it wasn't on purpose. What was it about her that made him so fucked up? He was starting to question his sanity. Letting out a sigh, he looked at Slim.

"I didn't mean to hurt her feelings, Slim," he managed to

Taming Lucca

pant out.

Slim leaned back against the railing on the porch across from him. His eye was already blackened and his nose was bleeding. His knuckles were scraped. Bone saw the blood dripping off them when the other man lifted them close to his face to inspect them.

"Yeah, I figured that. What the hell happened anyway?" Slim asked with confusion. "She seemed fine when Lisa came by earlier today to show her the cabin."

"She was here earlier today?"

"Yeah, Lisa brought her."

"Huh, I wondered how she knew where to run to. She burnt dinner." Bone leaned his head back against the wall. "I thought she was mad. I didn't know it was something she didn't realize she'd done." He sighed, remembering her eyes filled with tears just before she ran out of the room.

"Fuck. That was stupid," Slim said, chuckling. "Damn, my nose won't stop bleeding. If I didn't know better I'd swear you used your brass."

Bone looked at him, smugness filling him; at least he'd made Slim pay for not letting him apologize to Molly. The door opened near him and he looked up to see Lisa and Molly stepping out onto the front porch. His chest twisted with unease when Molly glanced at him from beneath her lashes.

"Damn, Bone, did you have to bust my old man's nose," Lisa demanded, walking over to bend down next to Slim. Molly watched him, her face clouded with dismay. Her hands were twisting a bit of her shirt into a ball and then releasing it. The sight made him feel even more like an asshole than her tears had. He had thought they were past the point when she was too nervous to speak after the last few days together but she seemed to have reverted.

"Come here, baby," he said, wanting her near him so he

Michelle Woods

could tell her he hadn't meant to hurt her feelings. He held out his hand to her and she took it as she knelt next to him. After a moment of staring at each other, she gently took his face in her soft hands, tilting his head to examine the swelling.

"Does it hurt?" she asked. A grimace twisted her face as she watched him.

He grunted. "Yeah, a bit, but that's not what I need to say to you." He cupped her cheek gently. "I'm sorry. I didn't know you couldn't cook. I've never known a woman who couldn't."

She turned bright red and tried to withdraw from him. Bone dropped his hand from her face, covering her hand on his cheek with his, stopping her from removing it.

"I'm going with Lisa to Titus, so she can teach me," Molly blurted out in a rush. Bone felt a visceral denial rise up inside him at the thought of Molly not being here with him. It made his voice gruffer than he intended when he growled.

"Can't she teach you when she gets back, and you can stay with me?" he demanded.

Molly knew she shouldn't give in to his demand; Lisa said to let him know he can't walk all over her. She steeled her spine to fight him. She wasn't a pushover and he wasn't allowed to treat her like a damned doormat.

"No, Bone," she said. "I'm going to Titus with Lisa. I need to learn how to cook."

He looked ready to argue with her before he seemed to make a decision and groaned with disappointment. Molly felt his hand squeeze hers where they rested against his cheek.

"Will you stay at the house tonight?" he asked earnestly, needing her to give him at least that much.

She nodded, helping him up from the porch. "I'm going home to make sure he's okay tonight. Come get me in the morning," she told Lisa, who nodded as she helped Slim into

Taming Lucca

the house.

Molly walked with Bone leaning on her heavily, his arm over her shoulders with hers around his waist as they made their way slowly back to Bone's cabin. Molly suspected that he might be pretending to be hurt a bit more than he was.

When they entered the house, she took him up the stairs to his bedroom. He took off his boots and his shirt, and then he sat down on the bed, reaching out and wrapping his arms around her when she was going to leave the room.

"Stay, please. I won't try anything. Just let me hold you tonight if you're going to be gone for three days," he begged.

She wasn't sure she should allow it, but she wanted to stay with him too, so she nodded her head.

"Thank you," he whispered, watching her as she moved away to take off her shoes and slipped off the shorts she'd been wearing.

Feeling nervous, she stepped closer to the bed, her body oddly warm all the sudden. When she was close enough to the bed he groaned, dragging her onto the bed with him, burying his face in her neck. She should protest, she knew, but she didn't want to.

"Goodnight, baby," he said, kissing the back of her neck when he had her in the position he wanted her in. Lying there spooned against him with his arms tightly wrapped around her, it didn't take long before she fell into a deep comforting sleep.

Chapter 14

Waking up with Bone's arms wrapped around her to the sound of the doorbell, Molly glanced at her watch sitting on the bedside table. She groaned when she saw that it was ten. Damn, they had overslept. She tried to sit up so she could move off the bed but Bone grunted and his arms tightened, trying to pull her back into the bed.

"Damn. Why is she laying on the doorbell? I have a damned headache," Bone grumbled.

Molly wiggled, trying to get him to release her so she could go let Lisa in while she packed and got ready.

"Let me up, Bone," Molly said, pulling on his arm.

"No, I like you where you are, babe." Bone looked at her through a curtain of hair, his eyes half closed, giving him a sexy half-lidded expression that made Molly want to lay back down and beg him to touch her. Knowing she couldn't do that, she smacked his arm with a light tap.

"Damn, woman, no need for violence!" Grumbling with displeasure, he let her go. Molly got up, grabbing her shorts and sliding them back on before heading towards the door.

"Molly," he called before she reached the door.

Turning, she looked at him. He was sitting up with just the sheet covering his lap. She stared at the tanned flesh of his

Taming Lucca

chest with a light dusting of hair that made her mouth water, her eyes unfocused. Her brain suddenly processing the pile of clothes beside the bed, she realized he must have taken off his pants and shirt before he fell asleep the night before. Molly was flooded with heat and her knees almost gave out thinking of all that maleness he was flaunting.

He looked so good, good enough to eat with only a sheet covering him. Molly didn't know why she felt so lightheaded all of the sudden. Her hand reaching out, she held the doorframe beside her for support.

"If that's not Lisa, baby, don't let them in without letting me know. I'll come down and let them in." Nodding, she peeled her eyes from his chest and almost ran down the stairs to let Lisa in, her legs trembling the whole mad dash down them.

Throwing open the door without looking, she saw Slim and Lisa waiting on the porch. Slim was sitting on a two-seat wooden rocker that sat right outside the door with Lisa on his lap. They had apparently realized that they weren't going to get let in quickly and decided to wait on the bench.

"Morning, Molly," Lisa said cheerily, smiling brightly. "You ready?"

"No, we overslept, so I still have to pack." She watched as they rose to their feet.

Slim grinned and whispered something to Lisa, who giggled. Then Slim bent her back over his arm and kissed her passionately. Molly watched with no small amount of envy at the love the pair obviously shared. She wanted that.

Living with Bone probably wasn't the way to find it though. As Brandy had warned her, Bone was not a one-woman man. Slim finally set Lisa away from him, slapped her ass with a whoop, and called over his shoulder as he walked away, "Gotta run, babe. I'll tell Rock to be here to leave with you

Michelle Woods

girls in an hour. Don't leave till he gets here! And call me tonight, we'll have phone sex again."

Molly blushed at such a blatant statement and Lisa laughed as she took in Molly's red cheeks.

"Sorry, that man is shameless. Now, let's get you ready to go." She giggled before she followed Molly into the living room.

As they entered, Bone came down the stairs wearing just his jeans. Molly stood near the door watching him, her body suddenly focused on the sexy abs that he slowly scratched over with his hand. Tearing her gaze from the mind-boggling view, she met his eyes with her own seeing in their brown depths satisfaction and more than a little desire. Molly tried to shake off the tingles that ran up her spine making her almost breathless. Lisa chuckled next to her, making her realize she was staring at the man like she'd been in the desert for days without water, and he was an oasis.

"Hi, Bone," Lisa managed to get out around her muffled chuckles.

"Morning, Lisa," Bone replied, a smug smile covering his face as he stood at the foot of the stairs.

Molly shook herself and began walking towards the stairs, trying not to look at Bone and his beautifully defined golden abs. When she neared him at the bottom of the stairs, her face still slightly red, his arm snaked out grabbing her, causing her to fall against him.

She lifted her face to protest, but his mouth landed on hers with a possessive kiss. Her arms went around his neck of their own accord, and her body softened, leaning into him. A moan of pleasure escaped from her as he devoured her mouth with brutal intensity. Then just as suddenly as he'd grabbed her, he let her go.

"Breakfast, ladies?" he asked with a slick grin.

Taming Lucca

"Sure. Come on, doll, let's get you ready," Lisa said with a snicker. Molly put her hand to her lips but nodded, following Lisa up the stairs.

Forty-five minutes later they entered the kitchen again with Molly's backpack filled with some of the clothes Lisa had brought her on her second day in Devils Falls. Bone was at the stove and turned to smile at them when they entered.

"Ladies, pancakes are on the stove. I ate while you were getting ready. I've got to get up to the clubhouse, we have church in an hour," Bone informed them as he set two heaping plates of round flat patties on the counted in front of them.

Molly's brow furrowed slightly; they were having church? She didn't really see Bone as the religious type. Most religion had been lost when the world was taken over by the ocean.

"Slim have someone riding out with you to Titus?" he asked with a questioning look directed at Lisa. While they were talking, Molly sat down looking at the odd little circles and wondering if they were any good or if they were tasteless like oatmeal.

"Yeah, Rock's coming with us."

Lisa was sitting down in front of one of the two plates with the patties they were calling pancakes on them. She jumped up to grab something in a small jar from the counter near the sink, then sat down beside Molly.

"Good, I'll send a few prospects over to head out with you too. We need to be careful with the Jackals stirred up over the other night," Bone said, his eyes on Molly.

His hands had begun to rub Molly's shoulders as he spoke to Lisa. He leaned down, his lips caressing her neck while his teeth slid up to nip her ear gently.

Michelle Woods

"Eat, babe. And you be a good girl and stay with Lisa and Rock." He paused, giving her neck little nips that left her gasping for air. Molly knew she should protest but she couldn't seem to manage it. "Got your phone?" he asked between the sucks and nipping bites along her neck.

"Yes." Molly almost moaned, feeling her body liquefy as desire burned inside her.

"Good, call me so I know you're okay. See you in three days." He gave her neck one last hard, almost punishing, nip before nodding to Lisa before heading up the stairs.

"Damn, girl," Lisa laughed with glee. "Bet you're nothing but a puddle of goo after that blatant claiming." Molly stared after the man, wondering what the hell had just happened.

"Yeah," Molly squeaked. Suddenly remembering what he'd said a few moments ago, she looked at Lisa questioningly and asked, "He goes to church?"

Molly was confused when Lisa almost fell over laughing at her query.

Bone walked out of the house about twenty minutes later, seeing Molly and Lisa still sitting in the bed of Slim's beat up old truck waiting on Rock and the prospects. Unable to resist getting another kiss from her sweet lips before she left, he headed towards the truck where they were sitting.

He walked up to her moving in close and nudged her legs apart to stand between them. Wrapping his arms around her waist, he pulled her to the edge of the bed pressing against her. She melted, not bothering to fight his embrace, which pleased him immensely. Her arms lifted to his shoulders as he looked up, meeting her eyes.

"I'll miss you, babe," he told her before he leaned forward, kissing her lips softly. He didn't want to embarrass her too much, so he didn't deepen the kiss like he wanted. As he pulled back he felt a thick sense of satisfaction pour through his chest when he saw the heavy-lidded look of desire on her face. Possessiveness roaring through him, he felt suddenly lightheaded from the need he had for her.

"Wow, that sweetbutt's hot. When you're done, Bone, I'd like a go with her," a voice from behind him said and rage unlike anything he'd ever felt thundered through his veins.

No one was touching his Molly.

Bone gently let Molly go before turning around. He felt her stiffen slightly as he disengaged and was pissed that she wasn't relaxed and soft like she had been a moment ago.

That motherfucker had better shut the fuck up quick or he was going to end up eating a bullet. He turned to see one of his least favorite brothers standing a few feet away. With the red haze filling his eyes, he walked toward the man with a purposeful stride, ready to rip the fucker apart.

"Bone, no, please don't get into another fight," he heard Molly plead, but he was almost to the idiot who thought he had the right to suggest that he might be allowed to touch Molly. Only a heavy hand landed on his shoulder and he turned, intending to knock out whatever fucker had dared to stop him until he saw it was Duck.

Shit, Duck would wipe the floor with him; the man was deadly in a fistfight.

"Rash, this is a misunderstanding. You need to get to the shop, you've got bikes to fix." Duck stared at the thin man with oily brown hair and grease smeared over his cheek and hands.

"A misunderstanding? Bone don't play with the good ones, Duck." He chuckled with ingratiating crudeness. Bone's hands clenched into fists and he growled. Bone's body tensed. readying itself to beat the little fucker into the ground, but he

Michelle Woods

was held back by Duck's restraining hand.

"It's different this time. Molly's not a sweetbutt. Don't make this mistake again, Rash. Got me?" Bone watched the man surveying Duck for a moment before he finally nodded.

"Yeah, I got it. I'll head to the shop. See you." He took off jogging in the general direction of Trick's shop. Bone's hands unclenched slowly as he watched him running down the path.

"That one's going to be a problem. I can't put my finger on what bothers me about him. He's been leaving the shop at odd times. Trick just told me today that he's been seen leaving or not been there when they needed him for a few weeks now," Duck said in a low voice to be sure no one heard him. Bone didn't really hear him because he was too focused on the fact that the idiot had thought he would get to touch Molly.

"He'd better stay away from Molly. I'll kill him if he fucks with her. I don't want that fucker to have a chance to fuck this up. Have someone start following him. Call Tick, ask him to take care of it," Bone growled quietly to Duck.

"She's not patched, Bone. You can't kill him for messing with her without one," Duck said, meeting his eyes with disapproval. This surprised Bone because Duck usually didn't care about much. Bone met the man's eyes and he realized that Duck really didn't like Molly living with him without a patch.

Bone knew that he wasn't going to patch a woman because he was too much like his father. One woman might be enough for a while, but eventually he'd stray. Ignoring the disapproval, he shook Duck's hand off and walked back to Molly, who wrapped her arms around him. He kissed her again lightly before pulling back.

"See you, babe." He turned, walking back to where Duck stood looking grim, and they headed to church together.

Chapter 15

Taking a bite of the apple she'd just bought, Molly watched Lisa flit from one aisle to another inside the huge department store. Molly hadn't realized that department stores even existed anymore until Lisa had dragged her here today. Apparently someone in Titus had revived this place and the clothing factory down the road about twenty years ago.

Turning, Lisa called out, "Molls, what do you think of this one?" She was holding a red and black slinky dress with thin straps and a flared skirt.

"It's okay. Looks like the other six only a different color." She munched another bite of the apple feeling bored sitting here. Lisa insisted they look at everything and Molly just wasn't the shopping type, likely because she'd never had any credits to spend. Molly snorted. She had eaten well lately, she realized as she crunched on the delicious fruit. Better than she ever had behind the wall, that was for sure.

Looking up at the dress Lisa was holding as she inspected it, she wondered how much longer it would be before she could convince Lisa to head back to the hotel they were staying at. After all they'd been here for hours; even Lisa must be getting tired of looking around.

Michelle Woods

Even when she was a young girl she'd been bored by fashion. Her mother had tried to teach her about Hillie fashions and she had wanted nothing to do with the hip new looks. It was likely the beginning of the end of their relationship, Molly realized. As soon as her mother realized she wasn't going to be a mini version of herself, she'd wanted nothing to do with Molly. Yep, Molly would take an engine to fix over a fancy wardrobe any day. It wasn't that she didn't like to dress nice, she did. It was that she just wasn't into spending hours on it.

Lisa came over with a huff. "How can you say that?" she demanded.

"Umm…it looks the same."

"No, Molly, this one has thin straps that cross in the back. The last one had thin straps that tied around the neck leaving the back exposed." She stared at Molly as if she was trying to figure her out.

"Sorry, not really into clothing much, Lisa."

"Ugh…you're no fun to shop with." Lisa looked around searching for Rock and the two prospects that had been their shadows since yesterday. At first Molly had been a little freaked about it, but now that she realized they were just there to keep them safe, she wasn't upset about it anymore.

"I want to head home. I've gotten enough stuff to sell at the stall. This dress was something I was getting for me to sex it up for Slim." Molly couldn't help the raised brows and the little laugh that came out.

"What?" Lisa asked, her brow furrowed.

"Do you really need to sex it up for him? He seems pretty sexed up already." Molly let out a giggle at her own joke.

"Wise guy! Ha, yes. Every woman needs to keep her man all hot and bothered. You remember that, missy," Lisa grumbled as she made a motion with her hand to Rock, who was leaning against the wall with the two prospects sitting nearby. He nodded, and they came over.

"What's up?" Rock asked.

"We want to head back home early."

"Thank goodness!" said the younger of the two prospects. "I want to get home, there's a bonfire tonight."

"Slim didn't tell me about that," Lisa said.

"Last minute, two patched-over clubs are coming," Rock said with a serious look.

"We still want to get back. If we leave now we can be back before they even set up," Lisa said, checking the time. It was two-thirty Molly saw as she looked at her own watch. It had only taken three hours to get here the day before so they would be back by five-thirty.

"All right, but if your old men are pissed, I'm blaming you two," Rock said gruffly.

"I don't have an old man," Molly whispered to Lisa with confusion.

Laughing, Lisa hugged her shoulders. "Huh, guess he misunderstood with you living with Bone. He never lets women stay at his house. If he has sex, then the bitch better be ready to leave after the deed's done. I've actually seen him throw, literally throw, a woman out his door once when she tried to stay the night with him. And I think it's likely Bone talked to him before we left. Seen him standing with Rock before we left." Lisa smiled evilly. "Oh, don't looked so pale, she was always trying to act like she'd bagged Bone since he'd let her hang around the club after they'd already had sex. She was a bitch."

"He won't allow me to sleep in the guest room," Molly confessed, blushing at the admission.

"Course not, Molls, you're different. He really likes you." Throwing her arm around her shoulders again, Lisa took her to the counter to buy the rest of the stuff she was purchasing

Michelle Woods

before they both followed the men carrying their bags out to the truck.

Forty minutes later they were pulling the stuttering truck to the side of the road. Lisa was cussing a blue streak, making Molly blush because 'fuck' was popping out of her mouth every other word. Lisa beat on the steering wheel with one hand.

"I don't think that's helping, Lisa," Molly said as she got out of the truck. Rock had pulled over behind them and was already off his bike and walking up to the truck when Molly moved in front of it.

"What happened?" he asked Molly as she lifted the hood.

"Not sure," Molly replied, looking at the engine and trying to work out what might be wrong in her head.

"Shit, I'll call Trick, he can send someone out to fix it." Rock took out his phone as Lisa came up beside the open hood too.

"Are you calling Trick or Slim, Rock?" Lisa asked, her hand shielding her eyes from the dying rays of the sun. Molly was twirling the possible issues around in her head trying to figure out what was wrong with the engine so she ignored them both.

"Yeah, give me a sec. Bone and Slim are not gonna be happy that we're sitting out here on the side of the road with the Jackals acting the way they are lately," Rock growled. "Damned cage!" he exclaimed, kicking the front tire before he took out his phone and began dialing.

Molly was fiddling with a loose plug and finally tuned in to what they were saying.

"Wait, Rock, I might be able to fix it. No sense in calling Trick till I see what's wrong, that way he can bring the parts if we need them." Molly was standing on the front bumper peering into the engine.

"You can fix it?" Rock asked, his disbelief clear in his voice.

Sighing, Molly just nodded, going back to her mental checklist of things. From the corner of her eye, she saw him shoot a questioning look at Lisa, who shrugged.

"Can't hurt to let her try, Rock." Rock nodded and put his phone back into his pocket, sitting down in the grass to wait. Lisa sat down with him after grabbing an apple. Molly turned back to the engine, ignoring them again while she set to work.

Thirty minutes later Molly found a hole in a hose that fed the radiator. She used a tire repair kit she found in the small toolbox Rock had pulled from beneath the seat when she'd asked for tools. She tested to see if the patch would hold and poured some water into the radiator from the bottle she'd been drinking earlier, then shut the hood.

"That should hold till we get back."

"You really fixed it?" Rock asked in disbelief.

Molly didn't answer because she was annoyed by the surprise in his voice. Instead she just walked to the driver's seat and turned the key.

"Huh, I better text Trick not to bother coming to fix it then," he grunted, still looking at her like she'd grown another head.

Sexist men were such dicks!

Molly narrowed her eyes at him as she headed around to the passenger side of the truck.

"How would he even know we were broken down, Rock?" Molly demanded with her hands on her hips, her teeth clamped tightly together.

"Mighta texted him about ten minutes ago," he said with a sheepish smile on his face as he took out his phone to text Trick again.

Michelle Woods

"Really! I told you I could fix it," Molly huffed, then turned back around and got into the truck. "Whatever, let's just get back, I'm tired." Sitting in the cab with her arms crossed, she waited for Lisa to get back in so they could get home. She was tired and now she was pissed off to boot.

Bone wasn't having a good time. He'd been sitting by the fire for almost twenty minutes with the party in full swing, and all he could think about was Molly. He'd been thinking about her all damned day. It hadn't put him in a good mood.

Trick and Tank had teased him earlier over his distraction when they were getting ready for the bonfire. It was pathetic that he was sitting here like a bump on a log. Bonfire night was rowdy fun that he should be enjoying. Hell, women were all over the place, but he wasn't interested in any of them and he couldn't figure out why.

He watched a blond with decent tits dancing without her top and holding a whiskey bottle in her hand. Normally he would be all over that or one of the dozen other women here, but instead he was sitting on his favorite bench with a beer in his hand just watching, feeling bored out of his mind and wondering what the hell Molly was up to right at the moment.

"Not the same when you've got a woman, is it?" Slim asked, plopping down beside him on the bench seat.

"I'm not patchin' her, Slim. Quit trying to make me give up my balls like you and every other man with an old lady," Bone grumbled. He wasn't pussy whipped, damn it. He just wasn't feeling this shit tonight.

"Well, you're the one acting like you have an old lady, Bone. Fuck. If this had been a week ago, you would have already picked out one to take home. Hell, sometimes more than one, and yet here you sit, looking bored." Slim chuckled while taking a swig of his beer.

Bone's hand tightened around the beer bottle and his jaw clenched because Slim was right.

What the fuck was wrong with him anyway?

Molly wasn't here, and she wasn't even going to allow him in her pants anytime soon. He turned to look at a blonde wearing a low cut top and cutoff jeans he'd been absently watching about ten minutes ago.

Shit, he should just take that chick back to his cabin. She was his type a few days ago. He could screw her and forget about Molly. It wasn't like Molly would even know, she wasn't here, and she hadn't called him today like he'd told her to, which pissed him off to no end.

That was why Trick and Tank had been teasing him all day. He'd been checking his phone every fifteen minutes to be sure it was working, like a fucking girl. Even as the thought filled his head, he heard a jeer coming from nearby.

"Yep, he's been acting as ball-less as you and Dog all damned day!" Tank bellowed out a laugh, and that was the last straw. Growling, he tossed his bottle into the trash bin nearby. He was done acting like a pansy-assed fool. He wasn't letting her change him. He was taking that bitch home and fucking her tonight and to hell with Molly.

Bone just hoped his cock got on board because right now it was limp as a wet noodle. Anger boiling up inside him at the reality of his uncharacteristic behavior, he stood, walking over to the chick without comment to the two yahoos yucking it up.

"Want to go to my place and fuck?" Bone asked without any delicacy.

"Fuck," Tank said.

Slim was standing beside him. "Go dance for a minute so I can talk to Bone for a sec," he said before the woman was

Michelle Woods

able to say anything to answer him, pissing Bone off.

"What the fuck?" Bone asked as the woman moved away a bit to dance beside the fire.

"Don't do this, Bone. You're going to regret it," Slim said, meeting his eyes earnestly, holding his shoulder.

"Look, you may be okay with being a dickless wonder when it comes to any woman except Lisa, but I'm not going to be one," Bone growled, anger coursing through his veins, a steady thrum of hard beats that made his head ache.

"Asshole, I have a dick, I just don't let it rule my freaking brain. I care too much about Lisa to hurt her like Stick does Brandy or your daddy did your mother." Slim shoved him hard, causing him to stumble back a few steps.

Before Bone was steady he grabbed him again, getting right in his face. Bone was enraged at the mention of his parents. His hands gripped Slim's arms where they held him by his cut. This wasn't the same fucking thing, Molly wasn't here, and she'd never know. Shit, for all he knew she wouldn't even care.

"I'm trying to stop you from doing something I know damned well you'll regret when Molly finds out about it! Now man up and don't make the mistake Bolt made with Tina last year. We all know how that turned out." Slim gave him a knowing look, then shook him like a rag doll. "Don't be an idiot and think that no one will tell her, Bone. We both know someone will. You can always count on family to gossip like old women," he shouted at him as he shoved Bone again, only this time Bone shoved back causing him to stumble a bit.

"Fuck you! I'm not patchin' her or any other woman."

"Fine, but I will help her when she leaves your sorry ass over this!" Slim yelled, walking away without looking back, heading towards his cabin.

Bone didn't like the fact that half the men around the

Taming Lucca

fire were staring at him now, most them patched-over club members. His jaw hurt he was clenching it so hard. He knew that Slim had hit a sore spot comparing this to how his father had treated his mother. This wasn't the same because he hadn't made any promises to Molly.

So why the hell did he feel so guilty all the sudden?

"Damn, that was awkward," Tank said as he looked at Bone. "But he's right you know."

Then he walked away too, heading towards a group of dancing women near the beer. Pissed off about the whole damned scene, he walked over to the woman he'd spoken to earlier demanding, "Well?"

"Okay," the blonde said, smiling drunkenly.

He grabbed her hand, dragging her back to his cabin, still not turned on at the thought of screwing her. When they entered the cabin that still smelled like Molly, he almost told her to get the fuck out, but then he thought about the jeers he'd have to deal with if he did.

"Strip for me," he told her as he plopped down on the recliner Molly preferred, feeling her scent fill his head. Guilt ate at him and he was barely interested in the woman who stood in front of him. He dispassionately watched the blonde giggling like a fucking teenager as she began a slow strip tease. Seeing her taking off her top didn't even make his cock twitch. His mind began to wander as he stared at the woman getting naked but didn't really see her. His mind was on Molly as it had been all day. He was thinking of Molly sleeping in this recliner the other day while she was sick; he felt his cock begin to rise and he felt his breath catch a little.

She'd been leaning on the arm, her legs curled beneath her, her hands folded under her head with that dark fall of her hair covering her face. Molly had been so beautiful and she'd turned him on more lying here in this recliner than the

Michelle Woods

blonde did with her large tits bared while she danced for him.

The blonde was moving slowly towards him half naked, still giggling. She cupped her tits and shook them at him. The slight hard-on he'd gotten by thinking about Molly was gone and his dick was suddenly limp like a wet noodle. He wasn't going to be able to fuck her because she wasn't Molly, he realized and cursed himself as the biggest idiot on the planet because if someone told Molly about this, he'd have a damned hard time convincing her that nothing had happened tonight with this bimbo.

Fuck, just fuck, he'd really screwed up. Slim was right, damn him; that asshole should have tried harder to knock some sense into him. He opened his mouth to tell her to get the fuck out but before he could speak the door flew open and a loud gasp stopped him. Oh fuck, no. No, he couldn't be that fucking unlucky, his brain screamed, but when his eyes landed on Molly he knew that he was.

"Umm...I...I..." Molly stuttered while she stood in the doorway of the cabin staring in horror at the woman who'd been stripping for him a few seconds ago.

She dropped several bags she'd been holding as she stared with open-mouthed shock. He saw the pain that suddenly filled her eyes, then she turned and stumbled out the door. He jerked to his feet grabbing the clothes the woman had been tossing towards him and throwing them at her before heading to do the door to go after Molly.

Bone hadn't wanted to ever see that look on a woman's face. Pain shot through his chest because he was the cause of that look in Molly's eyes and he had never wanted to hurt a woman that way. He was a fucking idiot. Why the hell had he done this just to prove she didn't mean anything to him? It was just asinine.

Reaching the door, he realized that Molly had taken off

running towards the bonfire. His blood ran cold when he saw her retreating form moving towards the fire. The party was in full swing now with two other clubs here, and she wasn't fucking patched. His stomach was twisting into a knot because she didn't have enough experience with the club to know if someone touched her, to lie and tell them that she was.

He spared a quick look at the blonde who was now trying to cover herself with the clothes he'd thrown at her, barking out, "Don't fucking be here when we get back."

He was out the door before he finished speaking, running towards Molly's fading figure. As he ran after her, he realized he should have fucking listened to that asshole Slim earlier. Questions assailed him as he fought to keep his shit together and followed her.

Why the hell was she here tonight when she was supposed to be in Titus with Lisa?

He reached the bonfire where he'd lost sight of her, scanning the rowdy crowd, searching. He saw Tank sucking face with a red-haired woman he had pinned to a tree, but Molly wasn't anywhere that he could see. Uncaring that he was interrupting, he grabbed Tank's arm, jerking him away from the tree a bit.

Tank turned with a deadly face, growling out, "What the fuck?" Seeing Bone's face, he let the woman go, turning completely. "What's up? Trouble with the club?"

That was one thing he liked about his vice, he was always ready to take care of the club, but right now he needed his friend, not his Vice President. His head was pounding with the urgent need to find Molly before she landed herself into trouble because he was a fucking moron.

"Molly's here," Bone bit out, his eyes turning to look at the crowd, searching every figure for her in the firelight. Tank stepped up beside him, his head turning as he began to help

Michelle Woods

him look for her.

"Fuck, Bone. She shouldn't be out here in this crowd without a patch. It's rowdier tonight with the recent Jackal fights," Tank said, his face contorting grimly. Tank moved when Bone did without him having to ask, both of them looking for any slight figure with dark hair. They moved closer to the fire and Bone was really starting to panic because he didn't see her anywhere. They reached the far edge of the fire and Bone decided they'd find her faster if they split up.

"You go that way," Bone indicated the left side of the bonfire. "I'll go this way. If you see Dog or Slim have them help. You call me if you find her," Bone told him and Tank turned to begin moving away, but Bone caught his arm. "And Tank, if anyone's touched her you bring them to me. Got me?" Bone's voice was cold, his eyes murderous at the thought of Molly hurt any more than he'd already hurt her.

Then it occurred to him that she might be out there with another man to get back at him and he became aware of the depths to which his possessiveness of Molly went. If someone touched her, even to give pleasure, they were going to be a dead man. He wouldn't be able to stop himself from killing the son of a bitch.

Chapter 16

Molly realized when she entered the area near the bonfire, with tears she refused to let fall filling her eyes, that she shouldn't have taken this route to Aunt Mae's cabin. Lisa had warned her not to go to the bonfire without Bone, or her and Slim, because of the rowdy crowd. As she flew out of the cabin headed to Mae's place, she hadn't really thought about anything except for the pain seeing Bone with another woman had set loose inside her.

The last thing she thought she would see when she walked into the cabin was a naked woman in the living room with him watching the slut from her favorite chair. Ha, what used to be her favorite chair because now she wanted to burn the damned thing in the fire she was skirting.

Deciding that she was already halfway to Mae's and going back to the cabin wasn't an option, she figured she might as well keep going. It was likely that she could make it out of this crowd before anyone spotted her anyway.

Molly guessed the sight that had greeted her shouldn't have surprised her. She'd been warned that Bone wasn't a one-woman man and apparently according to Brandy, his was his father's son. Molly felt a traitorous tear escape the corner of her eye. It also shouldn't hurt so much that he was probably

Michelle Woods

screwing the slut right now while she ran away like a fool, but it did.

Molly ran through the darkness seeing people in small groups and others in pairs doing who knows what in the darkened areas of the party. She didn't know what she was so upset over anyway. Bone hadn't promised her anything and she was only his houseguest, not his lover. Of course she'd thought that she meant more to him than another easy lay but that had been a bad assumption.

Molly was so distracted by her thoughts she didn't see the pair of legs stretched out beside a tree until she was stumbling over them, almost falling but managing to catch herself on a nearby tree before she fell. She felt the slight scrape of the bark on her palms and she felt another tear escape her eyes, damn it.

"Watch where the hell you're stepping mother fu——shit, Molly," Dog said and rose from the ground, pulling a woman with him. He looked around behind her for a second as if he expected to find someone trailing her. Molly turned to see what he was searching for and all that greeted her was darkness.

"Where's Bone?" he demanded, his face contorted into a grim look.

"Are you okay, honey?" the woman asked as she took in what Molly knew was probably a miserable expression on her face. Molly didn't know what to say to either of them. How did you tell someone that the man you're living with was currently screwing a blonde bimbo? Molly didn't know but she managed a reply.

"He's, umm——busy right now," Molly replied to Dog, not able to answer the woman because she had no idea if she was okay or not.

Dog stared at her for a long moment then asked, "Busy?

Taming Lucca

With you running around out here?"

"Yes——umm, h-he w-was with a wo——well, he's just not interested in me right now," Molly managed to stutter out without bursting into tears in front of the couple.

She looked at her feet, not wanting to discuss this anymore. She just wanted to get to Mae's so she could hide from the fact that Bone was with another woman and she was an idiot for thinking she was anything more than a passing fancy for him. Hadn't she learned anything from her ordeal with Luzen?

"Did he see you coming to the bonfire?" Dog asked intently.

"I–I guess," Molly replied, looking up at him and shrugging her shoulders.

"Then trust me, he's not busy anymore no matter who he was with." Dog watched her for a moment, seeing her teary eyes and destroyed expression. He frowned; reaching into his pocket, he pulled out his cell. He tapped on it a few times and nothing happened.

"Damn, Terry baby, did you bring your phone? Mine's dead." Dog looked at the woman with a soft look that made Molly want to cry even more than she had a moment ago.

Why did she have to feel so attached to a man who obviously didn't feel the same way? She hated that she cared that he'd had a woman in what she'd thought was their cabin. It was enough to make her want to throw things. She almost felt giddy thinking of throwing something at the asshole's head. Ha, that would serve his ass right if she beaned him in the head with a shoe or something.

"No, I left it at the cabin," the woman, Terry, said while looking at Molly with sympathy.

"Damn, Bone is gonna be looking for her and if he doesn't find her, all hell's gonna break loose."

"Um——I really think you're wrong, Dog," Molly said. It was likely that Bone was having a really good time with

Michelle Woods

the blonde right about now. The shithead. No, that wasn't fair, he hadn't promised her anything and they weren't in a relationship despite having lived together for a little over a week. She really didn't have a right to feel so betrayed.

"Ha, that's unlikely. I've known him a long time and I can say for certain that if he saw you, he's lookin' for you," Dog said before turning to Terry. He opened his mouth to speak when a hard arm wrapped around Molly's waist, and the smell of stale breath and beer assaulted her as a voice crowed with glee, "I caught you finally! You were running so fast."

Molly cringed at the high nasally sound of his voice.

"Now it's time for some fuuunn." He was slurring his words and his arm holding her tightened. Molly tried to pull away but it did no good; his arm was clamped tightly around her, almost too tightly. Molly could hardly breathe, but of course with the stale scent of his breath, that was likely a good thing.

"Fuck, let her go, asshat," Dog said, turning back and grabbing the arm holding her.

"Nope, caught this sweetbutt and now I'm keeping her." His breath assaulted her again making her want to vomit. Molly tried to pull his arm away from her, again unsuccessfully. Frustration at the night's events made her want to scream. Could this situation get any worse?

"Trust me, you want to let her go," Dog said, moving forward.

Bone's voice coldly came from behind the man and sounded deadly calm, almost flat. Molly tried to turn to look at him but the man's hold wasn't allowing it. She'd bet he was pissed to have to chase her. Well too damned bad. She hadn't asked him to come after her so it wasn't her fault.

"Let. Her. Go. Now." Bone's voice was almost arctic it was so cold, each word bit out through clenched teeth. The murderous tone made Molly want to cower away from him

Taming Lucca

because she was almost certain he wasn't going to be any less angry with her, but she wasn't the one who'd asked him to run after her. That was on him and he would have to get with his slut later. Stale Breath, who was holding her, loosened his arms around her waist allowing her room for some much needed breath and she gulped in a few deep ones.

"You her ol' man?" the man questioned, looking at Bone quizzically.

"No," came the flat reply from Bone.

"Good. I'm keeping her! I got to her first." Stale Breath was laughing and tightened his arm again around her waist. Without missing a beat, a gun was pressed to the man's head and she was let go. Molly turned and looked at the scene before her, a little shocked at the violence it promised.

"Fuck, Bone, put that away, man!" Dog yelled, pushing Molly behind him. Terry grabbed her holding her hand tightly. Molly stood watching, her heart pounding in her ears and her wide eyes trained on Bone and the man who'd grabbed her.

"He let her go. Come on, man, it's all good. Just take Molly back to the cabin," Dog tried to reason with him.

Bone didn't seem convinced and he looked at Dog with cold eyes. They were filled with deadly calm as he held the gun to the man's temple. Stale Breath stood frozen at the feel of the cold metal against his temple. Bone appeared to be getting ready to shoot the man, his finger squeezing slightly on the trigger. Molly felt her throat close off while she watched. She'd never seen anyone get shot before and she was feeling lightheaded at the prospect of watching Bone kill the man simply because he was drunk and wouldn't let her go.

"Bone, don't," Dog said again, trying to stop Bone from killing the man. Still holding the gun, Bone looked at Stale Breath without compassion, his hand steady as he watched

Michelle Woods

the man who'd sobered up quickly when the gun was pressed to his head.

"He touched her. He put his filthy hands on her and *she's mine*," Bone said, turning back to Dog with a crazy look in his eyes, his hand wavering slightly on the gun.

"I know, but you can't kill him. Not in front of Molly," Dog said, still trying to diffuse the situation without it ending in death.

Molly suddenly recognized that Bone had that crazy-assed look in his eyes because of her. She was astonished to realize that she wasn't afraid of him even though he stood a few feet from her with a gun pressed against a man's head. Bone's eyes met hers and she would bet he was seeing anxiety in hers as she looked back at him.

"Fuck!" Bone spit out as he lowered the gun. "Get the fuck outta here and don't let me see you around her again or you're dead."

Bone's teeth were clenched and his grip on the gun was tight. The man didn't have to be told twice and he took off, almost running away. When he was out of sight, Bone pushed his gun back into the holster on his belt and held out his hand to Molly.

"Molly, come here."

She stared at that hand, her own still clenching Terry's hand. She let go, standing up straight, meeting his eyes with her own. She wasn't going to let him drag her back to the house like she was an errant little girl.

"No!" Yelling, she moved to stand in front of Dog. "Dog can take me to Aunt Mae's. I'm not going back to that cabin." Tears still in her eyes, she raised her chin and held his gaze, determined to get her way.

"Fuck this! I will not have this conversation here," Bone said and he stepped forward, scooping her up and holding her hanging over his shoulder. At first, she was shocked to find herself slung over his shoulder but as he began to walk towards the cabin with her, she got really mad. How dare he!

She began to hit his ass, screaming to be let down. She wasn't pleased to hear the chuckles of Dog and Terry, who watched the display. He ignored the blows and continued to walk, his hand sliding between her legs holding her steady.

"Put me down, damn it!" Molly screeched.

"No!" he said, carrying her toward the cabin. She bit him on the lower back. He howled and his hand landed hard on her ass.

"Find Tank, tell him I found her," he called out to Dog. Then he was jogging with her on his shoulder towards the cabin. She wasn't able to do anything then except hope like hell he didn't drop her. She was feeling slightly nauseated and all the blood was rushing to her head, making her a little lightheaded.

Bone made it to the cabin without dropping her, thankfully. When they entered the cabin, Molly felt slightly bruised from the jabbing of his shoulder into her ribs as he set her down inside the door. As soon as she regained her footing, she immediately tried to run to the kitchen door to escape. He grabbed her by the arm spinning her around, his eyes a dark brown pool of serious intent.

"You go out that door again and I will beat your ass, Molly," Bone said with harsh honesty.

Molly didn't know what came over her in that moment but she knew that she was really pissed. She hated him in that moment and she didn't intend to be treated like a doormat.

"Fuck you!" she screamed, blushing bright red when she realized what she'd just said. Bone only chuckled, watching her intently.

"Oh, you will, don't worry, doll."

Michelle Woods

Molly saw red.

How dare he think that she was just going to replace the blonde without protest? Oh hell no, buddy, that was so not happening. Pain sliced through her and his actions filled her with rage. She wasn't a whore. She moved back from him when he reached out for her.

"No! Go find your blonde to take care of your sick needs. I will never allow you to touch me again!"

"Fuck, you think I want that blonde bitch when I can have you in my bed?" He stared at her in disbelief. "Not happening. You're the only one I want in my bed tonight," he said harshly, moving forward to grab her again.

Molly jumped back, her arms knocking away his hands as she began running up the stairs. "I don't want you to touch me!" she screamed over her shoulder as she headed to the guestroom. She knew that the door had a lock on it because she'd noticed it the other day when she was cleaning the house. Molly didn't hesitate, she ran towards the door as she heard him coming up the stairs behind her.

"Molly, get your ass back here," he commanded.

He sped up and Molly could hear the pounding of his boots as he thundered up the stairs behind her. He yelled when he saw she was headed into the guest room. "Don't you dare lock that door!"

Molly snorted. Ha, like she was going to listen to that!

She slammed the door just before he reached it and clicked the lock into place with a sigh of relief. She didn't think he'd destroy his own house to get at her, so she was safe for now. Her hands trembled as she stepped back from the door, her whole body feeling jittery.

She turned to the bed, throwing herself down on it and putting the pillow over her head to try and block out the sounds of him banging on the door and yelling for her to open it.

Did he really think she was going to let him in?

Molly shook her head, laughing scornfully; that was not likely to happen in this lifetime. He wanted to be all high and mighty by dragging her back here so he could suck it up. The bastard! Bone banged on the door bellowing for her to open it. He was banging so hard that it rattled the windows on either side of the bed.

"Molly, you open this fucking door right now! Damn it, I just want to talk to you, that's all! You need to listen to me, baby. Open the damned door!" Bone roared, slamming his fist into the door.

Fuck, Bone thought, running his hand through his hair, kicking the door and wanting to break it down, this was a shitty night. Not only had he fucked up with the blonde debacle, he'd also probably scared Molly half to death by pulling a gun. He remembered her wide-eyed expression as he'd held the gun to that bastard's head. That look on her face was the only reason that man was alive. He'd known that shooting him would likely scare her to death. She'd probably never seen that kind of violence and he hadn't wanted to be the reason she did.

Protecting her had become his purpose and he wasn't about to fuck that up like he had their budding relationship. Damn it, why the fuck did he try to prove he could be an asshole?

He'd made a promise to himself a long damned time ago never to hurt a woman the way his father had hurt his mother and then he went and pulled this bullshit like a freaking moron. What the hell had he been thinking when he'd dragged that woman here tonight? He hadn't been because he was just trying to prove that she didn't matter to his club. It was stupid

Michelle Woods

and he wasn't going to let it ruin what they'd begun to build.

Bone kicked the door again before remembering that the key to this door was in his dresser. Slamming his hand into the door once more, he turned and headed to his room. He stomped into the room heading for the drawer with purpose.

She was going to listen to him and understand that he'd made a mistake, and that he hadn't even touched that blonde. It wasn't like he'd even been able to get it hard for her with Molly taking up his every thought. Had she been five minutes later, the sweetbutt wouldn't have even been here and this wouldn't be an issue. Bone had already realized that he wouldn't be getting it up for any woman except Molly before she'd arrived.

Molly pressed her face into the pillow, her heart aching. Damn the man, he could have at least tried to get in for more than a minute before he gave up. Molly knew she was being ridiculous. Why did it matter how long he'd tried to get into the room? She'd wanted him to leave her alone and he had.

She couldn't help it though because the idea that he was probably already searching out that blonde to screw pissed her off. She felt angry tears begin to fall, sliding down her cheeks as she sobbed in despair. Her heart ripping in two with the unhappy reality of her situation, she wished that she didn't care if he screwed another woman but she did. It made the sobs come harder thinking of him with anyone but her. She balled her hands into tight fists in the sheet, her body quivering with the sobs that wracked her.

The door hit the wall with a loud bang, causing her to sit up and send a panicked look at Bone as he filled the doorway holding a key before tucking it into his pocket. She jumped from the bed intending to run into the bathroom to get away

Taming Lucca

from him, but he jumped forward, grabbing her and forcing her onto the bed with his weight pinning her to it. His face was inches from hers and she knew that she must look like a wreck with tears pouring over her cheeks and her hair likely a mess.

"I don't think so, baby," he said while holding her arms above her head.

"Let me go, Bone," Molly almost screamed. "Get off me." She thrashed on the bed trying to knock him off her. He held her easily, his body pressed against hers, his hands gripping her in a firm but gentle hold.

"No. Calm down, woman," Bone growled, his nose almost pressed to hers.

"Go find your blonde so you two can get it on and leave me alone! I've had enough of your manhandling for one night," Molly spat at him, still trying to get away from him.

Turning her head, she tried to bite his arm, her teeth snapping together when he moved it away from her. She realized when he growled at her to calm down that she wasn't going to get away. He was pinning her to the bed with his heavy weight. Unable to hold the tears at bay in the face of defeat, she sobbed, not caring if he saw her pain.

"Calm down, you little Hell Cat!" he grumbled, holding both her wrists in one of his hands to prevent her from biting him. He felt his dick swell against her as she wiggled back and forth rubbing it. He couldn't help the feeling of possessive glee the movements caused. He should be ashamed of the enjoyment he got out of holding her this way but he wasn't. She seemed to realize that he wasn't going to let her get away and the fight went out of her.

For a moment she lay still and silent beneath him before she

Michelle Woods

looked at him with tears in her eyes and he felt the way her body trembled as hard sobs came from her. Bone felt lower than pond scum because he was the reason for this and it fucking killed him to cause her such pain.

"Plea––please," she begged.

Huge sobs that made her whole body shake beneath him started pouring from her and it made him want to slit his own throat. Something inside him clenched as he watched the tears that poured down her face, and he just wanted it to stop. He lowered his lips to her checks following the tears with his mouth, trying to kiss them away, needing to make her hurt disappear because it was tearing him apart. It felt like claws ripping his insides out.

He'd done this to her.

He'd taken a strong, beautiful woman and made her hurt so bad she trembled with it. Hatred of his actions burned like fire pulsing inside him. He couldn't stop the wildfire of revulsion that seemed to consume him. Bone didn't know how to fix this, to fix them, but he knew that he had to find a way because the alternative was unbearable.

"Molly––baby, please. I can't stand to see you cry, it's killing me." Still kissing her face, feeling the wetness of her tears salting his lips, he was taken back to the nights he'd lain awake listening to the wrenching sobs of his mother when she realized that his father wasn't coming home, again. Those memories broke inside him like a tidal wave unleashing destruction inside him.

"Baby," his voice broke a little as he kissed her beneath each eye. "I'm sorry. So, so sorry, please stop," he whispered, knowing that the promise he'd made on those nights listening in the dark had been broken by his own need to prove he was the same bastard he'd been before he met her a week ago.

He didn't deserve her forgiveness, and yet he was begging

Taming Lucca

for it just as his father had so many times before him. It felt like he was being torn in two by the conflicting needs that slammed into each other over and over. One need was screaming that he should let her go, to let her find a man who deserved her, someone like Dog or Slim. The other roared that it wasn't letting her go, not ever. He knew which need was going to win before the fight even began. The gun he'd held to a man's temple tonight was an indication of what he would do to any man who touched her.

"Shhh—baby, it's okay," he whispered, his lips kissing her cheeks trying to make the tears she shed disappear.

Molly sobbed listening to Bone trying to soothe her. She felt him kissing her face, her eyes, and then he was kissing her lips, gently caressing them in tiny sipping kisses that made her feel so soft even as she almost hated him for those kisses. Her heart wanted him and his light caresses that teased her senses and it was betraying her. She didn't know what to do but she found herself tilting her head a little to receive the kisses and caresses of his lips without meaning to.

"Baby, it was a mistake, it will never happen again. I didn't even touch her." He kissed her forehead, trying desperately to make her stop crying. He let her wrists go, his hands cupping her face as he slowly thrust his tongue into her mouth in a gentle caress. Damn, she tasted sweet. His cock was already hardened with need despite his remorse at having hurt her.

Chapter 17

Molly couldn't stop herself from returning his kisses even knowing that she was cheapening herself by allowing him to use her for sex. Her body trembled beneath his, her hands shaky as they buried themselves in his hair. She was overwhelmed by the passion that filled her from just those lips gently caressing her own. A moan escaped her when his tongue began to thrust slowly into her mouth.

Molly had never felt like this with any other man. His caresses twisted her up inside creating a roaring vortex of needy desire that almost consumed her. She was no innocent, but the passion Bone made her feel was so much more than she'd ever felt with another man. Her hands tightened in his hair while his tongue thrust more forcefully into her mouth. Her body lifted off the bed pressing into his. She could feel the hard wedge of his thick cock between her legs, making her gasp as her mind shattered into a blissful kaleidoscope of unfulfilled desires.

Bone's hands traveled down, sliding beneath her shirt to cup her breasts and rub her nipples. Molly almost came apart at the light flick of his fingers on her breasts. Groaning, wanting more contact from him on her bare breasts, she pulled her hands from his hair and moved, trying to remove her shirt while he still pinned her to the bed.

Bone realized that Molly was trying to remove her shirt, and pulled back slightly to allow her hands to move the shirt up, baring her slightly rounded stomach. Unable to look away from that small bit of flesh she displayed, his hands fell from her breasts stopping her from removing her shirt as he tore his eyes from the skin she'd revealed to him. He had to be sure that this was what she wanted because if this went any further tonight, he was not giving her up, ever.

After making love to her there would be no way for him to allow her to leave him. He knew himself enough to know that much. If she let him have her that was it, she would be his, and his alone. His mind shuddered on those thoughts because he'd just thought of sex as making love even though he'd never made love. He was turning into a fucking pansy, but with her small soft body pressed into his hard dick, he didn't care.

"Baby, look at me," he said when he finally managed to look at her face to see her eyes tightly closed. Her eyes opened and they met his, filled with desire that made him want to forget what he needed to say to her and just rip her clothes off and love her, to own her. Fuck, now he sounded like Dog, but fuck if it wasn't what he wanted, to mark her in every way so that every other man knew to keep his fucking hands to himself.

"You need to be sure, Molly. I won't be able to back off after this. You'll be mine," he said, watching her intently. Waiting for her answer, his hands clenched on the bottom of her shirt wanting to just rip it off. There was so much more he wanted to say, that he was sorry for her walking in on him with the blonde, for being an idiot, for pulling a gun on a man in front of her, but at the moment the words were trapped behind a roaring wall of need for this woman and her body.

Michelle Woods

"Y-yes," she said, her voice raspy and soft, her eyes deep honeyed pools of desire as she lay looking up at him, her hands still buried in his hair.

"Good," he growled, moving back slightly to rip the thin t-shirt up and off her.

He stared with hunger at her small breasts covered in only a black lacy bra. He reached down pulling the front clasp of the bra, baring her breasts completely to his gaze. Growling with ravenousness desire, he leaned forward taking one large raspberry-colored nipple into his mouth, sucking it deep and then scraping it lightly with his teeth, his hand possessively caressing her other breast.

Molly arched beneath Bone in pleasure as his mouth caressed her breast while his other hand pinched her nipple. She'd never liked a man to touch her breasts because it always left her feeling awkward. It had never been something she enjoyed, but the feel of Bone aggressively sucking her breast while his fingers flicked her other nipple made her feel as if her body was going up in flames, and she was drenched with her own desire. She whimpered, holding him to her as her legs wrapped around his waist, and she clenched his shoulder, her nails digging into his skin.

"So good, baby." Bone kissed his way to her neck nipping her gently. "You taste so damned good."

He needed her naked and every inch of her pressed against him, now. His brain focused with pinpoint accuracy on that one goal. He reached down jerking his shirt off before his hands slid between them to unsnap her jeans and he began to tear them off her. When they were off he pulled back, looking at her lying in his bed with only black lace covering her slender body and let out a heavy groan.

Damn, she was fucking hot. He took in her little nipples pointing up at him, and her pussy covered with only black

Taming Lucca

lace. She was his fantasy come to life, and he needed to be inside her more than he needed his next breath.

He eyes caressing every inch of her bared body, he looked his fill for a moment. Molly moved her hands down from his shoulders, her soft hands sliding over the light dusting of hair on his chest. Her fingers found his nipples and she lightly pinched them, eliciting a grunt of pleasure from him.

His eyes focused on her little nipples and his dick throbbed. One nipple was rosy and slightly wet while the other was raspberry pink and looked neglected.

Umm, that would not do, he needed to make that better. Leaning forward, he took the tightly beaded tip into his mouth sucking gently at first but as her taste roared through him, his sucking became harder, needing to absorb as much of her as was possible.

Molly had never caressed a man so boldly; the few sexual encounters she'd had with the three men she'd dated were quick tumbles in the dark. With Bone Molly felt the need to mark him in some way, so that when he left her for another woman she would always be there between them. He suddenly leaned forward, his mouth covering her other breast, sucking it slowly at first then just as aggressively as he had the first. Gripping him, she cried out, wanting more. Her fingers twisted his nipples slightly and he groaned around her nipple. She felt satisfaction burst inside her as the sound left him because it meant he was as affected by her caresses as she was by his.

"Umm—such pretty berries, baby," Bone growled, his voice a husky timber that sent shivers down her spine. Goose bumps appeared on her skin and she felt like her head would explode from the sensations he was drawing from her body.

His mouth was almost devouring her nipple, but he wasn't willing to stop. As he felt her small body shake beneath his,

Michelle Woods

all he could think as he growled around her little nipple was Mine, all fucking mine.

It was a new thing for him to feel so possessive with a woman, but Molly was his. He knew that to his very bones because he wouldn't allow it to be any other way. Bone reached down between them to unfasten his jeans to let his aching dick free. Pushing them down and kicking them off, he kissed her again, smelling her scent filling the room. The smell of strawberries and sunshine consumed him, making him damned glad he hadn't brought the sweetbutt in here to pollute the room with her heavily perfumed scent. He knew that it was Molly's natural scent and he loved that it filled his room.

Bone allowed his hands to catch her hips when they moved back up her body. His mouth slid to her breasts again, moving between them, gently sucking one before releasing it to suck the other. Gradually moving his hand between her legs to slide beneath the black lace to caress her moist heat, he groaned at the soft wetness his fingers found.

"You're so wet for me, baby," he heatedly whispered as his fingers teased the tender lips of her sweetness.

He rubbed over her clit, hearing the little gasp she let out like music caressing his ears, and he needed to feel her around him. He thrust a finger inside her with a rumble of need, almost exploding like a fucking schoolboy with his first crush when her hips thrust up to meet his finger. Bone growled possessively, his mouth finding hers, his tongue thrusting deep to caress hers in a mimic of what he needed so badly from her. Setting a quick rhythm, he added another finger, watching her as she took it inside releasing a moan, panting in need. He worked her body till it was close to orgasm.

"Umm, you're so sexy, baby."

Pulling his fingers from her, panting from the feel of her

Taming Lucca

tight channel clenching at them, he wrenched her lace panties off. Moving between her legs to place himself at her entrance, meeting her eyes, he paused.

Molly watched between their bodies as Bone placed the head of his dick at her entrance. Wanting to feel him joined to her, she tried to press down to take him inside her. She needed him now, she was on fire, so close to her orgasm from his caresses.

He ducked, meeting her eyes, and asked, "Ready?"

"Yes…just do it!" she almost screamed, her need to come causing her voice to be shrill, and he chuckled, making her want to hit him. The bastard. Molly was almost mindless, her body was so close that it was teetering on the brink of an explosion that promised to be epic, and she didn't want to wait while he decided she was ready for him to take her.

As she felt him slowly parting her folds, she let out a gasp, her body tightening, and she gripped his shoulders, whimpering. Her hands clenched when he gripped her hips and thrust hard into her seating himself fully, causing a slight twinge as her body was forced to accept his large girth.

Bone stilled for a moment, feeling as if he was drowning. He was fully seated inside Molly for the first time. His brain shut down as sensations bombarded him, possessiveness the leader in the riot of emotions, followed closely by pleasure, making him feel the need to move.

Giving her what he promised the first day they met, "Lucca," he whispered, unable to prevent a short stroke into her. "That's what you should scream when you come around me, baby."

He wanted to fuck her hard and fast, but he needed her to know that she wasn't like any of the other women he had taken before her; she was different. He wanted to own her little body, wanted to erase every man who'd been inside her

Michelle Woods

before him. Thinking of another man touching her started that insane refrain in his head again, "Mine, Mine, Mine."

He began to move, unaware he was repeating that refrain out loud in such a possessive tone that Molly couldn't help feeling a bit consumed by him. She wanted to protest his growling claim of ownership but she didn't have the strength as her body trembled in orgasm and she began to thrash beneath him as she came apart.

"Lucca——" Molly screamed, and her mind followed her body into blissful abandonment.

Pounding into her, his body slamming into hers with heavy strokes, he grunted and groaned in satisfaction. Her body gripped his tightly and he felt the silken caress like a vice. Bone knew that nothing had ever felt as good as her body surrounding his did and the sound of the keening moan that didn't stop escaping her was enough to break him.

It wasn't long after the first orgasm hit her before she coming around him a second time as he pumped into her. While her second orgasm gripped him, he felt his balls tighten, and he knew he was close to coming. He kissed her and his movements slowed, trying hard to make their pleasure last. Bone knew when she twisted her hips a little as she moaned his name a second time that he was going to come and he almost fell on her as he felt his release. Letting out a roar of gratification that likely rattled the windows, his body slowly came to a halt. He groaned, resting against her for a long moment before he finally moved to his back. He brought her body with him so that he could stay connected to her, unwilling to give up the tight grip of her wet sheath on his cock.

Molly felt languid and happy as she lay on top of Bone where he'd dragged her after he came. She ran her hand up and down Bone's chest caressing him as he held her close, gripping her tightly.

"Fuck, I forgot a condom," Bone said suddenly.

"It's okay. I got the shot four weeks ago, so I'm good for about two and a half months," Molly said, tensing slightly as she lifted away from him, referring to the shot that prevented pregnancy.

"Why?" he demanded with a dark scowl covering his face.

"Um, I was seeing someone."

"Not anymore." Bone's voice was filled with angry jealousy as he gripped her hips and pulled her back down until she was resting on his chest, wrapping his arms around her tightly.

"No," Molly said, liking his neanderthal-like reaction a little too much. "Not anymore."

"Good." His hands began to caress her back, sliding up and down as he lightly began to kiss her neck. She moaned when he found a particularly sensitive spot, nipping and sucking on it roughly. She felt him harden slightly inside her, which shocked her. Luzen never wanted to make love so soon after they had been together. Bone was already moving his hand to her breasts to cup them while urging her to sit up so he could play with them.

Molly felt her body clench on him as she lifted, and he pushed his hardening member up into her with a groan, his mouth taking her nipple and sucking it deeply.

"You make me so horny with these sexy little nipples," he growled as he alternated between her breasts, sucking one for a few seconds before taking the neglected one in his mouth for the same rough sucking, his tongue curling around the tip, then sliding over it slowly. Molly was shocked that she was already beginning to feel needy again, her body slowly wiggling on his hardened dick. His hands clenched her hips as he pushed her up a bit then let her slide back down, causing her to cry out.

Michelle Woods

"Lucca," she whispered, desperately.

He pulled back and smiled with true pleasure at her keening cry of his name. He liked that sound on her lips, even with the possessiveness he felt eating him up inside at her mention of having been with another man so recently. He wanted her again mostly to stamp his ownership all over her body, every fucking inch.

"That's it, baby, ride me," he said, urging her to move up and down his thick length while his mouth took her breasts, moving slowly from one to the other. She rose and slid back down, grunting in desire as she set a light bouncy rhythm, her hands resting on his chest gripping tightly with her nails digging into his skin with every stroke. He gripped her hips helping to even out her pace, allowing her to feel every stroke of his dick, satisfied when it didn't take long for her to start clenching around him letting him know she was nearing orgasm.

"Lucca——umm, Lucca" she cried out as her orgasm washed over her, overwhelmed with the feel of him moving inside her.

Bone felt her shudder above him and she slowed to a stop making him feel desperate to feel her little pussy grip him. He pulled out, rolling away from her, landing on his feet beside the bed. Dragging her to the edge, he thrust hard into her, grunting at the hot, wet feel of her sweet body gripping his cock again. Growling, with her legs bent over his arms and his hands gripping her ass firmly, he set a hard rhythm that made wet slapping sounds with every thrust of his body into hers. It didn't take long for him to roar as he came, pumping into her with light thrusts before finally stopping.

"You okay, baby?" he asked as he gently pulled out of her, a little afraid he'd gotten too rough with her. She opened her eyes that had been closed and smiled a soft satisfied smile that made him ache. Yeah, that smile was sexy as fuck.

Taming Lucca

"Yes," she murmured, then as if she couldn't keep them open her eyes slid closed again. He moved her back onto the bed, gently arranging her then wrapping her in his arms as he lay beside her with a satisfied smirk.

He kissed her temple and whispered, "Get some sleep, baby."

Bone felt the little sigh that escaped her and knew that it wouldn't be long before he'd be waking her up to make love to her again. His need was sated for now but he would hunger for her again soon because his dick was already twitching trying to get hard. Bone knew it was crazy with the amount of sex he had on a regular basis to feel starved for her like he did. It scared the shit out of him that that fact didn't matter to his needy dick. He fell into a light sleep, his head filled with Molly and his mixed up feelings of possessiveness and need.

Chapter 18

Bone woke with Molly snuggled in his arms, her leg wrapped over his hip and her head resting on his chest. Warmth spreading through him, he grinned before slowly shifting her off him so that he could rise from the bed. As he stood beside the bed scratching his stomach, he glanced back at her in his big king size bed with her naked back bare to the waist and her hair falling around her. Her hand curled on the pillow he'd slid under her head, and he wanted to crawl right back in with her.

Satisfaction slid along his spine making his smile turn wicked; he'd worked her hard last night. He'd woken her twice to make love to her last night and he knew that the last time he took her at about three am she'd been worn out. Reaching out to run a possessive hand over her curved ass, he squeezed the flesh gently. She moaned and twisted a bit on the bed, murmuring something unintelligible that he would bet was something along the lines of leave me alone you horny bastard.

Reaching down to adjust his hard cock while mentally telling it he'd have her again soon, he moved into the bathroom, taking a quick shower instead. He pulled on a pair of jeans, not bothering with a shirt or boxers, and walked down the stairs.

Heading into the kitchen to make his baby some breakfast so that she could keep her strength up for the marathon of sex he would likely subject her to tonight, he paused when he heard a knock on the door. He opened the door to find Slim standing there with a slightly grim look on his face.

"You can't fucking have her!" he growled, not waiting for the man to speak.

His fists clenched and he glared at Slim. He wasn't in the mood for this shit. His and Molly's relationship was none of Slim's business. He thought the fight they'd had the other night had been enough to make him stop trying to interfere.

Fuck, had he just called it a relationship? He was turning into a pansy-assed idiot.

Feeling a little out of sorts with the riot of emotions that were dancing around inside him, he stepped back, allowing Slim to enter, surprised to see Trick, who'd been behind him, follow him inside.

"Umm, okay. I didn't come here to take her so we can agree on that point. Jeez, you're an asshole this morning. Wait, it's like twelve, you must just be an asshole," Slim said with a snort of laughter.

"Damn, Bone, we just needed to talk about your girl," Trick, the man who'd followed Slim in, said with a sigh, stepping back when Bone glared at him while taking a threatening step towards him. "Wait, we don't want to take her, we just want to use her for a bit."

Bone growled and jumped forward to grab Trick by the throat. No way were they asking to use her as if she was a pair of shoes or a flashlight. As if he was going to allow any man to touch her. Had they lost their fucking minds?

"No, wait, Bone. Not like that!" Slim yelled, grabbing him by the shoulders and slamming him back into the wall. Bone

Michelle Woods

growled and tried to take a swing at him.

Molly woke with a lazy stretch, feeling the slight soreness between her legs and realizing Lucca wasn't in the bed. Lucca was such a beautiful name she couldn't understand why the man didn't use it instead of Bone. She sat up when she heard raised male voices downstairs and wondered who was here. She moved again, feeling the slight twinge, making her remember the fantastic sex that had led to that soreness.

Bone hadn't stopped with taking her twice last night. After that first hard ride he'd let her sleep for an hour or two before she woke to find his head buried between her legs. He'd been lapping at her with hot sexy sucks of her clit that had almost blown the top of her head off. She'd come three times before he'd finally shown mercy and entered her. Then hours later she awoke again to him deep inside her, slowly moving in and out with light almost lazy strokes. He'd finally let her sleep after that with her cuddled to his side, his hand possessively cupping her breast.

Hearing a thud from below, she decided she better get up and take a shower to see what was going on down there. She entered the bathroom naked and glanced at herself in the mirror, letting out a gasp. She was sporting major love marks on her breasts and neck and she stepped closer to the counter, inspecting them. They surrounded her breasts and she counted five on each one, feeling a blush stain her cheeks as she tilted her head to discover four more on her neck. Wow, Lucca had been a little possessive, but for all she knew this was something he did with all the women he slept with.

That thought made her remember the blond bimbo who'd been in the living room with her shirt off. Molly felt her heart tighten in her chest when she thought of what she'd allowed Bone to do to her after she'd seen him with another woman.

Taming Lucca

Damn, he must think she was a bimbo just like that woman last night and she had no one to blame except herself.

Feeling slightly depressed because she didn't want to think of Lucca with another woman, she wondered if he was going to want her to move to the guest room now that he'd had sex with her. Lisa had said that he always kicked a woman out when he was done with her. Hell, he might even send her to live with Slim and Lisa, she realized, dismay gripping her hard.

Deciding that the only way to find out was to get her shower done and head downstairs, she sighed deeply. Then got into the shower and quickly washed off last night's sex marathon and got out. Molly dressed in a pair of cutoffs and a thin white shirt. Not bothering with a bra, she headed downstairs.

"She's a mechanic, Bone. A damned good one if she found that leak. I could barely find it, and I knew what to look for," Trick was saying as he leaned against the wall. "We can use her help at the shop."

"I will not have her working there! She is going to stay here," Bone was yelling at him when he saw Slim looking at her as she came down the stairs. She felt her heart jump a little when she heard him insist on her staying here, one of her fears alleviated somewhat by the words he'd yelled at the other two men. Turning, Bone stopped talking and ogled her for an uncomfortable amount of time, his face covered in a hungry look.

"Good morning," Molly murmured, her body frozen halfway down the stairs.

Bone stared at Molly in a pair of the smallest cutoff jeans he'd ever seen, her slender legs showing pale creamy skin that he remembered rubbing last night. His favorite part of her

Michelle Woods

was her sweet little nipples, which poked expectantly at her shirt as if begging him to take them into his mouth. Feelings of possessiveness and need mixed inside him to create a roaring vortex of desire and it was all he could do not to scoop her up and carry her back to his bed.

He realized suddenly that both Slim and Trick could also see his favorite little nipples poking hard against the thin shirt, and he didn't like that at all. His chest filled with a growl he didn't allow free as he began moving up the stairs towards her. When he reached her, he took Molly into his arms, his mouth covering her bee-stung lips, his tongue spearing through them to find the honeyed depths. Bone knew that his body was shielding her nipples from those assholes when his bare chest pressed against them.

Slim began to snicker behind him but he ignored him. He felt his desire to have her alone in his bed deepening. The only thing stopping him from carrying her back there at the moment was the knowledge that he'd worked her body hard last night and she needed a break. He pulled back, still holding her, and whispered, "Good morning, baby."

He ignored the laughter that rang out from below them. His eyes devoured her pretty blush and the way her eyes sparkled with unfulfilled desires. Bone liked seeing them lurking there.

"Lucca, why can't I work at the shop?" she asked quietly, watching him.

"No, Molly," he said, then added in a whisper close to her ear, "You're only allowed to call me Lucca when I'm inside you, remember."

Blushing, she put her hands on his shoulders and looked at him in disbelief.

"Really?" she demanded with horror; she was planning to call him that instead.

"Yep," Bone replied with a smile of devilment.

Taming Lucca

"Good morning, Molly," Slim called from the bottom of the stairs with glee. "We were just discussing you."

"I already told you it's not safe for her to be in the shop and that I'm not allowing it," Bone growled with displeasure. He was unwilling to allow her to be out in the open at the shop because if the Jackals discovered what she meant to him, they'd try to hurt him through her and that wasn't going to happen.

"I want to work in the shop. I'm not good with the house stuff," she said boldly without her usual timidness.

He watched her for a moment before letting out a sigh and asked with growing disappointment, "This will make you happy?"

"Yes."

"We'll keep her safe, Bone," Trick called up.

Molly looked over Bone's shoulder at Trick and Slim. The look on her face was so hopeful that despite the gnawing sense of worry her working at the shop caused him, he considered allowing it just to make her happy. Fuck, he was turning into a damned pussy.

"With three of us to look out for her nothing can happen to her. Tiny, Slim, and I will watch her like a hawk." Bone noted that Trick didn't include Rash in his promise. Bone realized that was a smart move on the other man's part because he didn't trust him with Molly after the incident the other day. Pressing his forehead against hers for a moment, his heart arguing with his head, he finally came to a decision.

"Fine, but baby, you stay with one of them at all times, and I mean it. There are a lot of men from other clubs that use Trick's shop. I don't like this idea and if you can't follow the rules I will revoke my decision."

"I promise, Bone," Molly said, a delighted smile lighting up her whole face making her even more achingly beautiful than

Michelle Woods

she'd been a moment ago. He knew he was going to regret letting her work at the shop but the pleasure it gave her was all he cared about at the moment.

"Go change, you're not wearing that." Bone indicated her cutoffs with a wave of his hand. Still smiling, she turned and began bounding up the stairs, excited that she would be able to do something she loved again.

"Okay, Lucca," she called over her shoulder as she returned to their bedroom.

Bone groaned at the sight of her ass almost hanging out of her cutoffs, his cock hardening. He didn't appreciate the low whistle Trick let out when she was almost at the top. Bone punched him hard in the gut when he could finally tear his eyes off her sweet ass.

"Lucca. Shit, she'll be patched by next week." Slim laughed with triumph, not expecting the hard blow to his stomach that caused him to bend over wheezing.

"Damn that hurt, Bone," he panted out.

"You'll get over it." Bone didn't bother to deny his accusation; this time he wasn't so sure that Slim might not be right about him patching Molly. He wasn't willing to look at that too closely right now. "Now you two assholes need to leave. You can come back and pick her up in an hour."

Bone walked towards the kitchen not bothering to wait on the two men to leave. As they left with much laughter, he began to get the pans out and make his woman some breakfast.

Molly entered the kitchen wearing jeans and a white tank top, causing Bone to frown. At least she was wearing a bra this time, but this outfit wasn't any less appealing than the first one had been. The jeans were tight and clung to her hips, and likely her ass, although he couldn't see with her facing him. The tank was ribbed and didn't show much but it was low cut enough that the tops of her breasts were showing.

"What's wrong?" Molly asked frowning

"Nothing. Only you're wearing that?" Bone forced himself to turn back to the eggs he was cooking at the stove. He knew that she was confused by his question and he glanced at her over his shoulder as she spoke.

"Yes, it gets hot in coveralls." She watched as he added some peppers and a few seasonings to the pan. She didn't know why he was so concerned over her wardrobe. Molly didn't know if she should ask if she needed to move into the guest room. She didn't like the idea that when she got back from the shop she might find him with another woman. Her chest ached a little at the thought.

Unsure how to ask, she settled for, "So, should I move my things to the guest room?"

Bone turned to her with a dark frown holding the spatula. His eyes narrowed on her and she could tell he was gripping the spatula hard.

"What are you talking about?" he demanded, and Molly noticed that the eggs had begun to burn on the stove.

"Umm...you're burning the eggs," she told him. He grunted, looking unconcerned as he turned back to the stove.

His movements jerky, almost angry, he lifted the pan to another burner, turning it off. He turned back towards her with an intent look on his face and the spatula in his hand. Moving around the counter, he slammed the spatula on it and then spun her stool around until she was facing him. Then he leaned forward, his eyes filled with a fire, holding her gaze as she leaned back into the counter trying to escape his intense look.

"You try that and see what happens, Molly." The words were said softly, but they weren't gentle or nice, they had a deadly ring to them. They were a warning and Molly felt a

Michelle Woods

shiver slide through her at the tone.

His mouth crashed onto hers, taking her lips in a demanding kiss that left her breathless. Bone's hands grabbed her shirt, wrenching it off her, revealing the pearl bra she was wearing under it. Surprised at this quick disrobing, she gasped and reared back, her back hitting the counter. He looked at her bra-covered breasts with a hungry gaze, making her glad she'd let Lisa convince her to buy all those sexy panties and bras at the market in Titus.

It had surprised her that Bone had given Lisa a pouch of credits for her; the amount inside the pouch had almost made her faint. A thousand credits were way more than she'd ever had to spend.

"Damn, that's a fucking pretty sight." Hearing him made her blush a deep red.

"Stop saying that, Lucca!" she cried out.

"Sorry, baby. It's going to take some time to break that habit. I've been using that word since I was fifteen. Thirteen years is a long time. Besides I like watching you blush, it turns all your silky skin rosy." He chuckled.

"Lucca," she pleaded, but she didn't know what she was pleading with him about. Was she asking him to behave or was she begging him not to?

His mouth came forward, sucking her breast, bra and all into his mouth. Molly couldn't contain the sensations that overtook her as she panted and leaned on the counter. Sucking hard, he moved his hand down, ripping her jeans down her legs. Molly let out a gasp because she still wasn't sure what had brought on this possessive claiming that Bone was currently performing on her. Moving between her parted legs, he dropped his own pants with a growl and tested her wetness with his fingers. Finding her soaked, he pressed his dick into her, sliding it in a little. She was ready, but she still flinched, jerking back from his invasion.

"Fuck, baby, I should have known it was too soon," he growled, the intense look that had been on his face moments ago clearing to something softer. He pulled back slowly, his hands gentle on her hips. He stepped back, pulling his pants up and zipping them over his painfully hard cock.

"Lucca, it's okay…please," she panted.

Bone couldn't seem to get his head cleared out ever since she'd uttered the words 'move to the guest room.'

Not fucking happening.

His brain had splintered at the mere suggestion that he not have her in his bed where she belonged. He knew that she likely had no idea that the words which had slipped past her lips had made him see nothing except a red haze of fury and feel nothing but the raw need to claim her.

Her body was trembling and he felt like a total asshole when he'd tried to enter her only to see her face grimace. He knew he'd overdone it last night and that her body would likely be sore this morning but her words had stolen those thoughts from his head like a thief in the night. He watched her from his position, seeing the hazy desires that swirled in her eyes as she looked at his zipped pants with a longing look.

He realized that she needed to be taken care of and dropped to his knees between her legs, burying his face in her sweetness. His head filled with her scent of strawberries and sunshine and his cock jerked against his zipper. He worked her clit with his tongue as she gripped his hair and moaned. Bone was suckling her little bud hard as she wiggled and let out little half signs of pleasure that were music to his ears. He'd never enjoyed giving a woman pleasure like he did with Molly.

Michelle Woods

It wasn't that he hadn't liked giving other women pleasure, it was just different with Molly somehow. Pleasuring her was like a drug. It thrummed through him making his cock swell to the point he wasn't sure it wouldn't burst from its confinement. He wanted to press his fingers inside her to increase the sounds that twisted his insides into knots but didn't want to hurt her, so he just licked and sucked her sweet little pussy until she came, letting out a keening cry.

"Oh–Lucca, yes–Lucca."

The sounds of her coming apart, her body bowing as she exploded into orgasm, was sweeter than any other moan he'd ever heard. He rose to his feet leaning forward to kiss each nipple through her bra, suckling gently on the tight buds for a moment before taking her lips. Bone thrust his tongue into her mouth, devouring her with long deep strokes.

Molly returned them timidly making small moaning sounds as he wrapped her legs around him. Her arms were around his neck holding him close. He kissed down her neck to her sweet breasts again, sucking and nipping at them until the ache in his dick became unbearable. His zipper was probably permanently embedded in his dick by now. Finally managing to pull away from her because his cock couldn't take any more pressure, he gave her one last gentle kiss on her forehead before stepping back.

He scooped her shirt up and held her it out to her. She took it with a little blush that made him want to start all over again. The only thing that stopped him was the knowledge that she needed to eat and change before Slim got back. He watched her slip the shirt over her head before walking to the sink. He leaned on the counter for a second as his cock commanded him to turn around and carry her back to his bed where he could ravish her again. Knowing she was too sore, he forced himself to wash his hands and put the omelets he'd made onto plates for himself and Molly before bringing them to the counter.

"Eat your breakfast, Molly. Slim will be here in a bit to take you to the shop, and you need to change that shirt. It's wet." His smile was wicked when he turned back to her. He hadn't wanted her wearing that shirt to work anyway, it was too revealing. It was probably a good thing that the wetness from his sucking her breasts inside her bra had made a wet spot on her shirt when she put it back on. It gave him a reason to tell her to change it without her getting stubborn.

He stood across from her watching her as she took a bite of the omelet he'd made her. She looked up from the plate at him with a heavy-lidded expression that made his dick twitch, wanting to revisit the damp hollow it had already explored quite thoroughly the night before.

"But—umm, don't you want me to take care of that?" Molly asked as she made a vague gesture at his lap, watching him carefully.

She felt an odd sense of pleased excitement over his reaction to her earlier suggestion that she sleep in the guest room. He had become angry and then he'd gotten possessive. Molly knew she shouldn't like that the way she did, but she did. Bone grinned and devilment entered his eyes as they met hers.

"You can take care of that later when you're not as sore, baby." She blushed a little and looked away. Molly shivered in anticipation before she picked up her fork and began eating the omelet with gusto. Good sex made her hungry as well as satisfied. Molly did worry a little about him going to another woman to satisfy him while she wasn't able to and that thought made her frown.

Michelle Woods

After she'd eaten, she walked to the sink intending to wash the dishes. Bone moved up behind her kissing the side of her neck, taking the dishes from her hands and whispering into her ear, "Go change. I got this, sweetheart."

Molly turned to look up at him. His eyes were filled with indulgence and his lips brushed hers gently before he shoved her a little towards the stairs. Molly headed upstairs tingling from the contact, wishing she wasn't so sore from last night. She changed into a black bra and matching tank top, inspecting herself briefly in the mirror before bounding down the stairs to find Lucca at the kitchen sink cleaning the last dish.

He set the dish on the drying towel next to the sink then pulled the plug to drain the water. She walked up behind him, wrapping her arms around his waist and hugging him. He reached down squeezing her arms as she rested her head on his back.

"Thank you for letting me work in the shop, Lucca," she mumbled into his back, pressing tightly to him.

"You're welcome, but baby, you can't call me Lucca around the club, okay?" His voice was gruff and she wondered what he was thinking.

"Okay, but can I call you Lucca when we're alone?" Molly replied, wondering what the big deal was. It was his name after all. Why did it matter that she called him Lucca instead of Bone?

"Yeah, you can call me Lucca when we're alone."

They stood there with her holding him and him holding her arms until Slim knocked at the back door. She squeezed him tightly one last time before letting go. She opened the door with a bright smile at Slim. Slim glanced inside at Bone with a knowing smirk that she didn't understand before motioning for her to follow him. Molly glanced one last time at Lucca

Taming Lucca

before following Slim to a truck that was parked outside.

Bone watched as Slim led Molly to the cage, wanting to walk out there and make her come right back inside where she'd be safe, but she was so happy now that he'd given in on the mechanic thing. With a sigh, he went upstairs; he needed to go handle the books for the club's finances. Damn, he wished that he wasn't so good with numbers; he hated the books.

Chapter 19

Molly watched Rash take the carburetor out of the truck they were working on. She'd been working at the shop for four weeks now, and everyone but Rash respected her abilities with all manner of engines. Rash, however, always acted as if he had to walk her through each step like she was an idiot, and it was maddening. She gritted her teeth again trying not to tell him he was a fucking moron. It wasn't nice to tell people they didn't have a lick of sense. She was a better mechanic than he was with one hand tied behind her back. She didn't know why the idiot couldn't see that.

Yesterday he hadn't even been able to tell the bike he was working on needed spark plugs until Tiny had pointed it out. Shaking her head as he walked her step by step through the removal, every word out of his mouth made her madder than a hornet's nest. She was not an idiot.

"See, this is where it connects," he said, pointing out the bolt that was clearly visible. Even if she had been a three year old she could have seen it. This was why the man made her want to murder him. He was so ridiculous, treating her as if she were mentally challenged. She never had this problem with Tiny, Trick, or Slim. They never acted like she had limited intelligence just because she was a woman. Hearing

Taming Lucca

him make another insanely obvious comment on removing the part, she rolled her eyes wishing that Tiny would hurry up and come back. He'd gone over to the diner to get them some lunch a half hour ago and wasn't back yet.

"I see," she said to make him think she was paying attention to what he was showing her as she let her mind wander to the last few blissful weeks.

Her relationship with Bone was better by the day and they were settling into a rhythm. She didn't know for sure but she hadn't heard about him with any other women. It pleased her to know that he hadn't slept with anyone but her since they began this relationship. Lisa seemed to think he wouldn't because of how bad his father cheating on his mother had hurt her. Brandy had even voiced her surprise at his behavior.

Lisa even said that he would likely just end it with her if he was going to mess around with other women because he wouldn't want to hurt her. Molly knew that those words had been meant to reassure her but they hadn't really done the trick. She didn't want to think of the end of their relationship. Right now they were spending most of their down time together. They went to work in the morning and around three she left the shop with Slim, who took her to his and Lisa's house on his way to handle whatever club business needed to be done.

Molly was becoming a proficient cook now that Lisa was showing her how to make a different meal each day. She always took half of what they made home to Bone. The minute she walked into the cabin each night Bone was all over her. He would make love to her sometimes twice before he would warm up the meal she'd brought and they would have dinner. She knew that it might not last forever, but for right now things were good.

"Look right here, Molly," Rash said, pointing into the

engine while turning to look at her expectantly.

Damn it, did he really expect her to go over there and look like she hadn't done this a million times before? When he just waited, looking expectant, she knew that he did. She managed, just barely, not to roll her eyes at the man's obvious idiocy and reluctantly walked over to the truck. Molly was standing next to him as she leaned over to peer into the motor. He reached around her pressing against her side and she started to pull away. A familiar voice tainted with a glacial tone came from behind them making her spin to face Bone.

"What the fuck is going on here?" Bone demanded.

Molly smiled, excited to see him standing in the shop's bay. Although she could have done without the scowl covering his face as he glared at Rash, who stepped back from the truck holding his hands up.

"Nothing, nothing, I was just showing Molly something, that's all," he said, taking another step back from Bone.

Molly sighed and walked over to Bone, wrapping her arms around him. He hugged her back drawing her to his side. Molly didn't want him to fight with Rash even though she wanted to punch him for treating her like a nitwit.

Bone looked down at her questioningly. She knew that he was wondering what the hell Rash had been showing her but she just shrugged and rolled her eyes. Even Bone knew that she didn't need any help with engines by now and she couldn't understand why Rash refused to acknowledge it.

"What are you doing here?" she asked, a little surprised to see him here.

"I came to pick you up for a surprise. Go get cleaned up, we're going for a ride," he said smiling at her.

She'd taken her first ride last week and she'd loved the freedom of it. She hadn't wanted to come back. Bone loved that she enjoyed riding with him and he'd told her that night

Taming Lucca

when they got back that one day when they had the Jackals sorted out that he would take her to his favorite camping spot near the city. She'd been pleased that he was thinking of their relationship lasting that long. Molly felt her heart pick up in excitement at the prospect of going on a ride with Bone.

"Give me about three minutes to clean up and ditch these coveralls."

Not waiting for him to answer, she ran into the back, hearing his chuckle follow her. She quickly shucked her coveralls. Entering the small bathroom, she walked over to the sink to wash up. In the mirror, she saw a smudge of grease on her nose, which she wiped off with a dismayed vigor. That was embarrassing, but she was a mechanic and it couldn't be helped. She refused to worry about Bone seeing her with grease smudges on her face.

She fluffed her hair and headed back into the shop to find Bone standing beside Rash. Both men were filled with tension as they glared daggers at each other.

Uh-oh, this looked serious.

Molly stopped near the truck Rash had been working on to watch them warily. Bone noticed her after a moment. He said something low to Rash, who nodded, and then Bone turned to look at her.

"Ready?" he asked her, a happy grin covering his face as if the moment with Rash hadn't happened.

Molly nodded, wondering what the heck that had all been about and followed him to his Harley. Bone turned to look at her as he climbed on the bike.

"You were wearing that under your coveralls?" he questioned as she moved to climb on the bike.

She looked down at the white tank and cutoffs, confused, as she straddled the seat, wrapping her arms around his waist, leaning into his back. "Yeah, why?"

Michelle Woods

"Nothing," he said flatly, cranking the bike. Letting go of the brake, he roared out of the parking lot. Feeling the wind moving through her hair, Molly let it go and just held Bone, enjoying the invigorating ride.

Thirty minutes later, they pulled up to a heavily wooded area where they turned off the road into a small cordoned-off parking area. Bone parked, putting the stand down while getting off the bike. After helping Molly off, he reached back into the box behind her seat removing a blanket and a basket.

"Came prepared, did you?" Molly questioned, watching him turn with the blanket over his shoulder, holding the basket in one hand.

"It wouldn't be much of a surprise if I wasn't prepared, woman!" he grunted, a slick smile on his face. Molly let out a little laugh at his expression before she allowed Bone to take her hand and begin leading her down a nearby path with a hand-carved sign that said Devils Falls. He stopped beside it, tying a red cloth on a little hook that was attached to the sign. He then began leading her past it still holding her hand.

"Umm——why did you do that?" she asked with confusion as she followed him up the path, hearing the soft sound of rushing water.

"So no one comes up here while we're naked, baby." His matter of fact tone made her blush. "We don't want anyone coming up here with us now, do we?"

"No," Molly said, her blush staining more than her cheeks at the thought.

A few minutes later they came out in a small clearing with a huge breathtaking waterfall that flowed down a sheer drop-off before falling into a small pool that flowed out and down to another drop-off.

Taming Lucca

"Wow, it's beautiful."

"Yeah, this is how the town got its name. They call it Devils Falls because it almost washes away the town when the storms are bad. It's also why we have a camp built on Devils Ridge about a mile away from here."

"Really, I thought Devils Falls was named that because of the Red Devils, not actual falls. How long ago did it flood the town?" she questioned.

"About ten years ago, it was when that big storm that went on for about three days went through. Most of the time the falls are drained off into the lower lands, filling that big aquifer that makes water for the city," Bone told her as they stood near the edge of the falls looking at the water rushing by. It was breathtaking and Molly was glad that he'd brought her to see it.

"Huh, I never knew about that when I lived in the city."

"Yeah, I'm sure it's not something most people wonder about, it's just there. Let's get some food in you so I can ravish you," Bone growled, kissing her forehead.

Molly felt another blush and wished she didn't do that every time the man mentioned sex but she couldn't help it. Thinking of sex with Bone always made her think of naughty things that she knew her mother would have scolded her for. Molly frowned a little wondering why she was thinking of the woman who'd abandoned her.

Bone was already spreading the blanket out for them to sit on. He let her hold his shoulder as she sat down on the blanket. He began unloading the basket, taking out fresh fruit, three sandwiches, and some of the apple pie Lisa had shown her how to make the other day, setting it all out on the blanket with relish, proud of his impromptu picnic.

Molly smiled at him, kissing his cheek. He grabbed her and pulled her into his lap facing away from him. She lay back

Michelle Woods

resting against his chest while he sat above her and fed her bites of fruit. Between the bites of fruit she ate some of her sandwich. Bone ate his while alternating running his other hand through her hair and feeding her.

She felt so relaxed here with him, and she continued leaning into him after she'd finished eating. He was running his hands over her stomach and up to her breasts beneath her tank, having already finished both of his own sandwiches. He cupped her breasts, his mouth moving to her shoulder with a possessive caress, his teeth grazing her neck gently.

She moaned, her head falling back to his shoulder. She crawled away from him a little before turning to face him, sitting again with her legs wrapped around his waist, his legs beneath her. He took her shirt and bra off, groaning at the sight of her breasts, leaning forward to devour them. His mouth roughly covered each one with a masculine grunt of approval, his tongue circling her areola, twisting it with his tongue, causing her to cry out.

Her hands buried in his hair, she grabbed his cut, pulling it off of him, laying it gently on the blanket beside them. Her hands were now able to caress his bare skin with abandon. She ran her hands over his back, moaning as he switched to her other nipple to give it the same treatment, feeling her body liquefy as desire burned through her.

Molly pressed herself down onto Bone's hardened member, wanting it to fill her with a need that shocked her. She was becoming a wanton little hussy, always needy and hot every time she thought about this man and his pleasure-giving member. Hell, just thinking about him at all made her body go soft and wet in seconds. He pulled back, urging her to move back a bit from him so he could unzip her pants. After accomplishing this, his hand slipped inside and she felt two of his fingers sliding into her wet sheath hard and quick.

Taming Lucca

"Fu––damn, baby, you're so wet," he groaned, sliding his fingers in and out of her quickly in a hard rhythm that had her moaning with pleasure as she gripped his shoulders.

"That's it, baby, come for me. Soak my fingers with your sweet juices," he growled, his voice husky and his eyes intently focused on her face.

She was so close as he fingered her that when his thumb slid over her clit, she burst into her first orgasm with a whimper. Her head was thrown back as she rode his digits, moaning her pleasure to the empty clearing.

He pulled his fingers out of her slick heat looking desperate. Bone began tugging on her shorts pulling them off her legs as she limply tried to help. She watched as he unzipped his own pants to free his dick, which sprang out pointing at her.

"You weren't wearing any panties." His voice was accusing as his eyes devoured her. "You know how much that drives me crazy, you wicked little minx."

He urged her closer, and his mouth covered hers as he moved her back into his lap facing him with her legs on either side of his.

Molly couldn't help the little giggle that escaped her. "You knew I wasn't wearing panties, Lucca. You told me not to."

"Put it in, baby. I need you," he demanded, pulling her down. Molly didn't hesitate, she wanted him inside her as much as he wanted to be in her. She felt him slipping into her, letting out a loud moan as her wetness slid down his thick shaft. She rose quickly and then dropped back down, his hands on her hips helping her to ride him in a fast rhythm that had them both near orgasm in seconds. She groaned, coming apart a second time while moaning his name, hearing him roar hers as he followed her over the edge into completion.

Michelle Woods

Twenty minutes later she was lying in his lap with her head resting on his thigh as his hands alternated running through her hair and playing gently with her nipples.

"Lucca," Molly said, looking up at him.

"Yeah?" he questioned with a gentle pluck at her right nipple.

"Have you and the club always been a family?" She looked up, meeting his eyes as he gazed down at her.

"Yeah, the Devils have always been my family. Dad was born into the club, but my mama was from Tidwell. They were happy for the most part till about two years after I was born when dad started hanging out at the clubhouse more often." Molly heard what he wasn't willing to say, that his father started messing around on his mother then. She saw the sadness that entered his eyes and reached up to caress his cheek, trying to remove that look from his face.

"It must be nice having a family." Molly sighed wistfully as she let her hand fall when he frowned down at her.

"You have a family, Molly," Bone said, gazing down at her.

"Not like yours. They weren't like the Devils are, accepting you faults and all. They wanted me to be perfect," Molly whispered, acknowledging the truth of why she'd never been good enough, even before the wallet incident.

"I meant we are your family, Molly. And anyone who didn't accept you as you are was an idiot. You're perfect." Bone's voice was impassioned and his glare was dark. His hands slid through her hair and he watched her, his face solemn.

"Lucca." She couldn't stop herself from leaning up to kiss him as he leaned forward to allow her to take his lips with hers. Their tongues mingled for a few lazy seconds before she lay back in his lap. After a while of listening to the sounds of crashing water and birds calling out to each other, she looked up at him again.

Taming Lucca

"My family, my real family, they didn't even try to help me when I was thrust outside the city. My mother and I had never had a close relationship, but I never expected her to betray me by refusing to help me when I needed her." Molly paused, her eyes filling with tears that caused Bone to look down at her with a scowl. "Carl told me that my mother could have given credits for me to take with me, but she refused."

"Molly, I'm sorry she hurt you, but I can't be sorry about what happened to you. I would never have met you if you'd stayed behind that wall." Bone was running his hands through her hair, his hand gently tugging to get her attention when it wandered over to the waterfall.

"Who's Carl?" he questioned in a deceptively quiet voice that almost made her laugh.

"Hmm––who?" she asked, pretending to not know what he was talking about. His eyes narrowed, and she could see little pinches in the corners of his mouth that told her he was clenching his teeth.

"Stop being deliberately vague and tell me, Molly!" his voice quietly demanding as he said it.

"Oh––that Carl." Again pretending to forget that he wanted to know who he was, she gazed at the waterfall, unable to prevent a slight smile.

"Molly," he growled, causing her to laugh.

"Relax, he's like a second father to me." She sobered, remembering her own father had disowned her, tears again threatening.

"Why did that make you sad, baby?" Bone asked, watching her closely.

"Before my mother left me in that cell to face my sentencing, she told me that my father disowned me. I never expected him to do that. How could he just disown me like that?" Tears filled her eyes. She clenched them, trying to stop them from

Michelle Woods

falling; she'd shed enough tears for them.

"Baby, what they did doesn't matter anymore. You're ours now. You know we'll always be here to care for you." Bone pulled her up giving her another soft deep kiss before settling her on his lap again.

"I know," Molly whispered. She did know that the club would be there for her even if she and Lucca didn't work out; she was family now, claimed by the club, and they always took care of family. It made her feel all warm and happy inside to know that what happened with her mother and father would never happen to her here. Even when she and Bone weren't an item anymore they wouldn't write her off.

They sat that way, with Molly resting on his lap, her eyes closed, him running his hands over her hair, with a slight breeze cooling their skin and the sound of the waterfall. Then when she was almost asleep she heard him say softly, "I want you to know that you're not just a woman I enjoy screwing. You're more, baby."

Opening her eyes, she met his as he watched her. "Yes, Lucca. I know." She closed her eyes again realizing that she really did know that after the past few weeks with him. She hadn't realized that she did until this very moment but she did. Just before she slipped into sleep her heart warmed again when she heard him whisper, "If I could patch a woman it would be you, Molly."

Chapter 20

Hours later with the sun setting, they roared back into town. Pulling up to their cabin, Molly was tired despite the nap she'd taken in the clearing beside the waterfall. They had made love again before they had packed up to head home. Feeling a warm glow in her chest, Molly realized that today had been one of the best days of her life. Bone made her happy, and she realized today in that clearing that she was in love with him. It didn't matter that their relationship might end up being just a fling for him, she was head over heels for him.

Bone cupped her elbow helping her climb off the bike, chuckling a little when she stumbled a bit because her legs were a little wobbly. She didn't have the energy to even glare at him so she just leaned on him heavily.

"Whoa, baby, you're almost asleep on your feet, aren't you?" he said as he steadied her.

"Yeah," she mumbled.

Bone smiled softly, his eyes gleaming with some unnamed emotion in the light from the porch before he leaned down and scooped her into his arms, holding her tightly to his chest.

"Grab the basket, baby," he said, turning towards his hog so she could reach it. She managed to get it unhooked and

Michelle Woods

held it on her stomach, leaning her head on his shoulder as he began walking into the house.

"Bone," a voice called out from the darkened path behind them as they started up the porch stairs. Bone turned to see Tank coming toward them. He stopped near the door setting her on her feet.

"Go on up to bed, baby. I'll be up in a little bit."

Molly kissed him lightly, turning to the door with the basket now held in her hand. He watched her as she stumbled a bit and it took everything inside him not to scoop her back up and make whatever Tank had to tell him wait. He couldn't help the warmth that poured through him as he remembered the time they'd spent up at the falls today. Molly was becoming so much more than just his lover and he didn't know what it meant but he was too damned happy to worry about it.

"I might be asleep. Goodnight, Tank," she said over her shoulder as she entered the house.

"Night, Molly," Tank said as he came up the stairs onto the porch, waiting until Molly headed inside before he spoke again. "It's those damned Jackals again, Bone," Tank grunted when Molly had shut the door.

"Fuck, what now?" Bone asked, leaning on the rail of the porch waiting for Tank to elaborate. He didn't want to deal with this bullshit tonight. He'd had a damned good day and this wasn't the way he'd planned to end it.

"They went after Train and his riders last night. I got the call around three; I figured it could wait till you got back. I sent Tiny, Rock, Trick, Slim and a couple of prospects over there to check it out. They called back to say it wasn't a random hit. They knew too much about the operation we're running at the Dixon farm. Knew the shift changes even though we keep it random, and they also had the layout. Train kept two guys for questioning. Tiny's waiting to work them over till we get there." Tank pulled out a cigarette and lit it up; after a few puffs he continued. "We've got to get to the bottom of these information leaks. It's pissing me off, damn assholes."

"Shit, give me a minute to call Duck to see if he'll keep an eye on Molly at the shop tomorrow. We'll get to the bottom of this before it gets worse," Bone said, standing and moving towards the door with an angry stride. His fists clenched and a muscle in his shoulders twitched, likely due to the tension that had overtaken him from the moment Tank started talking. "I'll meet you there in about an hour. I need to stop by the armory and load up."

He entered the house pissed that his lazy day with Molly couldn't end with him crawling into bed with her.

Stupid fucking Jackals.

He walked into his study and pulled out his nine millimeter. Putting the snub nose he'd taken to the falls back into the gun rack, he headed upstairs. He walked into their room to find Molly asleep on the bed wearing just her shirt and sexy black underwear lying on top of the covers. She'd obviously run out of energy before she'd even gotten done preparing for bed. Bone felt a slight smile curling his lips as he stood watching her sleep for a few moments.

Molly shifted slightly on the bed, her shirt riding up to reveal her slightly curved belly and he felt his dick beginning to harden making him wish he had time to take her before he left. Damn, would he ever see that woman and not want to fuck her silly, he wondered. He hoped not, Molly was so damned sweet. He was also surprised that even though it had been a month he hadn't thought of straying even once. He'd had several opportunities offered but he hadn't been tempted because he knew that Molly was waiting on him at home and the sweetbutts at the club weren't worth messing that up.

He felt a little odd after today at the falls because what

Michelle Woods

he'd said to her was true. He'd never considered patching a woman but with Molly he didn't know if he'd be able to avoid it much longer. His possessiveness would become unbearable if left too much longer. Sighing, he walked to the bed running a hand over her ass and gently squeezing it.

She startled awake, murmuring, "Too tired, wake me later."

Chuckling, he squeezed a bit harder, leaning down to kiss her long and hard, pulling back when she was panting and her eyes were open.

"Hey, baby," Bone whispered and brushed her hair away from her face. "I have to go out. I'm not going to be back till sometime late tomorrow."

"Oh, everything okay?" Molly asked, knowing he wouldn't tell her anything specific, but needing to know if she should worry. She sat up on her knees facing him with her arms wrapping around his neck.

"It's good, nothing too bad, baby. Just some business we need to handle," Bone said, his hand cupping her ass.

He pulled her closer and with a light squeeze and a growl he took her mouth again devouring her lips, thrusting his tongue roughly into her mouth, causing her to moan and cling to his shoulders, her breasts pressing against his chest.

"Damn, I wish I had time to take you again." A deep growl rumbling from him, he squeezed her ass cheeks again, making her moan and press herself more firmly against his hardened member.

"Umm——hurry and take care of it and come back so you can," she said, rubbing her hardened nipples against his chest, her smile wicked

"Fuc–sorry. Hell, with incentive like that, who could refuse," Bone said, kissing her one last time before urging her back onto the bed. He pressed the t-shirt up to reveal her bare nipples. With a groan, he ran his hand over those sweet

Taming Lucca

little buds and gave each one a tender suck before pulling the covers up and kissing her forehead. "See you tomorrow."

"Be safe, Bone," she said as she snuggled into the pillows, her little body wiggling while she tried to get comfortable, making him jealous of the damn bed. With one last long look at her lying there with her eyes closed, likely already asleep as tired as she was, he turned despite the ache of longing that twisted him into knots and exited.

He headed downstairs to call Duck so he wouldn't wake Molly if she was asleep. He needed to ask him to pick Molly up and watch her at the shop tomorrow. With Trick, Tiny and Slim with him working over those stupid Jackals, he wanted someone he trusted at the shop. Rash would be there but he didn't trust that bastard with Molly for multiple reasons. Today wasn't the first time the asshole had tried to cop a feel. Trick had talked to him about it a few days ago making him aware of the problem. Today he'd had words with the man and he really hoped that the asshole listened because he would kill him for messing with Molly, patch or no patch.

Pulling his phone out of his pocket at the foot of the stairs, he dialed Duck's number. The man picked up on the third ring and he explained what was going on, asking him to keep an eye on Molly. After Duck had agreed, he hung up, grabbed the rest of his needed hardware, and rode over to the armory to restock his ammo. Then he headed out to meet Tank. The quicker they left, the faster he could get back to Molly.

Standing beside a car she was doing a tune-up on, she picked up the pan she needed in order to let the oil out, listening to Duck. He'd shown up at the house this morning out with his cage when it was almost time for her to head. He said he'd give her a ride. She suspected when she climbed into the cab

Michelle Woods

of the large blue truck that Bone had asked him to keep an eye on her.

That suspicion had been confirmed when he stayed at the shop with his feet propped up on a tool chest while he leaned back in a desk chair he'd pushed out of the office. Molly didn't mind even though she thought Bone was being paranoid. At least Duck was entertaining and he was keeping Rash from making her insane.

"Molly my girl, you remind me of my older sister, you favor her quite a bit actually, thought it the first day I saw you," Duck said as he sat up a bit in the chair. She slid the drip pan under the car, sitting down on the sliding dolly that she used to move under the vehicles, staring at him.

"Huh, that's odd. You know the first time I saw you, I thought you looked a lot like my father." She used the dolly to move under the car, not seeing the way Duck looked thoughtful for a moment.

"My sister lived behind the wall. She was actually married to a really well known politician when the rains started sixty years ago. I was sixteen when the floods came and she was twenty-nine. Mom had me late in life. What's your surname, kid?" Duck questioned

Molly pushed the pan into place to catch the flow as she let out the oil before sliding back out, sitting up and leaning back on the car while the oil drained. Molly looked at Duck in surprise; could he be her great uncle? She felt her chest ache for a moment because if he was, that meant that she still had someone in her family who cared for her which would be nice.

Even though Bone and the Devils had become her family in the short time she'd been with them, she still felt a little like she didn't really belong anywhere because of her father disowning her. It was likely only because for so long her family and her life in the slums were the only things that had defined her, but now she was able to be so much more. A warm glow suffused her when she thought of the changes in herself and in the life that she lived now. She would never go back to being a timid mouse who bit her tongue to keep from telling off the people who were trying to put her down. Bone and the Red Devils had taught her that and she was damned glad that she'd ended up here despite the rocky road she'd traveled to get here.

"It's Daniels," she said, seeing a grin spread over Duck's face that stretched from ear to ear.

"Damn, that boy's in trouble now," he chuckled, confusing Molly for a moment before he continued. "You are my sister's granddaughter. I'm your great uncle. She married a Daniels and had one son." He chuckled. Molly stared at him with an open mouth, shock surging through her at his pronouncement. Duck looked up to watch Rash move over closer to them, calling out.

"Everything okay over here, Molly?" he questioned, looking at Duck with apprehension.

"Yep, you showed me last week how to tune the cars, remember?" Molly said, having realized weeks ago giving him credit for the knowledge she had got rid of him faster. When she looked back at Duck, she saw his raised brows as Rash moved away heading to the bay closer to the back room.

"It makes him leave me alone," she said, shrugging her shoulders, and Duck chuckled.

"Huh, smart girl. Now have I told you about my Freda yet?" he questioned as he lowered his bushy white brows.

He'd been talking to her about the pre-storm days for over an hour. He'd already told her about the television industry, and how people would near about sell their souls to get on it when he was young. It seemed odd to her to put so much

Michelle Woods

significance on being seen by millions of people. It was pointless.

She'd also been amazed when Duck had explained the Internet. It was a bit like the connected tablets that you could get from the city but the amount of information Duck spoke of being readily available to everyone and not just the rich seemed amazing. She couldn't imagine being able to access the amount of data he talked about with just a few clicks.

Molly laughed as he told her how when he was twenty, four years after the world had imploded when the storms had torn through, he'd walked into a deserted shopping mall with six other club members to look for food only to be shot at by Freda.

"That woman was a deadly good shot too, but at the time I just thought this crazy woman was shooting at me. She missed on purpose of course." She saw the faraway look in Duck's eyes and the smile he wore softened his whole face. "My Freda was one hell of a woman. She was mean enough to take on anyone. You know, she held off seven men in our house once. She was picking them off one at a time. By the time I got there to rescue her, she had killed all but two who were pinned down in the kitchen." Duck chuckled, his look far away. "I still remember her asking me what the hell took so long when I walked in the door like a madman, scared to death that she'd be dead before I could get to her." Smiling a sad but joyful smile, he sighed. "Damn, I miss that woman."

"How long has she been gone?" Molly asked.

"Four years. If I didn't know it'd just piss her off, I would have given up and went to join her, but I know that woman would be livid if I show up even a day before I'm meant to." Molly's heart ached for her new-found uncle but she was glad that he was still here. It was nice to know that she had one real family member who would care if something happened to her.

"Well, you'll see her again one day, Duck." She lay back down to slide back under the car to finish changing the oil. Duck's voice cracked a little when he said, "I know. I know."

Later that day Molly was working on a bike near the bay where Rash was talking on his phone with someone in a low tone. She didn't know what he was doing but as long as he was leaving her alone she didn't really care. Duck seemed to keep him from annoying her thankfully. He hadn't offered to show her how to do anything today which was kind of nice. Maybe she should ask Duck to come back once a week so she could get a single day of work done without having to watch Rash 'show' her how to take something apart.

Duck stood and said, "I'll be right back, sugar. I gotta take a piss."

She grinned, shaking her head because he seemed to like using vulgarities to get her to blush. She nodded, refusing to allow him to laugh at her like he'd been doing all day when she'd turn red at something he said. She went back to the tune up not paying attention to anything except the engine she was working on. She had her back to Rash, who was still talking on the phone, as she lifted the ratchet to remove the cams.

Suddenly she was grabbed from behind and a black hood was thrust over her head and pulled tight, hard male arms wrapped around her waist jerking her up. She tried to hit whoever held her with the ratchet, but a hand squeezed her arm hard causing her to cry out in pain and drop the ratchet. She kicked out trying to get away from the man who held her, but it was no use.

They lifted her, and she heard someone saying, "Hurry the fuck up before her other guard comes back." The rough voice wasn't one she recognized.

Michelle Woods

"Let me go!" Molly screamed, still trying to kick the man holding her.

"Shut the fuck up, bitch! Get the fucking door open and let's get the fuck outta here." The man who held her shook her so hard her teeth rattled and she felt dizzy.

"Fuck, don't hurt her!" she heard Rash yelling and wondered why he wasn't helping but then heard what sounded like a fist hitting flesh and realized that maybe he couldn't help her.

"Duck!" she screamed at the top of her lungs, knowing he was her only chance.

She felt a hard slap across her face that made her head snap back, and her cheek felt like it was already swelling from the blow. Pain radiated down the side of her face and she knew it was likely that he'd knocked her jaw out of place with that hard blow.

Molly was shoved into a vehicle and when she tried to resist, the only result was to feel another debilitating blow slam into her face. The blow made her dizzy and snapped her neck back. She didn't know what happened as she felt herself lifted and shoved, feeling the scrape of metal against her skin and then her head hitting metal. Suddenly, the world was fading away with her last thought before she passed out being that she'd never told Lucca that she loved him.

Chapter 21

Bone used his brass knuckles to knock the asshole in the face again. Blood sprayed from his mouth as his fist connected with the guy's face. Bone was starting to get pissed; they'd been beating this fucker for over six hours and he was out of patience.

"Tell me who the fuck is giving you information and we'll stop torturing you." He waited a few seconds.

The man spit blood on the floor; his face was a mass of cuts and bruises. Water covered his shirt and pants from the repeated dunking they'd done trying to get him to talk by almost drowning him. Bone nodded, and Tank began to push his head down into the tub again to hold him under when the man finally broke.

"Wait–wait, I'll tell you––please, not the water again."

Fuck, finally, but what a pussy, that water didn't even have parasites. Of course, they hadn't told the fucker that and he'd been dunked three times already. He'd likely swallowed some of the water despite his attempts not to and Bone figured he wouldn't want to chance drinking any more. He almost snorted.

"Who's the mole in my camp then, motherfucker?" Bone asked and waited for the man to speak, ready to be done with

Michelle Woods

this; he had a woman to get back to.

"It's Rash," the man choked out.

Bone stood there for a moment, not sure he'd heard the man correctly. A red curtain slid down over his eyes when he realized that Rash was the fucking mole. It poured through him with a cold chill because that little fucker was a member, not a prospect. He'd been sure it was one of the prospects in the inner circle but even the strange behavior of Rash recently hadn't led him to the conclusion that he was betraying the club. His head almost exploded with the knowledge one of his fucking members had actually betrayed them.

Bone's hands clenched into fists and he was numb when he felt his phone vibrate in his pocket. He growled, anger scalding him as he pulled it out to see it was Dog's number. His mind immediately went cold and a sudden sense of foreboding went through him.

"Yeah," he answered.

"Bone, they took Molly. Fuck, Duck's following them. I can't tell you how they knew when to show up. Fuck!" Dog said as soon as Bone answered.

Bone felt the coldness spreading, his hand gripping the phone tightened, and he stared at the man in front of him, his eyes almost sightless. All he could hear was a ringing in his ears as he held his phone with nerveless fingers and the world in front of him became hazy and out of focus.

He knew Tank was asking him what was wrong, but he could barely hear him over the ringing. Tiny took his phone from his hand, and he didn't protest when Slim pushed him over to a wall which he fell back against, unable to stand. His mind was racing over the fact that Molly had been taken. She was in the hands of those fuckers the Jackals. His Molly was in danger, possibly frightened or worse, hurt.

He heard Tiny yelling, "Fuck, fuck, how long ago?

Taming Lucca

Yeah—it was Rash! Stupid motherfucker, been giving them information for weeks." Tiny paused, looking at Bone. "No, Bone's losing it."

Slim asked Tiny what the hell was wrong with him from beside him and when Tiny responded, he let out a curse. He rested a hand on Bone's shoulder, his eyes solemn and his face drawn, his lips tight.

"We'll get her back, Bone. Duck is on their tail and you and I both know that he won't lose them. We'll find her," Slim tried to reassure him.

Bone's head suddenly cleared and he was standing again. The ringing was gone, and he looked at his brothers. His woman needed him right now and he refused to be a useless pile of shit while she was taken from him. Running his hands through his hair likely making it stand on end, he knew he must look like a mad man, but he didn't fucking care. He walked to the man tied in the chair.

"Where would they fucking take her? You've got ten seconds to tell me or I put a bullet into your head," he said, his nine millimeter resting on the man's temple. No one moved to stop him; they stood nearby watching grimly.

"I don't know. Please, I don't know!" Bone waited two more seconds.

"You have two seconds, asshole."

"They may have taken her to that abandoned train yard about ten miles from here. That's where we've been staying this week," the man shrieked, his voice so shrill he sounded like a woman, annoying Bone with the sound, his head already trying to add up the possibilities that this fucker was lying to him.

"Thank you," Bone said coldly before he pulled the trigger.

Turning to his brothers, dipping his hand in the water to wash the blood off his arm where it had splattered, he said

Michelle Woods

in a gravelly voice, "We ride. Someone take a cage so we can know if we're going in the right direction when Duck contacts us."

Bone turned and walked out of the little room they'd been working the Jackals over in. His brothers followed him out. Bone didn't know where his head was at the moment, but he knew one thing: those Jackals better not have hurt his woman, or today was the day he wiped them off this earth.

Molly blinked a few times, her head throbbing in time to her heart as she slowly became aware that she was in a small room. She glanced around seeing the walls, wondering if she would be able to find a way out. She remembered being kidnapped and with all the trouble the club had been having with the Jackals, she was sure that they were the ones who'd taken her. She saw that the room was furnished with only a cot that she was lying on, and some chains on the floor in one corner.

Easing off the bed, she got up and walked over to the chains trying to see if there was any way to use them. Her head throbbed again and she felt slightly dizzy from the blows to her face. She wobbled a bit as she knelt beside the chains moving them away from the wall. The chain was pretty useless but what she found along the wall beneath them wasn't, and she picked it up from the floor holding it with a smile. A Phillips head screwdriver wasn't much, but it would at least help her protect herself.

She moved to the door slowly, her feet moving at what seemed like a snail's pace as she became better oriented. Her head was starting to throb less and her dizziness was abating slightly. Molly was glad because she didn't want to be hindered by her ailments when she needed to get the hell out of this place before they tried to use her against Bone and the club.

Peeking through the crack in the door, she could see about ten men sitting or standing in the next room. Standing there made her realize that there was a lot of screaming from another room nearby. Molly felt fear spring up inside her when she heard the cries. What were they doing to whoever that was, she wondered, a chill slipping down her spine.

Molly stood by the door and watched for a while, her heart in her throat as her head finally completely cleared and she was able to think clearly. Her hands were sweaty around the screwdriver she held in a death grip. The men were moving around and she could hear them talk when the screams weren't drowning them out. Fear made her hands tremble and she decided after about twenty minutes that watching them wasn't helping her get out of here and she went to the walls searching for a way out.

Despite it being a small room, it took a while for her to work her way around the room searching for possible escape routes, likely because she was shaking so badly from adrenaline and fear that she was having trouble moving around. Molly wasn't sure how long she'd searched but she found a vent half covered by the cot. She bent down, sliding the cot out, trying to time the movements when she heard a scream start to hide the sound. When the cot was out of the way, she almost crowed in triumph because she would just fit through it.

She was about to start taking the cover off when she heard voices and movement. She lifted the cot back towards the wall setting it down gently, hoping no one noticed the sound. She quickly moved to the bed, laying down and closing her eyes, hiding the screwdriver inside her coveralls. There was a shuffle at the door, and something was shoved into the room with her.

Michelle Woods

"There, see, your bitch is still out cold. When she wakes up we'll all have a turn, and you can have whatever's left." There were more shuffles, then the door creaked closed again. "She might still be able to take it," the man's harsh voice called through the door and the wicked sound of his laughter caused a shiver to run down Molly's spine.

She opened her eyes to see Rash in a broken huddle on the floor near the door. Getting up, Molly carefully turned him over, seeing him blink at her through swollen eyes. His face was a mass of bruises and cuts that were bleeding heavily. Molly felt sorry for him and she felt bad that she had never liked him. He must have been taken because he was trying to help her and she'd always thought he was annoying and a little weasel-like.

"I tried to stop it, Molly," he said through cracked and bleeding lips, his voice hoarse. "I didn't know what they were going to do."

Confused by what he was saying, Molly pulled his hair back from his face watching him. Of course he hadn't known what they were planning, how could he?

"Shhh..." she whispered trying to soothe him. "You couldn't have known about this, Rash."

"Molly, I can't protect you now. I thought I could, bu–but I can't," Rash said, trying to convey something to her, but she wasn't sure why he'd thought he would be able to protect her against twenty or so men.

It must be that arrogance that made him think he was teaching her how to fix engines that had made him think that way. She tugged on him. She needed to get him on the bed because him lying in a heap on the floor wasn't going to be good for his wounds.

"Rash, help me, let's get you on the bed," she whispered, trying to tug him to his feet. After much shuffling and two almost face plants for Rash, she got him onto the bed. Her head was starting to pound again and she heard a slight ringing in her ears for a little while as she sat on the floor next to the cot panting.

Rash looked at her, his eyes filled with pain and despair. He whispered, "You need to find a way out, Molly. Just leave me and go."

"Okay, but we'll be back for you, Rash," she said, trying to soothe him.

Seeing his eyes close and hearing his labored breathing, she decided if she was going to get out of here she needed to get on it. She crawled to the end of the cot where the vent was located. She hadn't pushed the cot completely in front of the vent and it was visible.

She inspected the vent seeing that the screws were flat. Damn it. She didn't need this to top off the already crappy day she was having. Molly knew she could work the screws out with the screwdriver, but it was going to take a lot longer than she'd hoped.

Her mind on the need for her to escape so that she could get to Bone and then have them come back for Rash, she got to work, hoping no one checked on them in the next few hours.

Bone crouched beneath the trees staring at the large building about a hundred feet away. His knees sank into the leaves and his hands clutched his gun tightly.

He couldn't believe he was fucking waiting.

Waiting, while his woman was in that railway depot with those assholes, and she was possibly suffering or scared. If the rest of the crew wasn't here in ten minutes then he was going in without them, he didn't care. He wasn't going to sit out

Michelle Woods

here and allow her to possibly suffer while he waited on his brothers to get here. It just wasn't going to happen.

He turned to Duck, his eyes cold. He knew that the other man would know what he was thinking. Seeing a deadly calm in Duck's eyes, Bone watched him nod and without a word Duck checked his clip. Tank was sitting on his other side and he leaned forward looking at him and Duck, his face grim. Bone knew that he didn't need to explain because Tank would know what he was thinking.

"We need to wait, Bone. There are too many of them in there for the six of us to take down without back up," Tank hissed at him, his eyes filled with serious apprehension, but surprisingly it was Tiny who responded to Tank.

"If they're not here in ten minutes he's going in no matter what, Tank. You know that she's been here long enough to be awake now. And we both know what they can do to her in ten minutes." Tiny pulled out his piece checking the clip, his face set in a stoic expression.

"Fuck. This is insane. We need to wait," Tank growled, his head shaking as he spoke.

"You go ahead and wait, Tank," Bone said as he began moving after being reminded of what could be happening to his Molly right now. He sure as hell wasn't waiting any longer; those fuckers were dead.

"Fuck, I'll cover you assholes!" Tank said resigned. "I wish I'd brought one of those sniper rifles."

Duck stared hard at him, a scowl on his face as he watched him. Tank watched the other man back without speaking, his eyes boring into Duck's.

"What?" Tank questioned after a moment of this awkward staring.

"You're an idiot, that's what," Duck growled as they began to move towards the train depot.

Taming Lucca

"Well, it would be easier to cover you assholes if I had that sniper!" Tank hissed after them, and Bone saw Duck moving into a position near him shaking his head. Those two were like oil and water; he might have laughed at their banter if it wasn't Molly needing to be rescued.

Molly's hand slipped again as she turned the screw a bit more. Damn it, this sucked!

She had removed five of six screws, and this last one kept slipping. Growling a little in frustration, she turned the screwdriver a little more, inching the screw out. If she could just get it a bit more then she could twist it by hand as she had the others. It took another two minutes but she finally worked the screw to the point she could turn it by hand, giving a quiet crow of triumph as she pulled it out a minute later.

She pulled the grate away carefully trying not to make any noise and laid it down next to the cot. Molly glanced at Rash who was still lying there with his eyes closed. He didn't look like he was awake now so she climbed into the air vent moving through the tight space. Turning as best she could in the tight space, she pulled the grate back into place behind her. It wrenched her neck and her shoulder twisted painfully but it was better than them knowing where she was if they came in and found her gone.

It took her a few minutes to get her body untwisted before she was able to begin to work her way through the vent. She crawled along hoping that the vent didn't get any smaller because if it did, she wouldn't be able to fit. It was already scraping her shoulders every few feet where the sections were connected.

She had gone about three feet when she heard the yelling and gunfire start. She sped up hoping that they hadn't just

Michelle Woods

killed Rash when they found her missing. She also didn't know if they were going to figure out where she was and rush to the opening of the vent before she could get away. Molly could see light at the end of the vent and she crawled faster. When she was at the opening, she peeked through the slats to see if there was anyone around.

Not seeing anyone, she used her legs to kick the vent cover, hoping that the screws were rusted enough to allow her to kick it out. Molly kicked it a dozen times and she was fearful it was making too much noise but she kept kicking it. She hoped that the commotion inside would cover any ruckus she was making.

After about ten more kicks, it bent out at the top on one side. She kept kicking the other side until her feet finally busted the vent out but her leg shoved past a bent piece of metal scraping it. She hissed in pain, climbing out of the vent and looking at her leg, seeing that it was just a long scrape that bled slightly. It wasn't too bad but it would hurt like a bitch for a day or two.

Looking around to get her bearings, she spotted a van, some trucks, and about twenty bikes around the front. She thought briefly about running to them and seeing if she might be able to hot-wire one, discarding that thought quickly because if they knew she was missing that was the first place they were going to search for her. She saw a line of trees about two or three hundred yards away and headed towards them.

Molly knew that if she could escape into the woods she'd have the best chance that way. As she neared them, she heard her name yelled out. Glancing behind her as she ran, not stopping because she didn't know who it was calling out to her and she wasn't taking any chances, Molly was relieved to see Tank running towards her.

She stopped running and paused a moment before running

Taming Lucca

towards him. As she neared him she started hearing the gunfire from inside again. She realized that those shots she'd heard earlier had likely been Lucca coming to rescue her. She grinned a little because if he'd only waited a few more minutes, she would have been out of harm's way and the rescue would have been unnecessary.

Tank jerked her towards the side of the building, his big bulk in front of her as they worked their way around the building. The gunfire finally stopped and Molly heard silence as the echoing hollow sounds of gunfire disappeared.

She followed Tank into the train depot slowly, her leg stinging a bit when the adrenaline she'd been riding on faded. Molly was standing near the door when she saw Lucca standing in the middle of the room with Rash on his knees in front of him. Lucca was holding a gun to his head.

"What are you doing, Lucca?" she demanded as she rushed forward a few feet before she was stopped by Tank's restraining arm, which wrapped around her waist halting her.

"Baby," he said. His eyes, filled with relief, began running up and down her, landing on her scraped leg and then sliding back to her bruised cheek. "You okay?"

"Yes, I'm fine, but this isn't Rash's fault, Bone! He tried to stop them. He was out-numbered," she frantically blurted out, trying to get him to stop holding a gun on Rash. He had tried to help. It wasn't the man's fault that she'd been kidnapped. It wasn't like he'd arranged it or anything and she needed to stop Lucca from murdering him for not being able to stop the attack.

"You're sure you're okay, baby?" he asked without removing the gun from Rash's head.

"Yes, Lucca, I'm sure I'm okay," she assured him.

She looked at him, waiting for him to take the gun from Rash's head, but he only nodded, his eyes moving from hers

Michelle Woods

to Tank's.

"You don't understand what he's done, Molly. Just go outside with Tank," Bone said without looking at her, his eyes on Tank instead, the gun steady in his hand aimed at Rash's forehead.

"No." Molly couldn't believe he wouldn't listen to her about Rash. He was being unreasonable. She pulled against Tank's restraining arm trying to get him to let her go. Her nails dug into his arm but he held her tightly, not letting go despite the abuse.

"Bone, what happened to me wasn't his fault!" She knew she was screaming at him, but she didn't care.

His eyes were cold as they glanced back at her before slowly moving back to Rash, the gun never wavering. Molly could see the dispassionate look and her heart pounded in her ears.

Why wouldn't he listen to her?

"Tank, get her the hell outta here while I handle this," Bone growled.

Tank still had his arm around her waist and he dragged her toward the door ignoring her struggles as she tried to get away to stop Bone from killing Rash. It wasn't Rash's fault that she'd been kidnapped. She couldn't let him kill Rash over this. Her desperate thoughts were screeching at her to do something but Tank was easily overpowering her.

"No, Bone. You can't kill him. He tried to stop them."

It was useless to try to escape Tank. He lifted her and effortlessly carried her outside where he set her down, his back to the door preventing her from going back in.

"Tank, let me back in there. I have to stop him. It's not Rash's fault!" she yelled at him as she beat on his chest trying to get him to move from in front of the door.

"Molly. Molly, stop," he said, catching her hands to stop her from hitting him again, getting right in her face. "You need to let Bone handle this. Rash is the reason you were taken!"

He held her wrists in his hand, waiting a beat before letting her hands go. Molly blinked up at him, her body flooding with confusion. She watched somewhat dazed as Tank's arms folded across his chest and he watched her.

"Wait. What?" she questioned, her mind unable to process what he'd said.

Molly stood there, her stunned brain trying to accept this new information. She felt like she'd just been sucker-punched by the knowledge that she was in that little room because of Rash. She remembered Rash's words from earlier, 'I didn't know what they were going do'. At the time the words hadn't made any sense because she hadn't understood why he thought he should have known they were going to kidnap her. Now however, with Tank looking grimly down at her and Bone in that building with Rash held at gunpoint, it was crystal clear.

He wasn't saying that he couldn't protect her at the shop when they nabbed them as she'd thought, but that he'd set it up thinking that they would let him keep her like a damned pet. Her insides quivered and her hands balled into tight fists as she stared at Tank. Her brain was going over and over the things that could have happened to her because Rash was an idiot. He'd betrayed not only her but also the club. Molly couldn't seem to get a grip on the fury that flooded her when she thought about what he'd done.

Her hands were shaky as she leaned on the building beside Tank. She felt like her ears, which rang slightly with the buzzing of her pulse, were going to pop. Molly didn't care what Bone did to Rash because she could have been raped, or beaten, or hell, killed because of him. She stood there feeling slightly sick to her stomach as she thought about it. When she

Michelle Woods

heard the gunshot a short time later, Molly didn't even flinch. Rash had known the rules, you never betray family, and he'd done it anyway.

Bone stood with the gun to Rash's head as Tank took a struggling Molly outside, his chest aching that she needed to be removed from the room. He might not feel as cold and heartless if it wasn't for what Rash had done to Molly. Rash had sealed his fate with that choice. There was nothing he could do but kill him for his betrayal. He was glad that Molly was away from all this death; bodies littered the floor around the depot, and he was about to add another to the pile.

He wasn't sure how she'd ended up outside with Tank, but that question would have to wait. Bone had been frantically looking for her when they'd found Rash and he'd actually been demanding that Rash tell him where Molly was when she'd entered with Tank.

The heady sense of relief that flooded him when he'd seen her had literally made him lightheaded. He had managed to hold it together, even when he'd wanted to drop to his knees and just hold her tightly to him and thank every deity he could think of that she was alive and looked only slightly worse for the wear.

He wanted to explain to her why Rash had to die so that she didn't have that lost, almost accusing, look in her eyes but he needed to take care of this first. They needed to know what else Rash had told the Jackals about the club besides what they already knew.

Now that Molly was safe, Bone had to focus on the club. He was the president and despite his need to hold his woman close and know that she was safe, he needed to handle this business for the club first.

Taming Lucca

Bone knew that he might have just kicked the fucker out of the club without killing him if he hadn't tried to take Molly. Only there were some lines a man didn't cross and he'd crossed one with his complicity with this kidnapping. Rash had chosen to betray the club, and that alone was a killable offense.

Bone had never taken a brother's life lightly, but this time he didn't have a choice. Rash had no idea of the beast he'd awakened by taking Molly. Bone could still feel the slices of its claws in his gut when he thought of the wild ride to get here and the anxiety he'd felt kneeling in the leaves outside.

All Bone could think about was what might have happened to her had they not gotten here in time. Molly hurt was bad, but if they'd had time to rape her he didn't know if he would be able to live with that. Bone knew that the knowledge that he'd failed to get to her in time to prevent that would have eaten at him for the rest of his life. It was bad enough that he couldn't save her from getting taken in the first place.

Tonight there had only been twenty Jackals here. Thankfully they hadn't known they would be found so quickly and hadn't been ready for the Devils to come in guns blazing. This night could have ended with his and his brothers' deaths instead of him getting Molly back and taking out the trash that had somehow managed to ingratiate himself into his family.

His lips twisted into a grim smile as he looked down at Rash. The man was swaying slightly on his knees because he had been beaten pretty badly by the very club he'd been helping and it served his ass right. Loyalty was everything to an MC and this son of a bitch had betrayed them like they didn't matter to him at all.

After fifteen years with the club and five years spent earning his place, he'd thrown it all away just to get more power. Bone didn't get some people. You earned your power the right way.

Michelle Woods

You showed your worth and you earned the right to be more and fuckers like Rash just didn't get that.

It had taken Bone almost twelve years to earn his place in the club, two to even get beyond prospect and four more to become an enforcer. It wasn't like he had walked in one day and been voted president of the fucking club. He'd worked hard to get where he was and the club had voted him as president a little over two years ago. Rash only saw the power and he wanted it for himself but he wanted it now, not after he'd earned it, and because of that he was going to die tonight.

The stupid fuck.

"Show us that you still have some honor left, Rash. What else did you tell them about club business," Bone said, pushing the gun into Rash's temple. Rash swayed again, his eyes swollen almost shut from the beating he'd received. Bone wasn't sure how long it would be before the idiot passed out again.

"I only told them about the farms and Tidwell," Rash whined, looking up at Bone pleadingly. Bone curled his lip at the fool. He thought he would get out of dying tonight and Bone knew that wasn't going to happen but he remained silent, watching him.

"I swear that's all I told them," he moaned watching Bone with pleading eyes, not realizing that he didn't fucking care yet but he would. "I—I just wanted to move up in the club and they promised I'd have a say in their club if I gave them information. That's how it started. They offered me more and more, even promised I could keep Molly if I told them about the Dixon security. I couldn't help it, I wanted her. She's just so sweet." Rash began to sob.

Bone had heard enough. He wasn't sure he believed the man about what he'd told the Jackals but he would change up the schedules on all the normal routines for security. It would solve any issues brought on by this fucker's foolishness.

Bone's finger curled against the trigger. Seeing this, Rash began to tremble and Bone smelled the acidic scent of urine and realized that Rash had just pissed himself in terror. "Please—I tried to protect her. I didn't know what they were planning. Please."

"You think I fucking care, asshole? You think the fact that they betrayed you matters to me at all? You stole my woman." Bone leaned down snarling the words right in the other man's face, his eyes cold and his face grim. "How the fuck did you think that was gonna end, motherfucker?" Bone asked, not really wanting an answer.

The man sobbed and pleaded with Bone, his hands reaching out to pull on his leg. Bone watched the man fall apart with disgust, his bullshit meter full for one night. He pulled the trigger without a single thought to the fifteen years that asshole had spent with the club.

Rash's body fell down with the others at his feet. He glanced up at Duck who was suddenly standing beside him wearing the same grim expression he wore. Duck's eyes met his, and he nodded. They were done with this disaster, and it was time to take his woman home and hold her.

Needing to make sure that Molly had calmed down and was really okay, he turned to go outside, but Duck's hand on his arm stopped him.

"There's a water barrel over there; you should wash up before you go out to her," he said as he pointed to a nearby corner. Bone looked at his hands, which were covered in blood, and nodded. He didn't want to freak Molly out by coming outside with bloody hands after he'd just killed someone she thought had tried to save her.

His guts twisted when he thought about telling her what Rash had done. He didn't want to be the bearer of that news;

Michelle Woods

she'd been through enough tonight without adding that to the mix. He quickly headed to the barrel to wash up. He needed to hold Molly and make sure she was okay.

Chapter 22

Bone exited the building to find Molly leaning against the wall with Tank standing next to her. Striding toward her, she met him halfway, his arms sliding around her gripping her tightly. His chest rippled with an oddly soothing sensation when he held her. Relief flooded him and he felt as if he had just run a marathon.

He heard Tank say that the rest of the club was here, and he was going to go help with clean up. Bone nodded as he held Molly's trembling form. She was shaking as she pressed against him and he tightened his arms around her pulling her just a little bit closer, wanting to absorb all the fear she must have felt.

"I'm sorry you had to see that, baby," he said as he rubbed her back.

"See what, Lucca?" Molly asked, a little confused.

She hadn't seen him kill Rash even though she knew he'd done it. It bothered her that he'd been the one to kill him, but she could understand how he felt. If it had been Lucca who'd been hurt by someone, she would have wanted to kill that person. She wasn't sure where that mentality had come from because if you'd asked her months ago before she'd met the club, she would have said that she'd never kill anyone.

Michelle Woods

Being here with Lucca and the club had changed her and she couldn't say she was sorry about it. She was stronger now. Maybe that made her a bad person to some people, but she wasn't really concerned about what other people thought anymore. She understood that sometimes things didn't happen the way you expected, and you had to learn to roll with the punches or you weren't going to make it in this harder world outside the wall. There was a code, and if you violated that code you were taking your life into your own hands.

She realized that trying to live up to everyone else's expectations while living inside the wall had cost her what little bit of happiness she could have had when she'd lived there. She wasn't going to allow that to be her life anymore. She was stronger out here. She'd found a family that loved her, and she'd found a man willing to kill or die for her.

How could she be willing to give less than that back to him?

"Those men we had to kill, baby. I never wanted you to see something like that." Bone watched her face as she leaned back to look at him with a tender smile. Her heart swelling with the worry he had over her tender sensibilities, she almost laughed then because him killing someone who might have hurt her didn't bother her.

"You mean the men who planned to gang rape me later tonight? Those men?" she asked as Bone's eyes clouded with rage, his arms squeezing around her so hard that she couldn't breathe for a moment until his arms loosened.

"Yep, those are the men. Fuck–damn, sorry, baby," he grunted, pulling her closer.

"Bone, I don't care that they're dead," she said, and she meant it. They were going to rape her and possibly kill her, so she felt no remorse at their deaths. "Rash's death bothers me a bit, but I get it. He betrayed the club."

Taming Lucca

"You think I killed him because he betrayed the club?" he asked, looking at her with disbelief. His eyes held hers intently as she gazed up at him, her heart beating wildly suddenly at the dark promise she could see in his brown eyes. "I killed that asshole for one fu—damned reason and that's because he arranged to have you taken from me," he practically yelled at her as he leaned forward, his lips slamming down on hers. He kissed her with every ounce of passion he was able to muster. His tongue stroked hers with deep long thrusts that she returned until he pulled away, his gaze tender as he stared down at her. His hand caressed her sore cheek lightly.

"We need to get you home so you can see Doc about that cheek," Bone whispered, his need to be sure she wasn't seriously hurt gnawing at him.

"Lucca, it's fine. I just need some ice," Molly told him and pressed the other side of her face into his chest with a sigh.

"I still want him to look at it," Bone said sternly, watching as she looked up at him shaking her head in exasperation.

"I love you, Lucca," she whispered, knowing even as the words left her lips that this wasn't really the right moment to say those words to him. But Molly wanted him to know, even if he didn't love her back and they were standing outside a Jackals hideout. She didn't want to hold the feelings inside anymore because he deserved to know how she felt.

Molly knew that he cared about her or what happened to her tonight wouldn't have fazed him. It warmed her to her very soul that he cared for her enough to come after her when she was in trouble. Her own family hadn't even cared that much and she wouldn't worry too much about his ability to love her or not.

When she'd been taken tonight and she thought that she might not ever see him again, it hurt that he didn't know how she felt about him. It had made her realize she didn't want to

Michelle Woods

die without letting him know that she loved him. She needed him to know even if it didn't matter to him. Her body rested against his and she felt the sudden tension that filled him at her words. She waited to see what he would say, hoping that it wasn't a command for her to keep it to herself.

He held her tightly for a long moment before his lips met hers again, his arms clenching around her as he demanded, "Say that again."

"I love you," she whispered, laughing when he lifted her off the ground and spun her around in joyful excitement with a whoop of pleasure as joy cascaded through her. She kissed his cheeks and hugged him back. Bone let her slide down his body, his hardness pressing into her stomach as he leaned forward intending to kiss her again, when they heard Dog.

"Umm––sorry to interrupt, but Tank told me that I should see if you wanted me to take Molly home?" Dog said from behind them with a sheepish look directed at the two of them. "He says there are a few things inside that need your input."

Dog met Bone's eyes with a look that told him he needed to stay. Pissed that he couldn't just take Molly home to make love to her, he glared at Dog, who held up his hands in surrender.

"Hey, don't kill the messenger," Dog said with a weary chuckle.

"Damn, I guess you'd better go with Dog, sweetheart," Bone sighed, and gave her one last kiss while whispering a promise that he'd be home soon into her ear as he kissed it too.

Molly sat waiting in one of Doc's exam rooms. Dog had carried her to the chair she sat in, despite her protests that she didn't need a doctor. She shook her head thinking about his insistence that she not walk. Dog had set her down and

Taming Lucca

immediately left to go wake Doc up.

Molly had protested more than once on the way over here that she was fine but the words had fallen on deaf ears, so she was sitting in the cold plastic chair waiting for him and Doc to come back. Molly glanced up at the door when it opened.

Dog entered followed by a man that must be Doc. The man looked to be in his forties with sandy blonde hair and bright blue eyes that smiled when he looked at her. He was wearing jeans and a t-shirt that covered his lean corded body like a second skin and as he walked towards her she noticed that he had a slight limp.

"So little lady, I hear you've gotten yourself into trouble again," he said with a chuckle as he walked over to the counter picking up a blood pressure gauge and a stethoscope. Both were old fashioned and she stared in fascination at them.

Behind the wall, they could scan you with a little handheld unit and know what was wrong in seconds. Molly didn't know what to think of the equipment that seemed out dated and wondered if the little handhelds weren't available outside of the city.

Doc walked over to her, gently tilting her head to inspect the bruise that covered her left cheek.

"Hmm—that one's a doozy. Any dizziness?" he asked, frowning.

"Earlier when I first woke up I was, but I feel fine now, just sore and tired," Molly said, hissing as he probed her face with gentle fingers.

"Nothing seems broken," he murmured before he removed what looked like a pen from his pocket. "Watch this light for a second," Doc said, as he used the little pen to shine a light into her eyes and then had her follow it.

He checked her pulse and blood pressure, then asked if she was hurt anywhere else. Molly showed him the scrape

Michelle Woods

on her leg. He tutted a little before he went to a shelf beside the counter to get some alcohol swabs and ointment to treat the cut, covering the worst of it with a bandaid after it was cleaned and the ointment was applied.

He watched her for a long moment, making her fidget in the chair wondering why he was staring, before asking quietly, "Should I have Dog step out so that I can check any other injuries?"

She knew he was asking if he needed to check that she wasn't hurt inside from being raped. She felt an embarrassed blush stain her cheeks but she shook her head, answering him quietly, "No, they didn't have enough time to hurt me that way."

"Ah, well then." A bright smile broke over his face at her pronouncement. "I think you're fine, little lady. Dog, tell Bone to wake her a couple times tonight and ask the normal questions, name, day of the week, he knows the drill. I don't think she has a concussion, but it's better to be sure," Doc said to Dog as he turned away, going to a cabinet in the corner. He unlocked it with a key and pulled out a large bottle of pills. He took some out and put them into another smaller bottle and handed it to Molly.

"Take two of those when you get home, little miss. They will help with the pain and swelling. Ice will help too, and stay outta trouble. I've already seen you twice, not that I mind seeing such a pretty face, mind you, but next time I'd like it to be in more pleasant circumstances. " Molly blushed again and nodded as Doc turned back to Dog. "She'll be fine. I'm going back to bed."

Molly stood holding the pills watching Doc walk out of the room before she walked toward the exit herself.

"See, I told you I was fine," she muttered.

She shook her head at their overprotective behavior, even

Taming Lucca

though the care they showed her made a warm glow take up residence in her chest. Dog watched her walk to the truck following closely, causing her to turn and glare at the man. "You don't have to follow me like I'm an invalid. I won't fall down walking to the truck."

"I'm not going to be explaining why you're more beat up than you already are when Bone gets home tonight. I like my head right where it is," Dog said matter-of-factly as he helped her into the cab. With an exasperated sigh, she sat back in the seat waiting for him to get in and drive her back to the cabin. She watched as Dog walked around and got into the truck.

"You know this is ridiculous, right?" Molly asked when he got into his side, cranking the truck and driving away from Doc's. "I'm not fragile," she added, unable to keep the frustration out of her voice.

"Maybe, but I can't blame him for being a little freaked out, Molly. If it was my Terry, I would have flipped my shit just as badly as he did," Dog said, pulling up to the cabin.

He helped her out of the truck and into the house. Refusing to allow her to walk up the stairs, Dog scooped her up and didn't put her down till they were in her and Bone's bedroom, where he set her down.

"I'll bring you a glass of water to take your pills. Are you hungry?" Dog asked as he stood in the doorway.

"Maybe just a sandwich," she said, realizing that she hadn't eaten since earlier in the morning before the kidnapping.

"Okay, be back in a few minutes." Dog left to head downstairs and she went over to the dresser, pulling out one of Bone's Red Devil t-shirts and some of her sleep shorts, laughing a little at the realization that she hadn't worn a single pair of these. Normally she slept naked because that's what Bone preferred. She had a feeling if he came home to find her naked with Dog here she'd be witnessing a murder. A

Michelle Woods

smile teased at the corner of her lips as that thought occurred to her.

She was in the bed leaning on the headboard reading a book when Dog entered with a tray about twenty minutes later. He set the tray down and sat at the foot of the bed watching her eat. Annoyed that he felt the need to stare at her like she was a toddler eating its first solid food, she swallowed hard, glaring at him.

"You don't have to watch me eat, Dog. I won't choke," she snapped before rolling her eyes. She took another bite of the sandwich, expecting him to leave. Picking up the glass, she took a sip of the water to wash it down, a little unnerved by the fact that he was still watching her.

"Bone isn't like me or Slim," he finally said, his face serious as he spoke. "He didn't grow up with a dad who knew what a woman needed to make her happy, and it broke something inside him." He looked at the window for a few minutes before he looked back at Molly.

"I know that, Dog. I also know what happened with his family. Brandy told me," Molly said quietly as she waited for him to speak again.

"He went a little ape-shit tonight, Molly. If you'd been hurt worse, I'm not sure anyone could have stopped him from killing every Jackal he could find. I'm telling you this so you'll know. So you don't doubt that he cares deeply for you. He might not ever tell you that, but anyone who saw him tonight could see it. Bone never panics no matter what goes down, but tonight he did. Then he became deadlier than I've ever seen him." Dog scrutinized her intently as he spoke. He ran a hand through his hair, ready to say more, but she interrupted him.

"Dog, I know that Lucca cares for me. I know because I lived in the city where everything you did meant nothing if you didn't say the right thing or act a certain way. It's why I was never happy before I ended up here. Not many people wanted to know me. Not like Lucca and the rest of the club do. Do you know that my own family wasn't willing to help me when I needed help? That my dad actually disowned me? I only had two people I would call true friends inside that city. Now I have a family that would die to protect me, and I know the value of that. It's because of Lucca that I have that family. I know he cares for me. Dog, I won't give him up. I love him." Molly smiled slightly when his eyebrows rose at her knowing Bone's real name, causing her to almost laugh.

"I see. I just wanted to be sure you knew. I didn't want him to lose you because of something he was unable to say." Dog stood, taking the glass of water off the tray and setting it beside the bed on the table, then picked up the tray. "Take some of those pills Doc gave you. Bone will be back in a little while and he'll want you to be resting and the medication will help. I'll wait for him outside on the porch with the door open. Call if you need anything. I'll hear." He left the room.

Molly's head hurt and she was tired so she took two of the pills, falling asleep with a slight smile on her face at the thought of Bone coming home. She had a feeling that he would be randy when he got here and she really couldn't wait to be ravished by him.

Bone pulled up to the cabin about two hours after Dog had left with Molly, tired and ready to climb into bed and hold Molly. Tank had found Tick beaten half to death in another room in that depot. It explained why he hadn't reported in for the last two days. They'd also found six women shut into another room; two of the women had already been dead, and the other four were severely beaten and abused. One of the

Michelle Woods

women was able to tell them that they had been kidnapped from the surrounding area.

Slim was getting the women to a doctor they knew who worked near the depot. He'd help get them home when they were ready. It ticked him off that the Jackals had been kidnapping people from the surrounding area.

Climbing off his bike, he ran a hand down his face, feeling old all of the sudden. He was tired of this bullshit with the Jackals and he just wanted a chance to enjoy his woman. Fuck, it was hard to believe that only a few months ago he would have told anyone and everyone that he'd never be a one-woman man and yet here he was.

His mind circled back to Tick and the mass of bruises he'd been. He and Tank had taken Tick to Doc and waited while he'd gotten him situated. Doc said that Tick would be fine but if he'd been in that depot even one more day he'd have been dead. Tick had managed to tell them that Rash had texted him to meet and then he'd been grabbed. It made him want to revive Rash so he could make him suffer more before he killed him.

Bone headed up the walkway, seeing Dog sitting on the porch swing smoking a cigar while watching him.

"Tick gonna make it?" Dog questioned as Bone sat down on the porch and leaned back on the rail across from him.

"Yeah, Doc said he'll be fine. We settled the women in with Taylor in that small town about a mile from the depot. Fuck, I'm tired. Tank and Duck worked my nerves tonight after you left. I should have made Duck take Molly home." Bone leaned his head back looking at the star-filled sky before he finally rubbed a hand down his face looking back at Dog.

"Tank and Duck go at it again tonight?" Dog asked with a smile. Damned assholes, he knew that those two in the same room didn't work easy together.

Taming Lucca

"Ha, Tank found more toys in that depot. Duck, of course, called him an idiot again, which started them going at it. I swear Duck has never forgiven Tank for pissing on him that one time when he was three. Freda didn't help by telling that story to anyone who'd listen," he said with a reluctant chuckle.

Dog let out a loud laugh. "Shit, I had forgotten about that." Still smiling, he watched as Bone stared into the house looking for Molly.

"She's asleep. Doc gave her some pills to help the swelling. They put her out like a light. Just checked on her about ten minutes ago," Dog muttered and took a drag on the cigar, puffing out a few circles of smoke and surveying him with a knowing look.

"He say that she's okay?" he asked, his heart squeezing and his gut clenching as he asked the question that had been rattling around in his brain for two hours. He really should have asked Doc while he was there but Doc had been busy with Tick and he hadn't wanted to distract him.

"Yeah, she just needs rest. He said to check her for a concussion with the usual questions, but otherwise she's fine." Dog watched him as he scratched his head wondering when this shit had gotten so exhausting. He sighed in relief that Molly was okay. He couldn't stand the thought that she wasn't.

"Damn, that woman ties me in knots," he admitted ruefully.

"You should patch her, Bone," Dog said, watching for his reaction with a serious expression. He leaned forward slightly, the cigar in his hand, waiting for Bone to speak.

"I know," Bone said, knowing that Dog had likely expected an argument but he was done arguing over how much Molly meant to him. He wasn't going to keep being stubborn about it. Bone leaned his head back against the rail banging his head

Michelle Woods

a bit before he spoke again. "But I can't stand the thought that I may do to her what my father did to my mother. He broke her, Dog, and he didn't even know he did it. He couldn't see it."

"You're not your father, Bone," Dog said earnestly.

"I know that too, Dog," Bone said with his head tilted back resting on the railing.

Knowing that he needed Molly didn't make him a different man and that worried him. He was just as flawed as his father when it came to women. He'd been letting his dick lead him around for more years than he could count.

How could he be sure he would change for good? Hell, his father had been faithful for years before he started stepping out on his mother. His eyes scanned the stars as if seeking an answer written there but no answer was forthcoming.

"He did know, Bone. That's why he never touched another woman after she died. He found her journal after she died, and he realized what he'd done. But you won't be the man he was, Bone," Dog said firmly.

"You can't know that for sure, Dog," he said, watching as Dog snubbed the cigar on the arm of the swing, flicking it off the rail. "You'll be picking that up as you leave," he said, glaring at Dog with an angry scowl.

Damned smokers were nasty, throwing their butts down wherever they pleased.

"All right, man, chill!" Dog said with a raised hand. "I can know, Bone. It broke your mother, and you know what that looks like. I know you see it when you look at Brandy, we all do."

Bone was sure that he was right about him knowing what it did to a woman but he wasn't sure if that would stop him. He just didn't want to chance hurting Molly that way. He couldn't bear the thought of her crying her eyes out while he shredded her heart by stepping out on her.

"Dog, I need you to promise me that if I ever betray her like my old man did my mother that you'll take her from me. It won't be easy. I can promise you that I won't give her up easy." His eyes lit with a cold anger at even the thought of not having Molly in his life. "I will likely try to kill you, but she needs to be safe and happy." Bone ran a hand through his hair, pulling his knees up to rest his arms on them.

"I promise." Dog stood, walking over to him, laying a hand on his shoulder and squeezing it firmly. "You won't though. You're not that man; if you were, we never would have had this conversation. Now, go hold your woman and be happy she's safe. I'll see you at church tomorrow." He released Bone and walked down the steps, picking up the butt of his cigar and putting it in his pocket before heading down the path towards his and Terry's cabin.

"Dog," he called after him and Dog turned, looking back at Bone.

"Thank you," he said, meeting Dog's eyes with a grateful look.

"Anytime," he said and walked off, leaving Bone to head upstairs to his woman, feeling a little lighter somehow.

Chapter 23

Lisa held the mascara wand to Molly's eye applying it with vigor. It had been three days since the Jackals had kidnapped her. Bone had barely allowed her to be alone for more than a few minutes since that night. It was honestly becoming annoying that all manner of people showed up at the house to just say hello when she was there alone.

Sure they were.

At first she had just been a little amused by it, but after three days it was a little suffocating. Molly didn't mind company sometimes but every minute of the day was just too much. Not that she didn't appreciate his worry for her safety, she just wasn't going to allow it to get out of hand and she intended to talk to him about it tonight.

Right now Lisa, Terry, Brandy, and a colorful woman named Vivi were here helping her get ready for her first club bonfire party. Well technically it was her second but she wasn't counting the night that she'd run through the yards after finding Bone with another woman. She frowned thinking about that night. Trying to distract herself, she thought about this week.

Vivi had shown up this morning. Tick was here because he was still recovering but he was able to come to the party tonight. Lisa had dragged Vivi along to help Molly get ready. Terry and Brandy had shown up a few minutes ago, and now they were picking out the perfect outfit for her to wear tonight.

This was what was making her crazy. She was tired of everyone hovering around her all the time. She needed them to back off before she strangled one of them.

She was not fragile.

Bone woke her that first night with kisses, making slow passionate love to her before asking how she'd ended up outside with Tank. She had explained about the vent, and he'd started to laugh when he realized that if he had just waited a short amount of time she would have come right to them where they'd been crouched to case the depot.

He'd been unbearably overprotective since that night, at first refusing to allow her to go to the shop. That had lasted a day before she'd put her foot down and insisted that she be allowed to work. He'd relented after a thirty-minute argument. Even knowing that she had in effect rescued herself, he and everyone in the club were constantly buzzing around her as if she were unable to care for herself. It was foolish and was making her batty.

"Sugar, you got some heels to go with this dress?" Vivi asked as she stood in the doorway of the bathroom holding a red dress that Lisa had insisted she buy in Titus, even though she had objected that it was much too short.

"No, I'm not wearing that!" Molly cried with disdain.

Looking at the dress and remembering that it fell to just below mid-thigh, she shook her head. No way was she wearing that dress, even though all the other women wore similar clothing, only with property patches covering their backs. She stared wistfully at those patches wondering if Bone would ever give her one. She was hoping he might after what

Michelle Woods

had happened but she didn't know if it was wishful thinking on her part.

"Shoes?" Vivi held the dress up and asked again as if she hadn't just spoken.

"No," she said, looking at Vivi with an angry scowl.

She was not going out to a bonfire with a bunch of horny bikers wearing that, she thought firmly. Of course, one of those bikers was her horny biker if he knew what was good for him. She wasn't going to be a doormat like Brandy and allow her man to run around on her in silence. She felt a twinge of discomfort for thinking bad things about a woman who was trying to help her look amazing for her man.

"Molly, you look fantastic in that dress and I've told you that Bone will love it. Course he may kill someone for staring at you," Lisa giggled a little and a thoughtful expression broke over her face.

"Seriously I am not wearing that dress," Molly repeated to them before glaring at the other women who urged her to wear the dress without listening to her many protests.

Vivi ran out while Terry came into the large bathroom and took a curling iron to her hair. Terry styled her hair into soft curls that fell to her shoulders in a black cloud of sexy waves. When Vivi came back, she was holding a pair of red flats that she forced on Molly's feet.

Molly was flabbergasted when the women all ganged up, each doing their part to force Molly into the dress. When they were done, she stared at her reflection in awe. They had somehow managed to turn her into a sex kitten despite the livid bruise that covered the left side of her face.

Looking at herself for a long moment, she realized that she liked the look, and smiled at the women even though she felt a little awkward in the dress. It barely covered her thighs and floated around, giving her a sexier look than she was used to.

Taming Lucca

If it was only Lucca who saw her looking like this she would have been fine, but at the bonfire the whole club would see her.

"I can't wear this, it's just too short," she protested.

"Nope. You look amazing, and you are wearing that dress!" Lisa said, taking her arm. Still uncomfortable, she allowed them to usher her out the door towards the bonfire.

Music was playing loudly from the speakers nearby and when the women walked by heads turned. When they reached the group with Dog, Bone, and Tank, she was a little nervous. Bone and Dog were standing with their backs to them while Tank was looking off at the group of men standing about a few feet away who seemed to be fighting while others watched with roars and cheers. Tank suddenly looked back, seeing her and the other women coming towards them.

"You might want to turn around, Bone," he said, grinning with shameless desire.

Bone turned, looking her up then back down. He almost swallowed his tongue as he stared at Molly wearing a red dress that barely reached mid-thigh and her hair floating around her like a cloud. Rage burned inside him again when he took in the ugly bruise that covered the left side of her face. Damn, he couldn't wait for that reminder of her kidnapping to fade. Every time he saw it he was enraged all over again.

"Damn," he said as he came towards her, pulling her into his arms and half carrying her over to the bench seat that was nearby, sitting down and pulling her onto his lap. "You look good, baby," he said, his arms wrapped around her, hearing the other women laugh. He arranged Molly so that no one would be able to look up her skirt. No way in hell was anyone looking at her ass.

Michelle Woods

He knew that Dog and Slim must have told their old ladies that he was going to give Molly her patch tonight when they'd shown up at his house earlier. He'd left when Terry and Brandy had shown up about forty minutes ago and come out to wait by the bonfire. His woman was sexy without all this crap they had done to her, but with it he was barely able to contain himself long enough for her to enjoy herself. His dick was so hard he could pound nails with it.

"Thank you, Bone." She kissed him softly on his lips.

He grabbed the back of her head pulling her back in when she would have pulled away, growling as he took her lips in a devouring kiss. His hand slid up between her thighs a bit, unable to stop himself from seeking the wet heat he knew was waiting for him there. Fuck, they needed to go back inside so he could make love to her again. It hadn't even been an hour since he had taken her against the shower wall. He'd come home to find her just getting into the shower with her naked body turned away from the door as she tested the water and stepped in, her skin covered with water as she turned her face into the hot spray. He'd shucked his clothes and joined her in seconds.

Suddenly, there were hands tugging on her arms, and women's voices were wickedly declaring, "No, you are not messing up all our hard work. That can wait! Come dance with us, Molly."

Molly allowed herself to be pulled to her feet with a rueful laugh, following the women out onto the dance floor. Bone groaned as she moved away, but he smiled, his whole face lighting with happiness. Molly followed the women's steps, bumping hips as they laughed and held hands, dancing in circles and giggling like schoolgirls. Tank soon joined them, twirling each of them and laughing. Dog, who swung Terry up into his arms, spinning her around as she shrieked in laughter, followed him. Bone observed them, enjoying the merriment of his family and his woman, feeling joy spread through him as he watched.

Molly realized, as she laughing at the crazy antics of the wild group of bikers, that she was wearing that smile she had envied so much the first time she met Lisa. She almost lifted her hand to her lips to feel the wide smile; it was such a shock to find that she was wearing it. Molly was spun around again by Tank. She met Lucca's indulgent grin with that glowing smile, feeling truly happy for the first time in her life.

This was her family, this crazy group of rowdy bikers was actually her family.

She was grateful in that moment to her mother, who hadn't lifted a finger to stop her exile from the city. Molly never would have been as happy as she was right now if it hadn't been for her mother's inability to feel anything for someone besides herself.

Playing around a bonfire with bikers, and what the city rudely referred to as those bikers' whores, she felt lighter than she'd ever felt in her life.

Bone caught her eye and she saw that his eyes were darkened with desire as he watched her. She stopped dancing and began to walk towards him wanting to kiss him again.

That was when the laughter stopped, and someone yelled out, "Riders coming."

Bone stood, moving quickly towards her as Tank and Dog moved to usher the women towards the clubhouse. They all now wore grim expressions and a few of them were pulling out guns. The music was cut off, and she could hear the sound of bikes headed their way. Bone took out his phone when it beeped. He listened for several minutes, his hand holding her arm as he listened to whoever was on the other end of the line.

Michelle Woods

His face set in a grim line and he grunted, "Yeah. Okay. Only let five in."

He hung up, his arm wrapping around her waist as he moved with her towards the clubhouse. The other women were ushered into the clubhouse as well. They entered the common room where several prospects were drinking. Bone ushered her and the other women into a small room that was off the main room.

Dog and Tank followed them into the room with Terry, Lisa, Brandy and Vivi. Tank moved to stand next to a couch along the back wall as Bone pushed her down on it, moving to stand near the door with Dog, waiting. It was a tense few moments later when Slim entered with a forbidding expression. He leaned close to Lucca whispering something before glancing in her direction.

"I don't fucking think so!" Bone suddenly roared, causing Molly to blush.

Bone couldn't help the words that burst from him as a red haze of anger flowed over him like a cold chill at even the suggestion that he listen to anyone who wanted to take Molly away from him. One moment, he'd been sitting by the fire watching Molly dance, seeing her face creased with a happiness he wanted to keep there for the rest of their lives, and the next he was standing here listening to Slim tell him that the Blue Bandits were here claiming that they had a prior claim on his Molly.

"Just talk to him, Bone. I know that his request isn't going to happen, but we have to let him speak," Slim said with a dark look at him.

"Fine. He can say his piece and then he can leave." Bone looked at Molly then, his eyes caressing her possessively. "I'll

Taming Lucca

be back in a few minutes; stay here with Tank and the girls."

Molly watched them leave the room, shutting the door behind them. Standing, she moved towards the door. Tank sat down, putting his head back on the couch and closing his eyes. Terry sat down next to him, and Lisa leaned against the door with Vivi sitting on the couch's arm. Brandy was looking out the window trying to see who was here.

Molly knew that this new development had something to do with her from the way Slim, and then Bone, had looked at her, and she wanted to know what was going on. Standing near the door, she listened. It wasn't long before she heard raised voices and men shouting. Cracking the door, she peeked out, unable to see anything but the Red Devil cuts that were covering the men's backs where they stood between whoever was here and this room. She could guess who they belonged to, but she couldn't see much from the opening in the doorway.

"You can't have her!" Bone roared.

Another person spoke, but she couldn't tell what they were saying because they weren't yelling like Bone was. She heard Bone's response to whatever they were saying though.

"I don't care, Molly stays here."

That was it. She needed to get out there to find out what the hell was going on. She was out the door before Tank or any of the other women could stop her. She entered the main room to see Bone, Slim, Duck and Trick standing in front of the door to the room she'd been in. They were facing off against several other men who were standing near the door of the clubhouse. Bone was yelling at the man who stood in front of the group of men.

"You're not taking my woman!" Bone roared again.

Molly looked over the men wondering why any of these people would want to try to claim her. It didn't make sense,

Michelle Woods

she didn't know anyone outside the wall. As her gaze traveled over the men, she was shocked when she took in one of them and she couldn't help the name that burst from her lips when she realized why these men were here.

"Carl?" Molly gasped.

Her eyes fixed on the man in the back and to the left of the man in front, Molly was shocked as she stood for a moment watching him with her mouth hanging open.

Chapter 24

Bone's gaze snapped around and he stared at Molly standing just outside the door of the room where Tank was supposed to be watching her and the other women. He wanted to walk in that room and beat the shit out of Tank for letting her come out here. The Bandits had come here to try and take his Molly, not that he was just going to let that happen. Since he wasn't going to allow them to take her, this confrontation could get ugly fast.

He glared in fury at Tank, who came out of the room to stand behind Molly. His fists clenched and he wanted to punch Tank when he shrugged and muttered 'sorry.' Fuck, this wasn't going to end well and if something happened to Molly he was going to make Tank regret not watching her.

Molly watched as Carl's bushy brows formed a scowl when he saw her standing behind Bone and his brothers. Bone had turned to look at her with a similar scowl. He looked at Tank, who stood behind her, with fury. Uh-oh, this was getting kind of ugly, she thought as she watched the men. "Molly, go back in there and wait with Tank. I will handle this."

"No, Lucca," Molly said as she moved into the room, avoiding Tank who tried to catch her before she could move away from the door.

Michelle Woods

"Carl, what are you doing here?" she asked the man she thought of as a second father.

"Molly, get back in that room right now!" Bone snapped harshly, his hands landing on her waist. He tried to move her back from the other men with a forceful abruptness. Her hands came up, landing on his shoulders. Carl moved to stop him from forcing her back into the room.

"No!" Molly screamed in Lucca's face, even as the man who'd been standing in front of the small group moved to stop Carl from trying to grab Lucca to keep him from manhandling her.

"Lucca, stop it!" she demanded, glaring at him. "I will handle this myself!"

Lucca looked pained, and then he leaned forward, his forehead resting on hers with a resigned sigh. His arms were around her waist, his hands resting on her hips.

"Just don't leave me," he whispered agonizingly, and she realized why he was so panicked by her being involved in this situation. He was afraid she was going to go with Carl as he was obviously insisting. Molly felt a tenderness blossom inside her at his worry over something that would never happen. She wasn't going anywhere.

Molly smiled gently and whispered back, "Never."

Turning back to the other men, she took in the tensed bodies and the restraining hand on Carl's arm from one of the men who'd come here with him. She needed to defuse this situation, she realized, and quickly before it exploded into violence. Bone had allowed her to turn in his arms, but he refused to release her and he was holding her hips to keep her near him.

"Let's sit down," Molly suggested with a gesture towards the couches near the fireplace. After a long pause, Carl moved to the couches, as did the man who had been standing in the

Taming Lucca

front of the small group of men.

"Now tell me what's going on," Molly said when they were settled with her on Bone's lap on one couch where Bone had pulled her there the minute she sat down, and the other two men on the couch across from them.

"You're coming with us, Molly," Carl burst out with a dark glare at Bone.

"No. I'm not leaving the Red Devils, Carl," Molly said with a frown at his forcefulness.

This was very unlike Carl. He was usually an easy man to get along with. Carl was still glaring at Bone, and he began to speak again, only the other man interrupted him.

"Maybe we need to listen to her, Carl. She wants to stay, we should hear her out. Then we can decide what needs to be done," the man with dark blonde hair and bright green eyes that met hers with a surprisingly kind look said. He had a weathered look about him with crow's feet at the corners of his eyes and laugh lines on his face. He was handsome with a build similar to Bone's. She nodded at him. He seemed to at least be reasonable; perhaps talking to him would solve this dilemma.

"Thank you. Umm—and you are?" Molly asked, wanting a name.

Feeling a rumble beneath her, she heard Bone speak. "His name's Death Rider. He's the Blue Bandits Prez." He looked at Death with another fierce look.

"Uck...really?" she asked, without thinking of the insult she was dealing the man.

"Molly!" Lucca screeched at the same time Death roared out a laugh.

"I see she's a handful, huh, Bone," he said, still laughing.

With a sigh, grateful the man had a sense of humor, he replied, "She definitely keeps me on my toes. Though she

Michelle Woods

isn't normally rude."

He glowered at her darkly, unable to believe that in a tense situation like this one she had actually said that. Most bikers didn't take well to being insulted, and Molly had just unintentionally dealt the man one. Thankfully, Death had never been easily offended.

"Sorry, it's still quite a change to not have real names for people, and you have to admit yours doesn't sound friendly," Molly said sheepishly, blushing slightly.

"It's okay. I can't say that I am super friendly," he said with a devilish grin before continuing. "I'm here because one of my riders has a prior claim on you." He indicated Carl with a nod of his head.

"The hell he does!" Lucca's grip tightened on her as he clutched her to him.

"Calm," she said, running her hand down his arm to soothe him. The Bandit Prez watched the byplay with a thoughtful expression in his eyes.

"Molly, how can you want to stay with this animal?" Carl demanded with a thrust of his hand toward Bone as he glared at them all.

"Carl, what are you on about? Luc——Bone is not an animal," she said, shocked by his behavior. Carl was normally a very reasonable man but right now he was acting completely unreasonably. Carl stood intending to move closer, only to be stopped by a restraining hand from the man beside him.

"He left the proof of it on your cheek, Molly!" Carl boomed, and finally she realized what he was so upset over. She laughed with true mirth, realizing that this would be much easier to fix than she had anticipated.

"No, Carl. Bone would never hurt me. Not ever. It was the Jackals that kidnapped me a few days ago who did this." She indicated her cheek.

Taming Lucca

Bone was clutching her to him, and he'd growled when Carl yelled at her. He did not like another man taking that tone with her. Molly ran a hand down the arm that held her again with a soothing murmur before she continued.

"Bone killed the men involved with that debacle," Molly told him firmly and Carl sat back down watching her. His mouth hung open for a moment as he seemed to process her words.

"He–you mean he didn't hit you?" he asked, a little bewildered as he sat back in his seat.

"No, he didn't hurt me. Carl, you know me. Would I ever stay if someone was hurting me?" Molly firmly questioned, watching as Carl's face cleared a bit, losing its dark scowl.

"I thought I did, but then I saw your face and thought that he'd hurt you. Then you were refusing to leave, so I wasn't sure." He watched her face as she beamed at him. "You really want to stay with him?" he asked again.

"Yes. Luc––Bone makes me happy," Molly said, feeling Lucca's lips caressing her neck with tiny kisses.

Smiling, she looked up at him, and he looked down at her with a look that told her that he loved her. That look stole her breath for a moment and she was a little dazed when Lucca turned to look at the Bandits President.

"I will not negotiate. You can leave without my woman. She's mine."

Shocked by his declaration, Molly turned to look at him, a little awed. He just watched her as he pulled her forward, planting a gentle kiss on her lips that were still parted.

"Well then, I guess that's settled," Death said with a loud laugh of disbelief.

"Wh––what–I thought you said this club wasn't a place for a woman," Carl said, confused as he met Molly's eyes when Bone finally released her.

Michelle Woods

"That was before I knew she was property. Clutch, if she's property, the only way we leave with her is if they're all dead." Death's voice was resigned as he quietly spoke to Carl, and he looked at him with a quiet apprehension. Molly knew that if Carl protested, Death Rider would go to war with the Red Devils.

"Can I speak with Carl alone?" Molly asked, trying to avoid the need for the two clubs to war with each other.

"No," Lucca growled as his hand clenched on her upper thigh, holding her on his lap.

Lucca wanted to keep her close; it was cute. She felt a little giddy at the possessive way he was acting which likely set all women back a decade but she didn't care, she liked it. He was afraid that if she was alone with a man he knew she thought of as her father in many ways, he might somehow convince her to leave him.

Bone felt panic setting in as Molly insisted on talking to Carl. He hadn't had the chance to give her his patch yet and tell her that he loved her. He'd had the whole night planned before these yahoos had shown up to ruin it. Now she didn't know and if she talked with Carl, he might convince her to go with him because he thought she was just another piece of ass to him and she wasn't.

"Lucca," she whispered, waiting until he met her eyes. "It's okay. I'm just going to talk to him."

"Molly, baby, we haven't talked yet. It was something I was going to take care of tonight. I..." She placed her hand on his mouth, stopping the flow of agonized words as she frowned at his insistence that she listen. She wasn't going to leave him. She didn't understand the fear that had him acting like a madman. He should know that she wasn't leaving him.

She loved him. Didn't the insane man know that meant she was here to stay?

Taming Lucca

"Stop. It's okay, just let me talk to him and we can talk about us later," she said, dropping her hand from his mouth.

"Promise you won't go with him," Bone demanded.

"I promise," she quickly responded.

He nodded curtly, then helped her get up, holding the skirt of her dress down to preserve her modesty. He stood beside her. Carl stood with Death, and she looked at Lucca to see where they should go to talk; he indicated another room off to the side of the bar. She walked towards the door he indicated with Bone close behind. When they all reached the door, Bone stopped her again, looking into her eyes with a serious expression.

"I will let you step in there to talk to him, but the door stays open." His voice was set in stone, and she didn't bother arguing with him.

Nodding, she walked into the room seeing that it was a stock room for the bar. As Carl walked by Bone, he stopped him too, saying, "You hurt her, even emotionally, and I will kill you." His voice rang with finality.

Molly sighed and sat down on a crate, pulling at the hem of the skirt to keep it in place. Bone was still being overprotective, but as she watched the two men in the doorway, she saw grudging respect fill Carl's eyes as he nodded and stepped into the storeroom.

"So," Carl began as he took a seat on a crate near her. "You love him," he said without preamble as he looked at her.

"Yes," she said simply, not surprised he could read her so easily.

"I see." Carl ran a hand across his face, waiting a beat before saying, "He didn't hurt you?"

"No, I already told you that the Jackals did it and now they're all dead," Molly said, waiting for Carl to say what was on his mind.

Michelle Woods

"And you're okay with the fact that he killed them?" Carl watched Molly carefully.

"Yes, I am. They were about to gang rape me, Carl. I can't feel much remorse over them being dead," she told him, her voice wavering a little on the last words.

Molly was a little scared that he wouldn't like this new person she'd become and she would disgust him. It wasn't that she would change back into the woman she'd been before she left the city, so much as that she wanted to know that at least one person from her previous life still cared for her.

"You've grown out here, haven't you, kid?" he questioned, a slight smile coming to his face as he examined her.

"Yes," Molly said frankly, waiting for him to say something.

"I can see I was worried for nothing. When I finally got to the Bandits yesterday to see if you made it, I almost died when they said you hadn't. Then Death and Max began checking around and heard a rumor that a new female mechanic had started working at Trick's Auto Repair in Red Devils territory. I knew it had to be you. I insisted we come here to find you. When we rolled into a nearby town we asked around, found a woman who was willing to talk, and when we asked if she knew you, she said 'Oh you mean the one that they're beating?' I freaked when I heard that." Carl paused here, meeting her eyes, and she knew that he'd been even more worried when he heard that story.

"Death said that it might not have happened the way the woman thought. He knew Bone, and it didn't sound like him, but I wasn't in the mood to listen. When we got here, Death told me that he was going to do all the talking and perhaps we could just pay them for you. Then you'd be able to come with us without a huge fuss. But your young man wasn't about to allow that." He chuckled a bit as he said the last.

Smiling, Molly said, "I imagine not."

Taming Lucca

"Yep. I was, of course, ready to kill him to take you away from here. Then you told me you weren't willing to leave, and I lost it a bit. I couldn't understand why you would want to stay with a man who beat you." Molly's heart squeezed a little at his words.

"I wouldn't."

"I know, but when you look all bruised up and the man's acting like a Neanderthal, what was I supposed to think?" Carl leaned back against the wall behind him smiling.

"Well, not that, Carl. Bone and the Red Devils have become my family now." Molly leaned forward a bit still tugging at her skirt.

"Well, at least I can be secure knowing that he won't let anything happen to you."

"No, he won't. He's actually driving me crazy being overprotective. He has everyone stopping by to check on me. All. The. Time." Her voice was filled with her frustration at his highhandedness, and Carl let out a loud booming hoot of laughter.

"Oh, sweetheart, I've missed you. It breaks my heart knowing that I won't be escorting you off on one of your adventures anymore." Carl's eyes filled with sadness as he spoke of the times they had gone to abandoned buildings looking for the manuals she loved so much. Strange how it had only been a month or two and yet it seemed like a lifetime ago.

She stood, walking to him where he sat on the crate, and motioned for him to get up. When he did she hugged him, wrapping her arms around him tightly. His arms held her and they stood that way until they heard a possessive growl from the door, and Molly turned slightly to see Lucca standing there glowering into the room at them. He couldn't possibly be jealous of Carl, she thought with a smile as she pulled

Michelle Woods

away.

"Carl, you're welcome here anytime you want to visit," she said as she stepped back.

"Umm—Molly, they usually don't let another club's members hang about. I don't think they're going to allow me to come any time I feel like it." Carl's face had clouded with warning.

"They will. Won't you, Lucca." She was still watching him standing in the doorway.

"Yeah—fine," he said, exasperation filling his voice. She heard the snickers of the men behind him as he said it. Knowing that his easy agreement would earn him relentless teasing, she laughed.

"Wow, that's surprising." Carl raised his eyebrows in amazement.

She replied knowingly. "No, not really."

Chapter 25

Molly stood beside the bonfire watching Carl and Bone arm wrestle. It was funny that the two men had been trying to best each other like school boys for the last two hours. She felt a light touch on her shoulder and turned to see Terry standing beside her.

"Dog told me that if you want, he can distract Carl long enough for you to drag Bone back to the cabin." Molly let out a giggle, then looked at the two men who were each straining to best the other.

"Nah—I know how to handle this, just watch."

With a twinkling smirk, she walked over to the makeshift table that the men had set up to prove their manhood. She leaned over Bone's shoulder and whispered in his ear.

"I plan to go back to the cabin now. I'm going to take off my clothes and play with my nipples like you taught me until I'm so hot I can barely stand it. Then I'm going to play with my—," Molly's voice was low and husky as she told him what she had planned. The whole while she was counting in her head and laughed when she only got to six.

That was when Lucca's hand hit the makeshift table, and he crowed, "You won. I have to take Molly to bed now."

Jumping up from the chair, he scooped Molly into his arms

Michelle Woods

and turned, running towards the cabin without missing a beat. Terry's laughter followed as they flew past her.

"Well, that works too," she called, as chuckles and wolf whistles and an annoyed huff from Carl followed them back to the cabin. Bone stomped up the porch stairs and inside, carrying her to their room. He set her down, but when she went to wrap her arms around him, he stopped her.

"Wait, baby, I have something to give you."

He then walked out of their room, leaving her standing at the foot of the bed a bit bewildered. He came back a moment later holding a medium-sized box but stopped in the doorway, looking at her standing beside the bed in her red dress.

Damn, she was beautiful.

His chest ached as he took in the sight she made with her hair a little wild after he'd run to the house with her. That red dress clung to her body in all the right places and made him so randy he was surprised he had been so intent on besting her pseudo father at everything. He had almost forgotten tonight was supposed to be about Molly. He'd wanted this to be a perfect night for her. Only Bone wasn't willing to wait to claim her so that he could give her the perfect night she deserved. He needed to know that she was his and that every fucker who saw her would know it too.

"That's for me?" she asked, a little breathless.

"Yeah, baby. It's for you." He handed her the package, laughing as she jumped up and down in excitement.

"I love presents," she cried with such innocent joy he found himself grinning widely. She sat on the end of the bed, and he growled hungrily as he saw that skirt flip up, showing her panties. She began to unwrap the package with a childlike glee, ripping the paper and opening the box. She gasped as she pulled it out.

"Lucca," she said, clutching it to her chest with tears

forming in her eyes. Bone wasn't sure if they were tears of joy or not. He watched her carefully, waiting to see if her reaction was happiness or if he'd fucked this up. His heart was in his throat as she clung to the soft leather of the property patch and he sighed because he wasn't good at this shit.

"Will you wear it, baby?" he finally asked gruffly.

"Of course I'll wear your property patch, Lucca. I love you," she said, looking at him as if he had lost his mind.

"Good. Now, get naked."

Laughing at his immediate about face from unsure to confident male, she laid her new patch carefully across the nightstand, surprised to feel hard male hands land on her panty-covered ass.

"Lucca," she moaned as he pushed her forward, her hands landing on the bed.

"Sorry, baby, but I need to take you like this. I've been thinking about it all night." His hands slid along her body to the tie at the neck of the dress, undoing it so that the top half of the dress fell to her waist. He growled as he filled his hands with her naked breasts. His mouth came down on her neck nipping and sucking as he flicked her nipples, causing her body to flood with desire. She moaned and pressed herself back into him, feeling his hardness press into her butt. She wanted that inside her so badly, she thought, wiggling a bit.

He moved one hand to undo his jeans, jerking them down as his other hand squeezed her nipple and his mouth caught hers when she turned to look at him. His tongue slid along hers as she cried out with need and rubbed herself against his dick. He slid under her skirt to caress her liquid heat through her underwear with his hardened flesh. Grunting, he pulled away, his hand sliding inside her panties to find her slick wetness. Two of his fingers slid into her easily and he grunted in satisfaction when he felt her grip them. He began to roughly move them in and out, hearing her whimper as she pressed back into him.

Bone's dick was throbbing so hard he thought he might come just feeling her slippery juices as he fucked her with his fingers.

Damn, she was so ready.

Unable to wait any longer, he pulled his fingers out of her sweet body and ripped her panties off with a single brutal tug. Then he pressed his hard dick into her slowly, sliding into her narrow glove, groaning at the feel of her tightness squeezing him. When he was fully seated in her hot channel, he let out a growl. Grabbing her hips tightly, he began to thrust into her with hard, long strokes.

She began to make loud wailing cries as he pounded into her over and over with so much force he was afraid he was going to hurt her, but he needed it hard tonight. The threat of losing her again after she'd been kidnapped had him almost out of his mind.

He felt her body clench around him, almost making his eyes roll back into his head, as she let out a scream and came surrounding him. He thrust harder as he growled, unable to stop his rough lunges. It didn't take long before he was grunting as his dick exploded inside her. Fuck, he thought, as he fell forward crushing her into the bed. He moved to collapse on the bed beside her after a moment, not wanting to crush her.

"Sorry, baby. Give me a little bit, and we'll take it slow."

Sitting up, she turned over to look at him, giggling a bit. "That was amazing, Bone."

"Hey, what happened to Lucca?" He gently ran his hand down her face.

"Well, you did just bone me good, Bone," she said with a large grin covering her face.

Taming Lucca

"Fu—shit, who told you?" he asked, feeling his face flush because he hated that she knew why he was called Bone. Damn family should learn to keep their mouths shut. Of course that was wishful thinking; they were like a bunch of gossiping old women, the damned assholes. Bone was expecting it to be Tank but when Molly spoke, he figured he should have known.

"Terry," she said, letting out a light laugh. "I can't believe that you got your name from getting caught screwing some chick when you were supposed to be watching the bikes as a prospect."

"Yeah, like that mistake doesn't follow me around every day without you knowing about it. I outta have Dog spank her for that."

"Please do. I think she kind of likes it," she said in a loud, laughingly fake whisper. That had Bone guffawing out a loud snort.

"I just bet she does." He leaned forward and pulled her to straddle him as he lay back across the bed, filling his hands with her breasts. He leaned up, taking one into his mouth, sucking it, running his tongue over the tip teasingly, then pulled back to admire his handiwork. "Maybe I should spank you instead."

Molly leaned forward, a blush staining her cheeks, and took his ear into her mouth nipping it. "Maybe, I might like it, too," she said coyly. His hands slid around to cup her ass. Pushing his hardened dick into her already slick passageway, his hands squeezed her while she began sliding up and down his thick member.

"Oh, I think you would, baby," he said as he gently tapped her on the ass, causing her to moan loudly, her body squeezing around him. She realized that she most definitely did like it.

Epilogue

It had been six glorious months since she'd been patched by Bone, and she was still deliciously happy. She was currently at the shop changing the spark plugs of a fat boy Harley she was working on. Bone was insatiable, and she loved every minute of his passionate embraces. She had turned into a regular hussy since she came to live with the Red Devils.

Smiling, she continued to work, thinking of Lucca.

"Stop smiling like that, it's freaky," Tiny grumbled, walking from the back room into the bay where she was working. This was a lot of words for Tiny, who spoke little and mostly in one-word sentences.

"Going to Tammy's. Want so–" His voice trailed off when they heard what sounded like a woman screaming in the front office.

"Please…please––" the woman begged. "I just need to talk to her, please."

They heard Trick say something that was muffled by the door, so it just sounded like a rumble of noise. Molly stood up, dropping the rag and old spark plug on the tool chest. Walking towards the office, she didn't notice that Tiny was right behind her until they were almost to the door, where he quickly got in front of her. She shook her head.

Taming Lucca

Her new family was still a bit overprotective, but she wouldn't give them up for the world. She just followed behind him with another shake of her head.

"You have to let me see Molly!" The woman's screech was desperate and a little familiar.

Molly walked into the office behind Tiny, who had stopped dead, staring at the woman who was trying to get past Trick to the shop. Trick's hands on her shoulders were holding her back as she desperately tried to push past him.

"Racheal!" Molly exclaimed, take in the figure that grappled with Trick.

Hearing Molly, Trick stopped trying to prevent the woman from entering the shop. What shocked Molly wasn't that Racheal was here. No, it was that she was nothing but bruises.

They covered her face and what she could see of her impressively large chest. Her lip was cut, and she had a large half-healed slash on her arm that looked like she'd been cut with a knife. The taller woman limped slightly when she came towards Molly. She fell into Molly's arms, sobbing with relief.

"My God, who did this to you, Racheal?" Molly demanded, holding the sobbing woman. Tiny moved near her, and she glanced at him. The look on his face was scary; she hadn't seen Tiny ever look like that. Molly rubbed her hand over Racheal's back trying to soothe her.

"M-my husband," Racheal finally stuttered out, still sobbing.

"Where can I find your husband, darlin'?" Tiny asked in a deadly cold voice before Molly could ask anything else.

Racheal raised her head looking at Tiny with tear tracks on her face and a surprised look gracing her tanned complexion.

"Plot nine row twenty-eight in that little capsule they stuffed him in," she said, meeting his eyes.

"Good girl," Tiny said as he watched her stand up straight,

Michelle Woods

looking between Molly and Tiny.

"He does realize that I killed him, right?" she asked Molly with a confused expression that caused Molly to laugh.

"Yep, that's why he was asking where he was, Racheal. We don't let things like a woman being abused go unpunished out here like they do inside the wall." Molly looked fiercely at her friend.

"Well, Carl said you were different, but I never believed him until this moment. I like it," Racheal said, then after a moment she continued. "Carl told me to come here, that you'd make sure I was taken care of. Pearl gave me all her credits, so I can pay you for a place."

"No need for you to spend any of your credits, darlin', you can stay in my cabin. I'll stay in the clubhouse," Tiny said, shocking Molly.

First that he'd used so many words at once and second for offering a perfect stranger the use of his home. It wasn't like the mostly private man to offer something like that to someone he didn't even know. Hell, Racheal could be a thief or she could sell his stuff or about a hundred other things that should make him at least hesitate before giving her his home on a silver platter.

"I'll still be paying," Racheal insisted, and Molly could see that the strong backbone the woman had always had wasn't broken, just bruised a bit. This discovery filled her with relief; she'd been scared to death that what her husband had done to her would make her timid, but she should have known better she supposed.

"Fine. But you're staying at my cabin," Tiny said between clenched teeth, daring any of them to contradict him.

Racheal cocked her hip, her hand landing on it, reminding Molly of Miss Pearl, Racheal's mother, which made her laugh a bit because Miss Pearl was fantastic. Molly had a feeling

Taming Lucca

Tiny had no idea what he was getting himself into and she couldn't wait till he figured it out.

"I will if I decide to," she said, looking him up and down.

"You will be staying there, Racheal. So go ahead and decide to," Tiny said with bite.

"Maybe I will and maybe I won't, you do not have a say! I don't even know you." Racheal looked back at Molly. "Is he for real?" she asked just before a roaring motor shut off out front, and Molly knew that Bone was here.

Molly turned to see him enter the door with a grim expression that turned into a deep smile when he saw her. He stood there, his face creased in that happy smile, his eyes not even moving away from her to Racheal despite her being the reason he was here.

"Yes, I think he is, Racheal," she said as she sashayed to Bone, who took her hips in his hands and kissed her with a deep rumble of pleasure at the greeting. Bone's hands slid into the back pockets of her coveralls squeezing her ass. Molly couldn't help the little moan that escaped her as she melted against him.

"Not this again," Tiny said at the same time Racheal muttered, "Wow, Carl was right, you've got a hottie and you know how to use him." Racheal laughed when Molly turned, still standing in Bone's arms. Molly felt a laugh bubble up inside her because she was definitely different than she'd been when she lived in the city.

"Wouldn't want to disappoint Miss Pearl," Molly said, chuckling wickedly as Racheal bent forward with her mouth hanging open, shock clearly written all over her bruised face as she watched Molly.

"You wicked, wicked girl!" she exclaimed with a little wink at Molly.

Molly felt a flood of relief because that little wink told her

Michelle Woods

that her friend was going to be okay. Racheal wasn't going to fall into despair and stop living life because something bad had happened to her. She'd make it out of the darkness she'd suffered and Molly would help.

"Molly's not wicked, just easily corrupted," Bone said, smiling at Racheal then with a bit of deadly intent. "Do I need to take care of that for you?" he asked, indicating Racheal's bruises.

"Nope. But if it did need to be taken care of I'd be doing it, not you," Tiny said moving forward, meeting Bone's eyes with a look that seemed to speak volumes. Molly wondered what that look meant as she heard Bone's reply.

"I see," Bone said, looking thoughtful.

"Ha, well, both of you are outta luck cause I already handled it," Racheal said, glaring at Tiny. Molly knew that Tiny had no idea who he was playing with and she almost snickered when she thought of the wild ride he was going to take if he persisted on this path. Poor man had no idea what he was asking for.

"Racheal can stay in our guest room, right Lucca?" Molly said, trying to break the tension and earning a deadly look from Tiny. She didn't acknowledge the look; she wasn't forcing her friend to stay somewhere she didn't want to and he could like that or not, she didn't really give a damn.

"Tha——" Bone began, but Racheal interrupted him.

"I will stay at his house," she said, indicating Tiny. "What's your name anyway, grim?" she asked.

"Tiny," he replied, looking at her with a hungry expression.

"Huh…sure wouldn't tell too many women that, sugar," Racheal said, earning her a glare from Tiny and laughter from everyone else.

Taming Lucca

Sitting in the swing later that night with Bone's arms wrapped around her under the blanket to ward off the slight chill that had entered the evening hours, Molly sighed. It had been an eventful day. With Racheal showing up and the story she'd told Molly about what had happened to her, she wanted to dig up her husband and kill him all over again.

She didn't give a damn that Racheal had killed him because the bastard hadn't deserved to live. She'd told Bone some of the story when she'd finally left Tiny's cabin an hour ago and he'd let her cry for her friend. That was how they'd ended up sitting out here in this swing with her wrapped in the blanket with Bone holding her.

"Molly, every time I try to make a date to give you this, it always seems something goes wrong. Today with your friend showing up hurt, and the day before that when I had to go on a run up to the Dixon farm, and the one before that where the pipes burst in the clubhouse and I had to help handle that. So I'm just going to give this to you and hope that you'll forgive me," Bone said as he pulled a small box out of his pocket, handing it to her.

She clapped with glee, not caring that it was today he gave her a present. It was special because Bone was giving it to her. She tore the wrapping off of the box and opened it, tears filling her eyes. Bone reached into the box, taking out the diamond solitaire and holding it up to her.

"Will you marry me, baby?" Bone asked gruffly.

"Oh Lucca," she turned to him with a glowing tearful smile. "Yes, yes, I will marry you."

"Thank God," he said before slipping the ring on her finger.

His arms came around her and he was kissing her deeply. His hands held her against his chest as he pulled back a little, looking at her with a tender expression that told her more than the patch and the ring that he loved her. Molly didn't

Michelle Woods

care that he'd never said the words to her because his actions told her he loved her.

Words were meaningless. After all, how many times had her mother said those words to her and yet she'd abandoned her at the first sign of trouble. Bone might never say that he loved her but every step of the way he'd been there for her and that was why she was sure that he loved her. Dog was right; he might not ever say it but he cared deeply for her and she was damned glad that she understood. She had her shitty family to thank for that, she realized, and she was glad for their abandonment because it led her here to the Red Devils, and Bone.

Bone kissed her nose and rose with her in his arms carrying her up to their bed. Molly wrapped her arms around his neck wondering if there was ever a more perfect night as she was carried away to be ravished.

Other works

Claiming Racheal
Out at B&N and Amazon

Out March 1st 2016 at iBooks
and Kobo For more information on
upcoming releases see my web site:
www.michellewoodsofficialsite.com
or friend me on Facebook:
www.facebook.com/romance.michelle.woods

Chapter 1

Tiny watched the feminine butt wiggle back and forth with every turn of the wrench. His dick throbbed, pressing against his fly and likely leaving a zipper impression in the damned thing. Shaking his head at his inability to focus on anything except her, he shifted slightly. He had been sitting in the corner of the shop on a crate watching Racheal work on an engine rebuild for over an hour.

Damn, the woman was sexy.

Even after three months, he was still preoccupied with her. He remembered the day he'd first met her. Racheal had arrived at the shop after escaping the city with the help of Carl, a guard there. She'd been covered in bruises having been beaten half to death by her husband, but his dick had still stood to attention the moment he saw her. It was her lips and that sexy as fuck ass that was still torturing him as his gaze devoured it. He was beginning to think he was obsessed.

Of course, remembering those bruises covering her silky skin made him want to commit murder. If he could have dug up the bastard who'd hurt her and killed him again, he would have tortured him for hours before he finally put him out of his misery. Tiny's fists clenched and his jaw tightened.

Racheal moved around the truck slightly to get a better angle with the ratchet she was using and this time Tiny groaned. She now had her butt facing him as she worked on the engine. Suddenly, he couldn't think about anything except walking up behind her, grabbing those hips and ripping off those coveralls to take her from behind in a hard pounding rhythm.

Fuck, he needed to get laid. Only problem was she was the only woman he wanted.

Racheal had a fine ass that made him lose his head, not that the rest of her wasn't fine too. Tiny was just an ass man. Most men loved tits, but not Tiny. Nope, show him a fine ass and his boner was like a steel rod in seconds. This is why he found himself across the room staring at her ass doing a little jig, aching with desire. His cock felt like it was going to burst from his pants at any moment.

Trick entered the bay walking over to where Tiny was sitting. He leaned back against the wall beside Tiny, propping his foot behind him and giving Tiny a wicked grin.

"You know that most women find a man staring at them for hours creepy, right?" Trick asked in a low voice as he chuckled at his own joke. Tiny ignored him and continued his perusal of Racheal as she worked.

"Yep," Tiny said, earning a raised brow and a look from Trick.

Really? Had he expected Tiny to reply to that ridiculous comment that was meant to annoy him? Tiny knew that it annoyed his friend if he just didn't rise to the bait and that worked for him. Most of the time he didn't let the man bother him, which in turn fucked with Trick's head and that gave Tiny all the revenge he needed.

"So maybe you shouldn't keep staring at the woman, it might be creeping her out. How do you figure you're gonna manage to get into her pants if she's freaked out about you watching her all the time?" Trick asked, looking at him questioningly.

"Nope," Tiny replied, hiding his grin when he heard Trick grit his teeth. It always pissed off his brothers when he didn't answer them the way they expected. He loved messing with family and they never disappointed, he thought, snorting. Trick looked at him for a long moment then turned away, watching Slim coming towards them from across the bay. Slim stopped beside them and smirked at Trick's sour expression.

"Let me guess, it's a one word day, huh," he asked before letting out a snort of laughter.

"Yep," Tiny grunted, grinning briefly at Slim before turning back to gaze at Racheal. Slim's smirk became a deep belly laugh.

"Shut up, fuckers!" Trick said, glaring at Slim, who bent forward laughing so hard he was turning red. Tiny watched him for a moment before turning back to see Racheal was leaning over, her abundant breasts revealed by the way her coveralls were unbuttoned, making him growl. He stared at the heavy globes, his mouth watering as he imagined sucking on their beaded tips.

Fuck, his cock was going to end up permanently damaged from his zipper if he didn't get his thoughts off Racheal soon. Tiny watched the way they swayed as she worked, his hands tightening on his knees, his fingers digging into his jeans. Really, that woman was just sex on a stick and he wanted a bite.

Or several.

"You know he only does the one word thing to piss you off, Trick. After ten years you should have figured that out by now," Slim panted out when he'd finally stopped laughing. "Damn, how stupid can you be?" he added, earning a dark glare from Trick that only made him grin harder.

Trick glowered at him before he exclaimed, "Fuckers!" and stomped back into the office with Slim's laughter following behind him.

"Dang, he's moody, huh?" Slim asked as he leaned against the wall taking the position that Trick had just vacated, his smile genuine as he glanced at Tiny, his shoulders shaking as he let out another chuckle.

"Yeah, I don't think he likes it when we make fun of him. Wonder why?" Tiny asked, his grin sly because he knew exactly why and he loved it. Leaning forward a little, he shifted around trying to take the pressure off his aching cock. He heard the crate beneath him creak a bit and hoped it wouldn't break because that was all he needed, a sore ass to go with his sore cock.

"Yeah, the idiot doesn't get that you do it just to piss him off. What do you think of these new rumors we've been hearing about the Jackals?" Slim asked, shifting slightly on the wall and looking at Tiny. He tore his eyes off Racheal's breasts with an effort, meeting Slim's eyes with his own.

"Not sure, they've been quiet since the kidnappings. It's strange they've been attacking us for more than six years, and suddenly we don't hear from them for almost ten months. It's making us all nervous." Tiny's grim expression was mirrored on Slim's face.

"Yeah, I know. Bone's been a little edgy. Tank too. I think we need to start checking up on the rumors we're hearing. I'm going to talk about it in church today." Slim ran a hand through his hair with a dark frown.

"Huh, I was just thinking the same thing earlier." Tiny watched Racheal walk toward the back room, pausing at the doorway with a glance over her shoulder at him before she moved inside. Dang, he wished he could follow her in there and just screw her against the bench table they had back there.

"Really, is that what you were thinking about?" Slim asked with a laugh as he stood up and looked towards the back room where Racheal had disappeared. "Seems to me that wouldn't give you a hard-on, but I'm guessing that Racheal's tits might."

"Shut it, asshole!" Tiny growled. Getting up, he ignored Slim's laughter, moving towards the back room following Racheal. He needed to ask her if she wanted anything to eat from Tammy's Diner anyway.

"Yep, when are you patching that woman?" Slim asked with a chuckle, most likely expecting the same denials he'd gotten from Bone, but he'd be disappointed.

"When she's ready," Tiny replied, glancing over his shoulder at Slim. His response earned him a surprised look from Slim. Tiny knew that he was obsessed with the woman, and he had been for three very long, very hard months. He wasn't going to deny that he wanted her for more than just a simple screw.

He wasn't messed up cause his daddy had cheated on his mother like Bone. Nope, he had his own demons. His father had beaten his mama to death and then killed himself when

Tiny was fourteen. It was lucky he hadn't been home because his father may have beaten him to death too. But that was the past. He was focusing on his future now, and that woman was his future, she just hadn't realized it yet. Besides, his father's madness had led him to Devils Peak, where he'd met Bone and Tank when he was twenty-two.

They'd only been prospects then, out on a run for the club. He'd struck up an instant friendship with the two younger men, and he'd joined the club a year later.

He was thirty-one now, and he'd been with the club for nine good years. He liked having a real family, and a stable life. He understood the pain Racheal carried in a way no one else ever would and he could wait until she was ready.

Even if his cock thought it was going to die before she allowed him inside her.

Tiny had been gawking again. Racheal Trenton frowned at her reflection in the tiny bathroom mirror in the back of the shop, feeling more than a bit upset that she wasn't the person she'd been a year and a half ago. Her hands gripped the sides of the sink and she felt her head throb. She was mad at herself for allowing Eugene, her abusive husband, this power over her emotions. Even three months after he'd forced her to kill him that horrid night, she was still in his grip. Her hands tightened and she wished she could throw something.

A year ago, pre-Eugene, she would have been teasing a hunk like Tiny to death before finally putting him out of his misery by sleeping with him. She looked at the haunted, broken woman gazing back at her from the mirror with dismay.

How had she become this woman, she wondered with increasing frustration. Her pulse thrummed through her throbbing with fury; her hand lifted to run over her face in exasperation. She didn't want to be like this, damn it. The face looking back at her was a woman who wanted to just hide away from the world.

Racheal turned slightly, frustrated to no end that crying was a regular occurrence for her now; one minute she was fine, and the next she was sobbing her heart out. It was a miracle when she made it through a single day without crying at least once. Sighing, she brushed her hair off her forehead noting the scar there with a grim expression.

She was better than she'd been when she'd first arrived in Devils Falls she supposed, but she was still a broken bird waiting to fly again. Her heart twisted when she thought of her mother. Pearl would be disappointed in her. Her mother had always stood strong no matter what happened, unlike her. She'd crumbled beneath the crushing load of misery that Eugene had dealt her.

Racheal glared at her reflection, anger boiling in her stomach. She didn't want to be this pathetic creature and she missed her mother, desperately. Pearl had always been the glue that kept Racheal together. Without her, Racheal felt like she'd been set adrift without a tether. Maybe that was why she'd latched onto Tiny; he made her feel safe.

Racheal felt tears that she refused to cry threatening.

Damn it.

She needed to get a grip. She splashed water on her face trying to compose herself. It wasn't that Racheal didn't like it here in Devils Falls, far from it. She loved being here with her best friend Molly, and Tiny's constant presence soothed her somehow. She snorted as that thought broke through her hazy minefield of self-pity.

She wasn't sure why, but ever since that first day when she'd met him, she was calmer as long as he was hovering somewhere nearby. Her mind didn't burst into panicked jolts at the slightest sound and she wasn't afraid of her own shadow.

He would linger nearby, his hazel eyes watching her every move and those thick arms of his crossed. His muscled five-nine frame coiled with deadly energy that she somehow knew would never be used against her. It made her want to run her hands all over him but she didn't because she wasn't ready for another man when the last one still left a cold pit of fear curled inside her. Tiny's sexy black locks, hell, everything about the man, made her burn with desire. She still couldn't believe that he'd let his hair grow out after she'd said Bone had sexy hair. If only she wasn't still broken then she might be able to accept the fantastic sex his dark eyes and thickly muscled body promised.

Shaking away the thoughts swirling around in her head, she opened the door to the bathroom. She walked into the hall looking down not really paying attention, lost in her own head, when the man looming outside the door of the bathroom moved. She jumped back, screeching in surprise, her heart jumping in her throat because she wasn't able to make out the figure in the darkened back room, and she almost fell. Hard male hands reached out and clamped on her hips steadying her. A gruff voice barked at her when she flinched away from the man.

"It's just me, darlin'." Tiny moved forward, his face entering the light from the one bulb in the hallway.

"Oh, you frightened me again," Racheal told him and watched him with relief, her heart still pounding with fear.

Damn Eugene, she really hated that man's influence over her.

It was his fault she was so damned timid that even here a man looming in the dark frightened her. It made her fists curl, her nails digging into her palms, and her lips tightened into a hard line as she looked at Tiny.

"You want something from Tammy's?" he asked, not commenting on the fact that she'd reacted like a frightened rabbit again. That was one thing she could count on with him, he never commented on her reaction to situations like these even though it wasn't the first time she'd freaked out on him.

"Yeah, a turkey sandwich wi—"

"Mayo, tomatoes, and hot sauce," Tiny rumbled out before she could finish speaking, causing her to smile. Tiny always remembered how she wanted her lunch prepared. It was kind of sweet and it made her feel warm and safe but like a horrid bitch, and all that at the same time.

"Thanks, Tiny," Racheal said smiling slightly. She felt her heart pumping hard and she didn't want him to leave. She rushed to ask before he could move away, "Are Bone and Molly coming back today from the run to Titus?"

"Yeah, they should be back before church." He was watching

her with a solemn expression. "Babe, are you okay?"

"I'm fine. Just missing Molly." Racheal looked down, unwilling to tell him that she was tired of being afraid of her own shadow, that she almost hated herself for it. He didn't need all that thrust upon him. He had enough to worry about without adding her problems to the mix. Racheal lifted her chin trying to look as if she didn't have a care in the world.

"Hmm——" he said, still looking at her in that piercing way of his.

He watched her for several seconds before he lightly squeezed her waist, making her realize that he still held her hips in his light grip. It surprised her that she hadn't noticed. She'd been excruciatingly aware of every touch by another person since Eugene, that rat bastard, had wrecked her. It shocked her a bit that she was allowing his touch and it hadn't even occurred to her.

"It's going to be all right, Racheal." He squeezed her again, then lifted his hand to brush a loose strand of her hair away from her face. "It won't be this way forever."

She was taken aback by the way he always seemed to read her without even trying. Looking up at him with tears in her eyes, she wanted to kiss him. Only she wasn't ready for the fire she knew it would spark in them both. She settled for reaching out and wrapping her arms around his waist pulling him into her for a tight hug. Pressing her face into his chest, she almost groaned with the relief it afforded her.

How was it that Tiny always soothed her?

Tiny held Racheal, his face buried in her apple-scented ponytail. His heart ached for the wounded expression on his woman's face when she'd stepped out of that bathroom. He held her, rubbing her back.

He was livid with himself that he'd startled her again. He needed to stop doing that, he was always causing her to feel even more misery than she already did, and he hated it. He just wanted to take care of her, not freak her out.

Racheal pulled slowly away from Tiny, quietly whispering, "Thanks, Tiny," before heading back into the shop with him trailing behind her silently. Racheal saw that Slim was working on the truck she'd been fixing. She walked over to stand next to him.

"Hey, that was my damned job!" she exclaimed, watching him pulling out the radiator.

"Well, you felt the need for a break so I took over. Snooze you lose, doll," Slim said, laughing as he set the radiator down with a clang. It had been slow the last few weeks at the shop, and it was causing them all to be a bit stir crazy. When she'd first gotten here, they had been short one mechanic for almost ten months and the repair backlog had kept them all busy. Now, with all the work caught up, they were all clinging to every job.

"Slim," Tiny grunted, glowering at Slim from behind her.

Uh-oh, she thought with glee.

Tiny was up in arms for her again. Smirking, she waited for Tiny to get Slim to walk away. She almost snickered at the sour look on Slim's face as Tiny stood with his arms crossed and a dark glower on his face.

"Her. Job," he gritted out.

"Damn it, can't you stop acting like a damned pansy for one damned day!" Slim exclaimed, glowering right back at Tiny. The two men had a five minute stare-down until Tiny finally spoke.

"No, I can't. I'm going to Tammy's and you're comin' too. I need help carrying shit," Tiny commanded, causing Racheal to snort out a laugh.

"Man, it's just not fair. I wanted to fix something this week," Slim whined, a large grin splitting his face. Yep, she really did love it here.

Tiny just watched him with his hang-dog expression till Slim threw his hands up, grumbling under his breath as he followed Tiny out the door. Slim turned to look at her once before they reached it, winking, and she knew there were no hard feelings despite Tiny's orders, making her smile.

Racheal really did like Tiny. He was always ready to take on her cause, even if she had stolen this job when Slim went to the bathroom two hours ago. She wasn't ashamed; she'd wanted to do the complete rebuild on this motor. She needed the distraction from her own ridiculous thoughts.

Racheal walked over to the engine and got to work, her lips twisted into a happy grin as she leaned over the motor.

www.ingramcontent.com/pod-product-compliance
Lightning Source LLC
Chambersburg PA
CBHW030032180626
46810CB00001B/325